Emmett the Empathy Man

Lindsay Woodward

ISBN: 978-1-9995855-0-1

For Carmel and Oliver.

Thanks for the inspiration. We made a great team.

.

EMMETT THE ILLUSTRATION

With a proud smile, Zack placed a piece of paper in the middle of the table and all three of them studied the image on it.

'Wow,' Jenny said. 'You drew that? That's really impressive.'

'Thanks,' Zack said, a little coyly.

'You've put in loads of detail,' Adam said. 'He actually looks real.'

'Is he how you imagined?' Zack asked.

There was a momentary pause as Jenny and Adam absorbed the image before them.

'I suppose I thought he might have had a few more muscles,' Jenny said.

Zack shook his head. 'Why would he need muscles? His special power is that he empathises with people. He doesn't need muscles for that.'

'He still needs to be strong, though,' Adam said. 'We want him to be strong.'

'He is, he's emotionally strong,' Zack replied. 'You can tell by his eyes. If you look, I've added in degrees of wisdom and compassion. Do you see?'

They all focused on the eyes of the man in the

illustration. 'They just look blue to me,' Adam stated.

'He's not meant to be a man that punches his way through life,' Zack explained. 'We said we didn't want that.'

'Do you think it's a bit lame?' Adam asked. He ran his hands through his short dark hair, thinking it through. He was the typical tall, handsome man who was never short of attention from the ladies. 'I don't mean your drawing, mate. You know you're a brilliant artist. It's just maybe this Empathy Man stuff is a bit crap.'

'I think it's got legs,' Jenny argued, sipping at her pint. She was casually dressed as always in jeans and a T-Shirt, and she had a pink stripe running through her bleached blonde hair. 'We all agreed, it's time for a change. The comic world is begging for something new. It's got too much about saving the world from catastrophic disasters. I really liked our idea of stripping it back and making it about a man who works with the little people.'

'I've been working on that storyline we brainstormed,' Zack said, bringing out a wad of papers from his backpack and placing them on the pub table. He handed a particular page over to Adam who scanned it quickly.

'Is that really what we came up with?' Adam said, throwing the paper back down. 'A kid being bullied? It's such four o'clock in the afternoon stuff. Were we really pissed last week or something?'

'It's touching on real life problems,' Zack insisted.

'I love that it's about the kid's journey,' Jenny added, scanning through the comic book sketches that Zack had drawn. 'It's not just about Empathy Man and how he has this incredible ability to understand exactly how a person's feeling at any given time, it's more about the lives of the people he helps. I think our readers are going to find it quite emotional.'

'Why has he got a cape?' Adam asked, grasping his pint firmly in his hand.

'Because he's a superhero,' Zack shrugged. 'We wanted

him to be recognisable as a superhero.'

'But he can't fly.'

'Neither can Batman!' Jenny stated. 'Nor Robin.'

Adam considered her argument for a second as he gulped at his lager. 'But they were the caped crusaders. This man,' he continued, pointing to the illustration before him, 'is more like the caped cry-baby. He'd be all, "look at me with my small arms, let's sit down and talk it through because I know exactly how you're feeling, I'm Empathy Man". Can you see how crap that is?'

'Stop being so negative!' Jenny demanded. 'Just because he's emotional and caring, it doesn't make him weak.'

Adam sighed and shook his head. 'Either way, I still don't get what he needs a cape for.'

'He has not got small arms!' Zack protested.

'No, I can see they're not small,' Jenny mused, studying the illustration again. 'But when you compare him to the likes of Superman-'

'You and your obsession with Superman!' Adam said rolling his eyes. 'Why does he have to be compared to Superman? There are far better heroes out there.'

'Like the Marvel ones?' Jenny scoffed.

'Name one bad thing about the Avengers. And they fight in the real world. I can't see you hopping on a plane to Metropolis any time soon.'

'Why do you always insist that our superheroes have to exist in known cities?'

'Because it's better.'

'Here we go again,' Zack sighed, sitting back in his chair.

'When I went to New York,' Adam continued, 'I saw that man dressed as Spider-Man. It made it a far more exciting concept that I was actually in Peter Parker's home.'

'I know, I know,' Jenny said, 'and then you walked down Fifth Avenue and you could picture exactly where Avengers Mansion would be.'

'Exactly! You don't get any of that being a Superman fan. Spider-Man is much better.'

'Don't you dare start! You are not going to win that argument.'

'How could Superman ever beat Spider-Man in a fight? I mean even I could beat Superman in a fight.'

Jenny sighed, shaking her head. 'Yet you still haven't managed to get your hands on any Kryptonite, have you? I told you they don't sell it in Asda.'

'If you notice,' Zack said loudly, trying to bring the conversation back to his illustration, 'I've drawn his legs deliberately bulkier than his arms. I did that because we said we wanted him to run really fast.' Zack pointed to the blue, Lycra clad legs in the picture.

Adam and Jenny looked down at the piece of paper again.

'Do you think that's too much like The Flash?' Jenny asked, thinking it through.

'We never said it was super speed,' Zack countered. 'I was thinking more Usain Bolt speed. The difference is, though, that he doesn't get tired.'

'This is lame,' Adam said. 'It would take him hours to get to a victim in need on the other side of town. The bully would have stolen the kid's lunch money, eaten the lunch and got home for dinner by the time Empathy Man gets there.'

'What about a super car? Like the Batmobile?' Zack asked.

'No, it wouldn't work,' Jenny said. 'Bruce Wayne was different. He was a genius multi-millionaire.'

'Same as Tony Stark,' Adam interjected.

'Yes, same as Tony Stark,' Jenny agreed. 'But Empathy Man is a simpler man. Okay, so as a GP he's clever, but he doesn't have the time, contacts or money to be developing super vehicles.'

'What about we have him driving around town in a trusty little hatchback, then?' Adam quipped. 'Or perhaps a

Smart Car? Something handy to negotiate the peak time traffic.'

'There's no need for sarcasm,' Jenny exclaimed. 'We just need to think it through a bit more. Oh, I've got it!' she said, clapping her hands with delight. 'We could have it so he empathises with vehicles. The speed of the vehicle would determine how fast Empathy Man could run. So a Fiesta would be slower than a Ferrari, if you see what I mean. He could only go to the top speed of the vehicle that he empathised with.'

'That's ridiculous!' Adam stated. 'How can he empathise with inanimate objects?'

'Why couldn't he?' Jenny retorted. 'At least it's consistent.'

'I like it,' Zack said as he started to scribble notes in his notebook. Zack was the smallest of the group, with floppy, mousy hair and a round, cheeky face. 'I'll reflect it in the next draft. Maybe, Jenny, you could update our character profile?'

'What's that?' Adam suddenly said, grabbing some more of the papers from the table.

'What?' Jenny asked, trying to look over at what Adam had picked up.

'We're not calling him Emmett!'

'You haven't?' Jenny tutted in Zack's direction.

'It's just a working name,' Zack shrugged.

'Emmett the bloody Empathy Man,' Adam exhaled. 'Who would ever fear that?'

'I needed to give him a name to help bring him to life. It's part of my process.'

'We agreed on just Empathy Man, with his real life identity being Dr Oliver Brown. That's his name,' Jenny said.

'Empathy Man just felt stunted. He needed something more.'

'Superheroes don't have proper names as their super names, Zack,' Adam stated, getting visibly irate. 'It's not

Steve Spider-Man and Ian the Incredible Hulk.'

'What about Dr Strange or Thor?' Zack retorted.

'Is he winding me up?' Adam asked, turning to Jenny with exasperation.

'Anyway, why can't we be different?' Zack added. 'No one's ever laid down absolute superhero rules. We can do what we like.'

'The problem is that we don't like it,' Jenny replied.

'Shit, hide it, hide it,' Adam said, quickly stuffing all the papers into Zack's bag, before throwing it haphazardly back to the wooden floor.

'Hi baby!' a stunningly beautiful woman purred before she leaned down to kiss Adam on the lips.

'Hi Cadence,' Zack said, waving in a rather pathetic way.

'Have you eaten already?' she asked.

'Yep,' Jenny said, quite to the point.

'What are you doing here?' Adam asked, shifting awkwardly in his seat. He looked up at Cadence, with her long, thin legs and flowing brown locks.

'I came to let you know that I'm going out tonight,' she replied, flashing her dazzling smile and perfect teeth. 'I've got VIP access to that new club in Soho. Do you want to come?'

'You could have texted that to me,' Adam said.

'If you don't come then I probably won't see you until tomorrow,' Cadence said, slipping herself onto Adam's lap. 'Is it wrong that I wanted a kiss goodbye?' She kissed him again.

'You know it's my Sunday with my mates,' Adam replied.

'Go if you want,' Zack nudged.

Adam flashed Zack a "mind your own business" look and then he turned back to Cadence. 'I only see them once a week, I see you every day.'

'Sorry, did you say VIB?' Jenny queried.

'No, VIP,' Cadence replied with confusion. 'Everyone

who is anyone is going to be there.' She turned back to Adam. 'Are you sure I can't tempt you, baby?'

'You know I'm not interested in all that celebrity schmoozing,' Adam said.

'You used to come out with me,' she said, pouting in a rather melodramatic way.

'Look!' Jenny said, pointing to the TV screen nearby them. 'Hamilton's just overtaken Vettel!'

All of them stared at the screen for a moment, but Cadence looked away again within seconds. She stared at Adam with her pouty lips, but he was now transfixed on the Formula One race before them.

'Just two laps to go,' he said. 'Come on Hamilton, keep the lead.'

'There was us thinking this was a boring race,' Jenny grinned.

Cadence sighed loudly so they could all hear, but not one pair of eyes moved from the screen. Then a few minutes later, as Hamilton was first to pass the chequered flag, Adam punched the air.

'Yes, that puts him ahead of Vettel,' Jenny said.

'Only by a few points, but we'll take it,' Adam replied. 'The perfect way to finish before the summer break.'

'As I was saying,' Cadence said, kissing Adam again to get his attention. 'We never go out together anymore. I miss those times.'

Adam sighed. 'What if I take you out for dinner tomorrow night? How about that?'

Cadence thought for a second, then she said, 'Okay, but I'm choosing where.'

'Anywhere that's going to make you happy.'

Cadence kissed Adam a final time before standing up in one easy motion. 'I'll have a think. Enjoy the rest of your afternoon. I'll be staying in my apartment tonight so don't wait up.' Then she glanced across at Zack and Jenny and muttered, 'See you.'

As she strutted out, all three of them watched her go.

Adam looked irritated, Jenny looked jealous and Zack was sporting an inane grin.

'You really are the luckiest man alive,' Zack said to Adam. 'Why have you not married her yet? She's clearly crazy about you.'

'I don't know,' Adam shrugged.

'Girls like that don't wait around forever, you know,' Zack added. 'Don't leave it too long and then miss out altogether, that's all I'm saying.'

'Are you going to propose?' Jenny pushed.

'Can we just drop it?' Adam snapped.

Suddenly a bulky man tripped up next to them, just about rescuing himself from hitting the floor.

'Whose bag is this?' he demanded to know as he regained his composure.

All three of them looked to the floor to see Zack's backpack wrapped awkwardly around the man's left foot.

'Sorry,' Zack said, very meekly.

'You made me spill my beer.'

'Sorry,' he replied again, ever so quietly.

'What are you going to do about it?' the man demanded.

Zack, with visibly shaking hands, pulled his wallet out of his pocket. 'Here you go,' he said, handing the man a twenty pound note. 'Have a few on me, to say how sorry I am.'

'Zack!' Adam warned with a disapproving look.

'What? He lost half his pint.'

'He'd drunk half his pint!' Adam argued, turning his stern face towards the man.

'Have you got a problem, mate?' the man said, his six foot body glaring down on Adam.

'It was me that left the bag on the floor and I know full well you spilt about three drops of that drink. I can see it's embarrassing but don't take the piss.'

The man scrunched up Zack's twenty pound note and shoved it deep in his jeans pocket, then turned on his heels, back towards the bar.

'Why did you give him that money?' Adam asked Zack.

'He spilt his drink.'

'He was trying it on.'

'He was the size of a house!'

'You know this would make a great story for our comic,' Jenny interjected. Both Adam and Zack stared at her with bewilderment. 'Poor, shy Zack gets bullied by an enormous oaf, who then goes on to steal his money. Empathy Man would feel your pain, Zack. He'd come running in and he'd clobber that oaf right across the face.'

'What, with his huge muscly arms?' Adam gibed.

'No, he's cleverer than that,' Zack argued. 'He'd punish the man by making sure he kept falling over all night, so he'd end up barely having a sip of his beer, pint after pint after pint. Empathy Man's all about the lessons.'

'He sounds more exciting by the second,' Adam tutted sarcastically.

'I bet you could use his help,' Jenny said, nudging Adam on the arm.

Adam thought quietly for a second, sipping at his lager.

'Well, I wouldn't say no to his help,' Zack said.

'Nor me,' Jenny agreed.

For a few moments, none of them said a word. They all just finished their drinks, pondering on what Empathy Man could do for them.

Then Zack said, 'I know it's my round, but will you go Ad? The big oaf's still over there.'

Adam rolled his eyes, then he put out his hand to reject Zack's offering of two ten pound notes. 'I'll get the next one. You've bought enough drinks today already. Even if they weren't for us.'

QUESTIONING JENNY

The next night Jenny was waiting in the centre of Miloworth, a small town about twenty miles north of London.

She'd arrived early and was patiently standing by the statue that stood firmly at the top of the high street. She always had a habit of arriving early on dates. It wasn't a deliberate decision, but no matter how many dates she went on, she found herself jittery with nerves and she ended up leaving her flat far too soon to try and get it over with.

Jenny was a shy girl who had never enjoyed meeting new people, so online dating had been big leap for her. She'd first decided to tackle the online world a few months before and, after a few sleepless nights panicking over whether she could actually meet a stranger all on her own, it had fast become a regular feature in her life. This was her seventeenth date, and her fourth just in the past two weeks.

She'd told all her friends that she was having the time of her life. She'd had multiple free dinners and plenty of drinks. But the truth was far different and Jenny had struggled immensely over the past few months. It was more about persevering to compensate for other issues in her life than actually enjoying what she was doing.

It was bang on eight o'clock and her date still hadn't turned up. Okay, so he wasn't even a minute late, but Jenny was getting fidgety. She exhaled sharply as she went through her plan of how long she'd wait for. She'd decided that he clearly wasn't going to show up.

It was three minutes later when she saw a man striding across the road towards her, and she recognised him straight away. At least he looked like his picture. That hadn't always been the case.

He had a confident walk, which was good, and he seemed quite neat and tidy, which Jenny always liked. And thankfully he was tall. Jenny was five foot six and she liked a man who was at least four inches taller than her. She didn't wear heels often but when she did she wanted to make sure that she would never tower above her date. That was very important. He was ticking lots of boxes so far.

'Hi, Jennifer is it?' he asked, reaching out his hand to shake. She always hated the first bit. Some went to hug her, a couple had given her a kiss on the cheek, most just smiled or waved, but this was the second man that had shaken her hand. This was far too formal for Jenny's liking.

'Hi, yes, you must be Elliot?' she said, shaking his hand in return like they were in some sort of business negotiation.

'You want to get a drink?' he asked.

'Sounds great.'

She walked beside him as they headed towards the pubs, which were luckily at their end of the high street. 'Have you had far to travel?' she asked.

'No,' he replied. 'I just live in the next town. Taxi took about five minutes. What about you?'

'I walked here. I only live a few roads away.'

'A proper local girl, then,' he noted.

They headed into The World's End, one of the more traditional pubs in town, and walked straight up to the bar.

'What do you fancy?' Elliot asked with a pleasant smile.

'Would you mind if I had half a Carlsberg, please?' she replied. Jenny had always been a pint drinking girl. Lager was her favourite tipple and she'd found it far more cost effective to go for the whole pint. But she'd never yet been able to bring herself to ask for a pint on any of her dates. She was too worried about what the reaction would be.

'You know that's just what I fancy too,' he said, turning to the barman to order a pint for himself and a measly half for Jenny, as requested.

Drinks in hand, they took a seat towards the back. Being a Monday, it was quite quiet. There was just one young group nearby the bar that Jenny surmised must have been students, but other than that they really did have their pick of the place.

'So, do you like Jen, Jenny, Jennifer?' Elliot asked the second they were sat down.

'Jenny. I've always been a Jenny.'

'Well, nice to meet you Jenny,' he said, clinking his glass against hers. They both took a sip and then there was a momentary pause.

'Tell me Jenny,' Elliot finally said, 'what do you do for a living?'

'I'm a Graphic Designer. I work at a little Marketing Agency just down the road from here. I've always loved art and I guess I'm quite creative, so I decided to study Graphic Design at university and I've been doing it ever since. What about yourself?'

'I'm an HR Assistant.'

'Really? What does that entail then?' she asked.

'What's your favourite colour?' Elliot suddenly said, much to Jenny's confusion.

'What?' she asked, not sure if she'd heard correctly. That was a severe change of subject.

'What's your favourite colour? Is it pink?' he asked,

pointing to the streak in Jenny's hair and then her fuchsia nail varnish.

'Actually, I like all colours. I think a rainbow is far more enjoyable than settling for one individual tone. But what about you? What's your favourite colour?'

'It's black. What do you like to read?'

Again, Jenny was silenced for a moment by another swerve in the conversation. She took a sip of her drink and then smiled as nicely as she could. 'I like comic books,' she replied, and then she waited for the comments.

This normally started a barrage of questions, such as 'Who's your favourite character?' or 'Did you like it as a kid or just as an adult?' and Jenny sat poised for whatever was coming her way. Comic books were her favourite subject in the world and it was always the highlight of her dates when the topic came up.

'What sort of music do you like?' was the next thing Elliot said, though.

Jenny found herself edging slightly to the side so she could see his hands. Did he have a list of questions that he was ticking off? This was most bizarre.

'Do you go on a lot of dates?' she asked.

'No. I only took the plunge online a few days ago. You're my first.'

Figures, Jenny thought to herself. Then she said, 'Superman's my favourite comic book character.' She was hoping he might get the hint that it was okay to have one conversation at a time. 'I've loved him since I first saw Christopher Reeve when I was kid. Don't you think he's just the best?'

'Who's Christopher Reeve?' he asked.

Jenny felt punched in the stomach. 'The man who played Superman in the films from the eighties. Well, technically the first one was 1978.'

'Oh yeah, I remember. I saw that once. Anyway, I asked what sort of music you like.'

Jenny sighed. She could see very clearly how the night

was going to pan out and he was losing points by the second. But she didn't want to make a scene so she obediently answered his question. 'Dance music, I suppose. What about you?'

'Yeah, I like dance music too.'

Jenny screwed her face up. Was he serious?

'What hobbies do you have?' he then asked.

Jenny fought the urge to roll her eyes. This was getting seriously boring. She couldn't resist the words that came out of her mouth. 'I like to read comic books while listening to dance music and watching Superman films.' She hoped it might at least make him smile.

But, with a completely straight face, all he said was, 'Sounds fun.' Then he went straight into, 'So what's your favourite film?'

'Tell me something about you. Tell me a story,' she said, desperate to get him off his pre-prepared list of questions. Maybe his mum had helped him. His profile said he was twenty-six, the same age as Jenny, but he seemed far younger.

'If you can just excuse me for a second, I actually need the toilet,' he said, diminishing any hope Jenny had of boosting the date to... well boring would be an improvement at this rate.

As he headed off to the loo, she grabbed her phone out of her bag.

Her heart started to flutter as she saw she had a text from Adam. Even though they'd been friends for five years, he had the most intoxicating effect on her.

Jenny had gone to school with Adam's younger sister, Lizzy, but it wasn't until Lizzy's twenty-first birthday party that Jenny had first officially met him.

Adam and Lizzy's parents had hosted a barbecue in their garden to celebrate their daughter's milestone. Jenny remembered vividly how another school friend had taken over cooking the burgers. He'd been showing off that he was a master of food and everyone was going to eat the burgers in the way that he liked them. He'd been incredibly annoying.

This lad was at his peak of arrogance when Adam arrived. Adam had been instantly unimpressed with this egotistical display, stating 'with great power comes great responsibility, mate, so you better make sure you don't give anyone food poisoning,' and Jenny had burst out laughing. No one else had appreciated the Spider-Man reference, but she'd loved it and that was that.

Within the hour they'd started debating who would win in a fight: Superman or Spider-Man, and then they didn't stop chatting all night. Jenny had never felt so comfortable with anyone in all her life.

After the barbecue, a whole group of them had decided to go clubbing and, much to Lizzy's surprise and Jenny's delight, Adam had joined them. They'd drank together, laughed together and danced together; in fact they were virtually inseparable all night. Then it was finally in the taxi back to Miloworth that Adam and Jenny first swapped numbers, promising to go to Comic Con together; which they did just a few months later. And they've gone every year since.

From that moment, Jenny hadn't been able to stop thinking about Adam, and even five years on she still couldn't get him out of her head. He was gorgeous, full of confidence and they had absolutely loads in common. They were as close as two friends could possibly be. But that was where it ended.

Because Adam had Cadence in his life. Perfect Cadence, the model. How on earth was Jenny supposed to compete with that? And not just a stunningly gorgeous model, but one with brains too, who'd gained a degree in Business Studies. So even when her good looks disappeared she still wouldn't fade away like a decomposing mushroom, she'd thrive like some sort of shark, forever snapping away at Jenny's potential happiness.

Cadence had been away working on the night of Lizzy's barbecue and it had been a good few days before Jenny had learned about Adam's relationship. That had been one of the saddest moments of Jenny's life.

Jenny always called Cadence "the bitch" in her mind. She wanted it to be true - she wanted to hate her – but, in reality, Cadence was actually really nice. She was very generous, always gracious and could be extremely thoughtful.

What a bitch.

All in all, Jenny believed she had no hope with Adam. In fact, she thought it was a miracle that he even knew she existed at all. But that still didn't stop Jenny planning her whole life around him.

She opened up the text message to see what it said. He'd so often text her when she was on a date, checking that she was okay. It was really sweet. He was such a nice man.

How's the date going? Hope it's better than the last one.

Jenny cast her mind back to her date last Friday with Jeff; the man who groaned about absolutely everything. The menu was too small, the venue was too noisy, the food was too hot, the coffee was too cold, the blue of Jenny's nail varnish was too bright. She'd wanted to scream. When he'd suggested that they go for drinks after the meal, she couldn't have come up with an excuse fast enough.

Then he'd had the nerve to text her on Saturday morning to say what a lovely night he'd had. Jenny certainly had no intention of texting him back.

Jenny considered her response to Adam. Even when she'd been having a good date, she'd not told him. She couldn't resist looking like she was truly single, just in case a miracle happened. What if Cadence was to fall off an unusually high catwalk and splatter tragically to an untimely death? Jenny would need be there to pick up the pieces, but she couldn't do that with a boyfriend hanging around.

Although what if Adam proposed soon? Six years: he and Cadence had been together for six years. Jenny couldn't see them ever breaking up. Everybody in the world loved Cadence. Even Jenny couldn't deny that he'd be crazy to give her up.

The bitch.

Jenny concentrated again on her phone. She had to text him back quickly, before Elliot reappeared. Although he had been quite a long time in the toilet. Maybe he'd escaped through the bathroom window? Without even meaning to, Jenny found herself crossing her fingers.

Tonight I met a man going for the record of how many questions he can ask me in one hour. He's doing well! I, on the other hand, am not. Maybe one day I'll have a date that's not a disaster. Hope you're enjoying your dinner date? xx

Jenny pressed send and then she waited. She had to admit that she was more excited by the idea of receiving Adam's reply than seeing Elliot again. But that wasn't fair on Elliot, really. No matter who else was there, Adam was always Jenny's top priority.

Her phone suddenly beeped again. He'd replied!

I've just contacted Guinness, they're sending round a record adjudicator now. You might as well make it a night to remember. I wish him the best of luck!

Jenny spluttered with laughter. She loved the idea of an official person standing over them, marking a tally for every boring question that Elliot could reel off. They'd state the rules clearly that Jenny had to provide a full and proper answer. There would be no cheating. Then it would get really tense at the fifty-eight minute mark when he had eleven more questions to fit in, but would there be time?

The smile was suddenly wiped from her face when Elliot waddled back to the table. He was absolutely soaking wet.

'What happened?' she asked, not sure what to do.

'The tap exploded. I've never seen anything like it.'

'Have you told someone?'

'I've let the barman know. It's pretty flooded in there.'

Jenny watched as water pooled on the floor around him. She couldn't imagine how anyone could get that wet from just a tap.

'I'm really sorry but I'm going to go,' he said. Jenny couldn't be sure if he was crying. He could have had floods of tears and she wouldn't have been able to tell the difference.

'Of course,' she said, standing up.

'No, you stay. Finish our drinks,' he said.

Jenny looked to the barely touched pint and a half in front of her. It did seem like a waste to leave them.

'Are you sure?' she asked.

'Let's do it again soon,' he said. 'There's so much more I want to learn about you.'

Jenny fought the urge to laugh. She knew she'd most definitely not be seeing him again, but she could never tell the truth to her dates' faces. 'Sounds great,' she said. 'I hope you dry off soon.'

With that he waddled away, leaving a small brook trailing behind him, and Jenny was left sitting on her own.

JENNY'S PINT

Jenny sighed. She'd had worse dates. She'd finally managed to get a pint out of a date and she didn't have to try and avoid a goodnight kiss. So actually, when she thought about it, the night had ended on a high.

She looked down at her phone that she was still gripping in her hand. At least it seemed Adam was up for chatting tonight. Maybe he and Cadence had gone for an early dinner and he was now at home again, being forced to watch a programme about fashion.

She decided to text him back. She knew there was no way she was going to admit that she was sitting alone, though. As much as she didn't want Adam to think that she was out on the date of her dreams, she also didn't want to look like a complete loser. It was only half past eight. Of all the dates she'd had, this had definitely been the shortest.

The Guinness adjudicator has just arrived. It's getting exciting! xx

She knocked back the rest of her half pint and waited patiently for a reply.

'Excuse me, sorry, but we're going to be closing soon,' a man said.

'Already? Oh okay, I won't be long.'

'It was your friend that got soaked in the toilet, wasn't it?'

'Yeah. What happened?'

'I have no idea. I'm really sorry. He said the tap exploded and the whole bathroom is now like a swimming pool, but I can't find a single thing wrong with any of the fittings. Everything seems to be working fine as far as I can tell. But I'm still going to have to close as I can't take the risk of it happening to anyone else.'

Jenny glanced around. She was now the only customer left. It really was a quiet Monday.

'But finish your drink. Please.'

'Thanks,' she smiled, suddenly feeling the pressure to down her drinks quickly.

Her phone beeped with a new message and her heart started to race.

Will you be named as the joint record holder or will it just be your date?

She reconsidered telling Adam that Elliot had gone. Maybe he might give her some sympathy. What if he was to come and join her, to help drown her sorrows?

She could be crying on his shoulder, and then he'd look down to see her sad face. She'd mutter something about how Elliot had broken her heart and Adam would see her in a whole different light. He'd focus on her lips, suddenly finding them utterly irresistible, and then he'd kiss her, deeply and passionately. After that he'd be forced to admit his true feelings, declaring that Jenny was actually the love of his life and no longer could he live in such denial.

What was she thinking? He had perfect Cadence. How were Jenny's little lips meant to compare to Cadence's luscious offering? It was like choosing between a beautiful, million pound yacht and a tiny, rotting fishing boat. Adam really couldn't be blamed.

At least she could text him. That was better than nothing.

No, the glory will all be his, but I'm proud to be a part of it. There are crowds around us you know, all egging him on. xx

Jenny looked around the empty pub. The man who had spoken with her had just locked the front door. It really was closing time.

She picked up Elliot's pint and started to sip at it. The man began to wipe the table next to her and she found herself transfixed by his efficient cleaning skills. She noted with a smirk how his cleaning was far more entertaining than her date had been.

'Was it your boyfriend?' he asked, looking across at her. 'If you don't mind me asking?'

He was maybe in his early thirties and quite good looking, with longish floppy brown hair and bright green eyes. He wasn't in the usual uniform, he was dressed in a smart shirt and grey trousers. Jenny made the guess he was management.

'Just a date,' she replied.

'Not a first date?' he said with concern.

Jenny hesitated. Did she really want to tell this stranger just how disastrous her love life was? The alcohol must have already gone to her head as she suddenly found herself saying, 'Sadly so.'

'Oh, I'm really sorry. What a way to cut it short. I hope you get to meet up again soon.'

Jenny was shaking her head before she could even think about it.

'Not so keen?' the man asked.

She couldn't believe she was chatting away to him, but he felt really easy to talk to. 'Not the one for me. Maybe it was a lucky escape.'

The man studied her for a second. Then he said, 'Do you fancy some company while you finish up? There's not much else for me to do here. The pub's closed.'

Jenny hadn't expected this, but he seemed like a nice man. It was certainly a better idea than her sitting on her own. 'Okay.'

'I'll just get myself a drink. Can I get you another one too?'

'A pint?'

'What else?'

Jenny smiled. 'That would be really nice of you, thank you.' She knew she had a virtual full pint still to go, but she also quite liked the idea of delaying the end of her night.

The man headed behind the bar just as a fresh message beeped on Jenny's phone.

Is it looking like he'll do it? I have my fingers crossed.

Jenny couldn't resist typing something back as quickly as possible before her new friend came to join her.

We're on question 304 now and he needs 501 to break the record. He can still do it, there's still time! xx

'I really am sorry about soaking your date,' the man said as he sat down opposite Jenny, presenting two full pints of lager.

'You didn't do anything.'

'I still can't figure out what happened. To make matters worse, though, the hand dryer suddenly stopped working and we couldn't find toilet paper anywhere. Nor any of that blue roll we use. It's like everything just vanished.'

'So he couldn't dry himself at all?'

'No, but he was really great about it. He seemed like a nice bloke. He just mumbled something about drying off on the way home. I suppose it is a warm night.'

Just as the man said those words, they heard what

sounded like a crash of thunder.

'That wasn't...?' Jenny headed to the window to take a look. 'Oh my God, the heavens have opened. It's pouring down! He's going to get... even more soaked.'

She couldn't help but laugh. Talk about bad luck. She walked back to the man, trying very hard to stifle her giggle.

'Don't think I'm a horrible person,' she said, biting her lip.

'It is quite funny,' the man said, joining her in a chuckle. 'He did look a right mess. Are you sure I haven't ruined your chances with Mr Perfect?'

'No. He was more like Mr Boring.'

'Or Mr Wet!' The pair of them creased up laughing again when Jenny's phone beeped back a message. She couldn't stop herself instantly looking at it.

I hope you're giving good answers. None of this yes and no crap, he needs detail!

'Is that him?' the man asked.

'No,' Jenny said, not able to wipe the "Adam's just contacted me" smile off her face. 'It's just a friend checking up on me. You never know with these dates, there's always the risk of meeting an axe murderer.'

'Very true. I tried it once, but it wasn't for me. It cut too much into my free time.'

Jenny rolled her eyes. 'Very funny. I'll just text him quickly back if that's okay? Report all is good.'

'Sure.'

I've been told to keep my answers down to no more than 10 words to ensure the time is optimised. This record breaking stuff is hard work! xx

'I've seen you around before,' the man said.

'Have you?' Jenny asked. Then she felt bad as she

couldn't remember ever seeing this man before in her life.

'I always play a little game with myself as to what colour streak you'll have in your hair the next time I see you.'

Jenny instinctively reached for her pink patch. 'It keeps life interesting,' she shrugged.

'I love it. You certainly brighten up Miloworth.'

Jenny smiled coyly. 'Do you live locally?'

'You could say that. I live upstairs.'

'Really?' She then felt even worse that she'd not noticed him before. 'Do you own this place?'

'No, I just manage it. The flat was part of the deal.'

'I'm done in there now!' a voice suddenly called from near the toilets. Jenny looked over to see a young lad standing there with a mop and bucket.

'Thanks Harrison. You can head off now. I'll pay you for the night, though. You've done a good job.'

'All right, thanks Nathan.'

'Is that your name? Nathan?' Jenny asked.

'Yes, sorry I should have said.'

'I'm Jenny.'

'Lovely to officially meet you, Jenny.'

'Likewise, Nathan.'

Jenny's phone beeped again and she grabbed it quickly.

If anyone is up for the challenge, I know you are!

'Good news?' Nathan asked, noticing Jenny's instant smile.

'No, he's just winding me up.'

'Did you tell him about Mr Wet?'

Jenny hesitated. 'Yes. I told him I'll be off home in a minute.'

'Oh right.' Nathan looked disappointed at this.

'Don't you want to get off? I must be stopping you from doing something?'

'Going home alone, like every night. I'd prefer the

company if it's all right with you?'

'Oh. Well, okay. Sounds good!' Jenny lifted her pint and clinked it against Nathan's. 'I'll just text him back to say I'm having a nice night.'

The press have turned up now. I might be on the BBC later! This is quite an unexpected night out. xx

'Do you like tequila?' Nathan asked.

'You can't beat a tequila slammer on a Monday night!' Jenny grinned.

'You're on!'

Nathan headed over to the bar, and Jenny followed him. She took a seat on a stool and watched as Nathan artfully filled up two shot glasses with a clear liquid.

'This is my favourite,' he said, although she couldn't see the name on the bottle. 'It's got a beautiful taste to it.'

'I'm game for anything.'

He placed one of the glasses in front of her before reaching in the corner and grabbing a salt pot and then two pieces of lemon.

'What shall we drink to?' he asked.

'To new friends,' Jenny replied. Then they clinked glasses before licking the salt, downing the liquid and finally sucking the lemon, all in the space of about five seconds.

Jenny shook her head as the sourness of the lemon curled up her tongue.

Her phone beeped again and she grabbed it from her pocket.

I've just recorded the news, hope to see you on the telly! Let me know how it all turns out. Got to go now, Cadence wants an early night.

All of a sudden a rage of jealousy exploded from Jenny's heart. It was one thing knowing the bitch was in his life, but a whole different thing having to hear about their sexual exploits.

She imagined Cadence being this fantastic lover that was so flexible, any position on earth was possible; the crazier the better. Adam probably couldn't get enough of it. Jenny was suddenly fixated by the idea that they'd done it in every room, five times a night, with Cadence constantly bringing all of Adam's fantasies to life.

What a bitch.

Then Jenny felt sad. She'd seen Adam without his top on just once at a football match a couple of years ago. She'd nearly fallen over. He'd got a far sexier body than even her own imagination had mustered up. But it was only Cadence who ever got to enjoy it.

Well, two could play at that game!

'You want another one?' Nathan asked, grabbing the glass before her.

'Do you want to go up to your place?' she said, very directly.

'What?'

'We both need the company. We're both free and single.'

He looked at her dubiously. 'Do you mean for a drink?'

'No, I mean for sex. Do you want to have sex?'

Jenny felt so soured with jealousy that she really wasn't thinking anymore. In all the dates she'd had recently, she'd only slept with one of them. He'd seemed a nice man and they'd gone out three times before she'd invited him back to her place. And then after that night he'd stopped texting her.

Not that she'd really minded. That could have been the weekend that the bitch slipped on spilt champagne at one of her snotty VIP events. It would be tragic how no one would notice her sprawled out on the floor, as her tiny little waist and wafer-thin legs would be far too small for anyone to feel beneath their feet. After a night of being trampled on, her injuries would be so severe that the only reasonable course of action would be to put her down, ending her traumatic misery. Adam would be so sad. Such a shame. It was important that Jenny kept herself available as a shoulder to cry on, just in case.

'If you want,' Nathan shrugged, although Jenny could tell he was hiding a huge grin that was desperate to smother his face. She could almost hear him chanting to himself *play it cool, play it cool.*

That was sweet. He seemed sweet.

It wasn't just Adam who would be having sex tonight!

JENNY AND HER COCKTAIL

For the hundredth time that night, Jenny glanced at the digital alarm clock on the bedside table next to her. It was just after six. Surely it was finally a reasonable time for her to make her escape?

She hadn't slept at all. She'd spent all night fretting about how she could have sex with a man that she barely knew. Twice. What had she been thinking? How on earth had she ended up in this situation?

Suddenly she jumped. She turned around, sure she had seen someone standing by the window in the corner of her eye. But no one was there.

'Are you okay,' Nathan asked, rolling over to hug her. Her startled jump must have woken him up.

'Yeah, I'm fine. I was just dreaming.'

'A nice dream, I hope?' he asked. Jenny just shrugged in reply. How could she dream if all she'd done all night was stare at the clock, waiting to leave without it looking like she really wanted to leave? No wonder she was seeing things.

He leaned in and kissed her gently, and Jenny noticed a tickle of joy across her body as his lips met hers.

She relaxed in his arms for a moment. He was a nice

man, and he certainly had a nice body. The sex had actually been very good. They definitely had chemistry. But she couldn't shake a fretful niggle about it all deep inside.

'I'd better get going,' she said, freeing herself from his embrace. 'Work calls.'

'I enjoyed last night,' he said with a smile. It was so warm and genuine, Jenny couldn't help but smile in return.

'Yeah, me too.'

'It was a bit unexpected, but certainly well received,' he chuckled.

She sat on the edge of the bed and suddenly felt utterly exposed. Even though he'd seen all of her naked body in quite a lot of detail the night before, she couldn't help the shyness that now closed in on her.

She located her clothes on the floor of the small room and she quickly darted to get them, ensuring that her bareness was kept to a minimum.

'Do you have time for breakfast?' he asked, sitting up.

'No, I'd better shoot off,' Jenny said, struggling to get her jeans on at speed. 'But thank you.'

'I could just make you a coffee.'

'No, it's fine. You get back to sleep. I'll let myself out.'

'Are you okay?' he asked as the smile dropped from his face. He seemed concerned.

Jenny didn't know what to say. The honest truth was that she didn't know how she felt. It had been really good, but she also felt guilty.

'I just hate mornings,' she said, evading the question. 'I'd better dash.' Then that was exactly what she did, escaping from his flat as quickly as she could.

For the rest of the day, Jenny tried not to think about her sudden, unexpected one night stand, but her tired mind wouldn't let it go.

She felt stupid, but not because of Nathan. He'd been lovely. He'd been a very caring man. All through the night he'd constantly made sure she was okay, and he certainly hadn't left her wanting more. No, she felt stupid because of her motivation.

Sleeping with a man to make another man jealous, who was never even going to find out about it anyway, had been a huge wake up call for Jenny. She'd acted incredibly irresponsibly. She barely even knew this Nathan. What if he had been an axe murderer? Where would she be then? Probably buried in a field somewhere with her body never to be found again, and that would just serve her right. She'd certainly have no one to blame then but her stupid self. Except, of course, Nathan the axe murderer, but absolutely no one else could be blamed.

She arrived home from work that Tuesday night exhausted. The first thing she did was pop two pieces of bread in the toaster before grabbing the squeezy cheese from the fridge. It was self-pity, comfort food time.

She threw on her pyjamas and then she ate copious amounts of cheese on toast in bed while watching trashy TV, only getting up to place more bread in the toaster.

By half past eight her eyes were drooping but her brain wouldn't switch off. Her overthinking of the night before had escalated her one night stand with a pleasant man, who did not turn out to be an axe murderer, into a brush with death because he actually could have been an axe murderer and it was just by pure luck that he wasn't.

She was so annoyed with herself and her reckless behaviour that she didn't sleep well again on Tuesday night, and by the time Wednesday morning came around she'd made the decision that her life had to change. Facing death head on had made her re-evaluate what was important.

She knew it was time to stop her silly fantasy. She had to accept that Adam was with Cadence and there was nothing she could do about it. He was in love. They were going to get married, have perfectly beautiful children and live happily ever after. It certainly didn't matter who Jenny was having sex with: axe murderer or no axe murderer.

Jenny was sick of the heartache of seeing Cadence all

loved up with Adam and she knew she had to start facing the inevitable. It terrified her to consider it, but before long, one Sunday afternoon, Adam would be announcing that he and the bitch were getting married. What was she going to say? She'd have to pretend to be happy. Surely it would be a whole lot easier if Jenny actually was happy.

She spent all of Wednesday telling herself over and over that her obsession with Adam had to end and it finally gave her some determination. The second she got home that night she opened her laptop up and she approached her online dating with a fresh pair of eyes.

As she scanned through the men she'd been chatting to, it became instantly obvious to her that she'd not really taken her online experience that seriously. Her criteria had been "as long as they're not too weird", and that was about it. Her standards had clearly been very low. No wonder she'd had so many crap dates.

With a whole new perspective, Jenny started to narrow down her selection process. She thought about what she actually wanted in a partner, rather than just someone to distract her until Adam came to his senses.

She'd only ever originally decided to try online dating after Adam had suggested it. He'd seemed concerned that she was in a permanent state of singledom. It was as if he'd hinted that there might be something wrong with her and the last thing she wanted was for him to start questioning why she appeared to be so anti-men. How could she explain that it wasn't that she didn't want a boyfriend per se, it was more that the only one she wanted was attached to a bitch. She was so in love with Adam that nobody else ever seemed to compare.

But, looking at her online dating decisions, it also seemed that she'd been avoiding anyone who may compare and she'd been choosing dates with men who were far from boyfriend material. At least being honest with herself was the first step to sorting the problem out.

Yes, Adam was always going to be the benchmark, but

at least if she tried to find someone who was just as good, she would finally have a chance at happiness.

As she started to dismiss men that didn't meet her new high standards, the whole experience became more enjoyable. Then, just a few hours later, she found herself chatting to a man who seemed to tick every box.

On Friday night, Jenny was waiting by the statue in Miloworth for her date. Gary, the box ticking man, worked in marketing, like her, he lived alone, like her, and he seemed clever and ambitious, just what she was looking for. This actually had potential, and so far they'd exchanged loads of fun, interesting messages.

Everything about this date was different. For starters, Jenny had been so excited about it, she'd actually left later than planned and she'd only arrived with about three minutes to spare. She'd also not told anyone that she was meeting him, which she never did. She normally told Adam everything about her dating life, but she didn't want to anymore. It was time that she left him out of it. She wasn't doing it for him now, she was doing it for herself, and so she wanted to make the judgement call all on her own.

It was now exactly half past seven and Jenny was looking in every direction to see if she could spot wonderful sounding Gary. The town was bustling with all the weekend party-goers and it made it difficult to pinpoint a man that she only had one picture of.

All that was going through her head was how much she wanted to finally meet a nice man; someone who would actually be there for her. She was sick of being single Jenny who was pinning all her hopes on a taken man. It was time for her to meet a man all of her own and she made a little wish to herself that tonight would be the night.

'Are you Jenny?' she suddenly heard behind her.

She turned around to see a tall, stocky man, who looked almost like his picture. He wasn't quite as handsome as she'd expected, but he still wasn't bad. 'Yes. Gary is it?'

He took a step back and very obviously looked her up and down. Then he grinned wildly. 'Wow, you're looking hot tonight, mama!'

She suddenly felt very coy. She had to check quickly that she hadn't accidentally put on her Halloween PVC cat suit with the way he was drooling over her. No, she was definitely wearing her denim skirt and sparkly top. It really didn't warrant the reaction, but it was flattering nevertheless.

'I've booked us a table at the Chinese, if that's okay?' he said.

Jenny hesitated. She'd already eaten. They'd talked about keeping it casual. Could she really eat two meals in one night? Also, what if she didn't like Chinese? What if she'd had Chinese the night before and didn't want it two nights on the trot? Why couldn't he ask her before making bookings! This wasn't exactly how she saw the night going.

'That's great,' she said, telling herself to get a grip. It was kind of him to put some thought into it. That was what mattered.

'Yeah, my mate works there,' he said. 'He can get us fifty percent off, so you can have whatever you like. Sound good?'

Jenny just nodded and smiled. She pushed the disappointment deep down inside of her. He was thrifty and that was a good asset. She had to focus on the positives.

'The table's booked for eight-thirty but I thought we could grab a cocktail first. What do you reckon?'

'Sounds great,' Jenny grinned. She wasn't really a cocktail drinker but it was a very kind idea. He was clearly making a big effort and that was far more important than the fact that she was hugely disappointed by absolutely everything so far.

He grabbed her hand and led her up the high street.

Jenny scanned her brain to think where they could be going. She couldn't recall any places in Miloworth that served cocktails. Maybe, after all these years, there was somewhere she didn't know about. Maybe he was leading her to a hidden gem!

No, instead he led her up to the top of the high street to where a lone pub sat. It was The Station, the only pub nearby the train station, and one of the roughest pubs in town. It certainly wasn't known for its cocktails, it was more known for its bar brawls and that stabbing six months ago. Oh well, maybe it had recently changed hands and had massively improved.

He led her in and they headed straight to the bar. It smelt like stale beer and the place was just plain tatty. Jenny also quickly spotted that she was the only female in there. She unconsciously grabbed Gary's hand tighter, having never felt more uncomfortable.

They reached the sticky bar area and Gary signalled to a man, who was roughly the same age as him.

'Mate!' the barman said, approaching Gary. Then they did this weird handshake thing. They obviously knew each other very well.

'What do you want then?' Gary asked, turning to Jenny.

'Are we still having cocktails?' she replied, totally confused.

'Of course.'

'Do they serve cocktails in here?'

'Baz will do whatever you want him to. Eh eh, within reason!' Both the men laughed but something about it made Jenny's skin crawl.

'Is there a cocktail menu?' she asked.

'Don't be stupid,' Gary replied. 'What sort of place do you think this is? No, you just tell Baz what cocktail you want and he'll do it for you. All right?'

Suddenly Jenny felt terrible pressure. She really wasn't a cocktail drinker. She liked lager, and the occasional glass of wine with food. The only time she'd ever had a cocktail was on her friend's hen do.

Then she tried to remember what they'd had. She'd liked it, so it was a safe option. Then the name of it popped into her head. 'Can I have a Cosmopolitan, please?'

'Of course. Anything you want. What's in it?'

Jenny panicked. She hadn't got a clue. It was a pink or red colour, that's all she could remember.

'I'm not sure,' she shrugged.

'Well if you want the bloody cocktail, you need to tell Baz what's in it,' Gary virtually shouted. 'Who do you think he is, Tom Cruise?'

Jenny knew then and there that she should just walk away. He really wasn't acting like the man she'd expected, and so far the whole experience had not been enjoyable or pleasant. But as the two pairs of eyes glared at her, waiting for her to speak, she felt compelled to carry on.

'Vodka,' she said, desperately trying to recall what had been in the drink she'd had two years before. Surely there had to be vodka in it. Vodka was in everything. She watched as Baz picked up a long glass and put two shots in it.

Then she felt very sure that there was something beginning with C in the drink. She was sure that she'd decided at the time, in her inebriated state, that the reason it was called a Cosmopolitan was because they wanted a trendy word beginning with C to match the alcohol. That made sense.

She scanned her eyes across the bottles at the back of the bar and she saw a drink that began with C. That must be it. 'Courvoisier.'

Without blinking, Baz grabbed the cognac and then he added two shots on top of the vodka.

'What else?' Gary demanded. It had been red. What could make the drink red? 'Come on, Baz hasn't got all night.'

'Blackcurrant juice,' she said, blurting out the first thing that came to mind.

Baz nodded and then poured blackcurrant juice into the mix. It looked totally wrong. It looked too dark.

'And lemonade,' Jenny added, her brain momentarily telling her that the clear liquid of lemonade would brighten it up. But, of course, it didn't.

It was pinker. She was sure it was pinker. She needed something whiter to brighten it up. That made sense. What could she have that was white?

'Come on!' Gary demanded. 'You wanted this cocktail, now you're telling me you don't know what's in it?'

'And milk,' Jenny said, the words coming out before she even had chance to properly think them through.

As the milk was added to the top of the disgusting mix before her, her heart sank.

'Anything else?' Gary asked, not batting an eyelid at her unusual concoction.

'That's all,' she replied, forcing a smile, realising that she had to quit.

Baz grabbed a straw and stirred the blotchy, fizzy, alcoholic nightmare that she was actually going to have to drink. She suddenly doubted that she'd got one single ingredient right.

'I'll have my usual,' Gary said, as Baz slid Jenny's cocktail over to her. She then watched as Baz poured a pint of Stella.

'You're not having a cocktail?' she enquired with envy.

'God no,' he said. 'I don't know how you drink that stuff. It sounds horrible.'

Jenny had to agree, her drink did sound horrible.

'How do you remember what's in it?' he asked as he passed Baz a twenty pound note.

Then the reality of the situation hit Jenny. Baz and Gary didn't drink cocktails. They didn't have a clue. Moreover, they didn't really care. She could have asked for anything. She could have said she wanted a Jen-Vodka-Special with vodka and orange and Baz would have done it for her. Why on earth did she try and actually work out what was in a Cosmopolitan?

Reluctantly, she grabbed her drink and she followed Gary across the uneven floor to a rocky table right at the back; right next to the pool table. She carefully placed her drink down before sitting on what she quickly found to be a very unstable chair.

'I take it this is a favourite place of yours?' she asked, as Gary sat down opposite her.

He shrugged. That was all he did.

'Are you going to drink your drink?' he said, glaring at her. She hadn't touched it yet. 'You asked for it,' he added.

She felt a rush of indignation but it was quickly diffused when she was poked in the back by a pool cue.

'Sorry love,' the man said. 'Do you mind?' She turned around to see that she was right in the way of a man trying to take his shot. She edged herself towards the wall to give him room, then she turned back to Gary, expecting him to suggest that they move to a different table, but he was still glancing between her and her drink.

Knowing she could avoid it no longer, she pinched the straw between her fingers. She put her lips to it and sucked ever so lightly. So light in fact that just a drop of the fruity burn fizzled her tongue.

Gary looked at her expectantly. 'Really nice,' she lied, trying to plan how she was going to get rid of it. Then she looked around in desperation wondering how she was going to get out of this date full stop.

This was Jenny's biggest problem in life: she was utterly useless when it came to conflict. She'd pretty much tell anyone anything if it made her life easier. She should have told Gary that she didn't like cocktails, or she'd never made one before, or the pub was a sticky hole that made her deeply uncomfortable. But honesty like that didn't register with Jenny. She believed far more in going along with it until she was able to escape unnoticed. Even though it meant that unless a miracle happened, she would be stuck on this date all night.

Her lack of confidence and need to please people had caused issues for Jenny on many occasions. Time and time again she'd sat quietly in the corner, unhappy with a situation, but too afraid to speak up. She always just let things play out as if life couldn't be changed, and then she'd go home and feel sorry for herself.

It was only through a broken heart that she'd ever found the inclination to deviate away from her norm. That was the day that Adam announced he was moving in with Cadence. Or rather Cadence announced it as she swooped in to interrupt their Sunday get together.

It had hit Jenny like a brick. She'd been floating along in her foolish fantasy that Adam really wasn't that serious about Cadence and it would surely end soon, and then they'd suddenly got a mortgage together. It didn't get much more serious than that!

As her heart snapped in two that day, Jenny was forced to re-evaluate her life. She'd decided it was time for a change. She was sick of being the nice girl that no one ever took notice of. So she bleached her hair and bought some new outfits and, practically overnight, her life changed.

People started to treat her very differently. Whereas she'd spent years trying to please everyone else, suddenly it seemed that people wanted to please her. It was like they saw her as more confident and edgy, and she had to admit that she felt more confident too. She still avoided conflict like she was running away from zombies, but at least she felt easier in social situations.

She'd never been able to decipher whether the change in her attitude had come from her new exterior or from a determination to overcompensate for her broken heart. Either way, it seemed that the perception of her as a shy girl vanished overnight. And, much more to her delight, her friendship with Adam flourished as well. They'd always been close, but suddenly they were virtually inseparable. From the moment that Jenny had taken herself out of her comfort zone, Adam had seemed far more engaged in her life.

She'd often find herself replaying in her mind that Sunday when she'd first presented her new appearance to Adam. He hadn't said much but he'd played with her hair all afternoon, and she'd loved it. He hadn't been able to take his hands off her. Okay, off her hair, but that was still intimate. Sort of.

Jenny sighed. A few minutes had gone by where neither Jenny nor Gary had spoken and Jenny found herself wishing for that miracle again. She had to get out of this date, but it wasn't like she could just say, "I'm having a crap time, I'm going home." Just the idea of it mortified her. She had to pretend she was having fun, as always. And she knew that if he suggested they meet up again she'd say yes and then just blank his calls and texts afterwards. She found that to be a much better way of handling things.

As she glanced to the window, looking for any sort of miracle, she could have sworn a figure in blue was waving at her. She took a second look, but he was gone.

Suddenly she was poked in the back again, but this time it was hard and the power of the cue thrust her forward. She banged into the already unsteady table and the force of it knocked her drink over.

As the red liquid shot across in Gary's direction, it soaked his white shirt. He went to jump out of his seat, but the instability of it made him stumble and he fell awkwardly to the floor.

As he fell out of view, all Jenny heard was him yelp in pain. She looked around the table to see him grabbing his hand in agony. But his hand wasn't right. It was bent upwards, in a direction it really shouldn't be in.

'You fucking bitch!' he screamed at her. She raced to his side to see if she could help but he blustered at her to get away. Then he yelled, 'Baz, call an ambulance!'

Before Jenny knew it, all their fellow patrons were surrounding them to see what the commotion was.

'Is there anything I can do?' Jenny asked, bending down beside Gary who was still curled up on the floor.

'Get out of my face!' he screamed.

She was very happy to do that. As awful as she felt for him, going to the hospital with him was the last thing she wanted to do.

She grabbed her bag and then stepped over to the bar, pushing past the crowd of onlookers. She could see Baz on the phone, most likely calling the emergency services, and she knew she wasn't needed.

Taking the opportunity to leave, she headed to the door as quickly as she could.

She got outside and took a deep breath. What an unfortunate but lucky escape. Then she felt instantly bad for thinking that. His injury had looked horrific.

She glanced back into the pub, when she was suddenly faced with what looked exactly like Zack's illustration of Empathy Man. It was just for a second. The instant she blinked, the image before her was gone.

Her week must have been more traumatic than she thought.

She headed down the street, deciding it was most definitely time to go home. She grabbed her phone to occupy her mind and she saw she had two texts from Adam. She quickly read them, trying to tell herself that she wasn't excited about hearing from him. But, of course, she was.

19:34

How's your week been? Same old boring one for me. Hope you haven't been too upset after missing out on the world record on Monday.

19:46

My mum says do you want to come to my gran's party next Saturday? It's at the social club in town.

'Jenny,' she suddenly heard. She stopped to look at who had called her name when she saw the warm grin of Nathan approaching her.

'Hi,' she said, unexpectedly happy to see him.

'Are you on your own?' he asked, looking around to see no one else near her.

She shrugged. 'Let's just say it's really not been my week.'

'I hope there's been at least one highlight?' he asked, although she could tell it was more for confirmation than anything else.

'Monday night ended quite well, I suppose,' she smirked, and as she said the words she knew they were true. Seeing Nathan again actually made her forget everything she'd been worrying about all week.

'Where are you off to now?'

'I was just going to go home.'

'Come and have a drink with me,' he said.

'Aren't you working tonight?' she asked, scanning his smart look.

'Yes, I've just been getting some change from next door. But I'm finishing at nine. I could get you a drink for now and then we could get a take-away together after that.'

Jenny looked at his kind eyes. Of all the dates she'd had, he was by far the nicest man she'd met.

'If you're sure?' she asked, but he was already nodding enthusiastically. 'Okay, great.'

She followed him into the pub and she sub-consciously placed her phone back into her bag. She'd not even noticed that she hadn't texted Adam back and, for the first time since Lizzy's barbecue five years before, Adam completely disappeared from her mind.

ADAM AND HIS MUM

Earlier that Friday night, Adam and Cadence had driven around to his parents' house in Miloworth, only about half a mile away from Jenny. Adam had a really good relationship with his family, even though his mum irritated him at times.

His mum had been nagging him all week saying that she hadn't seen him for a while. So knowing that Cadence was due to go out later that evening, Adam had jumped at the chance for a deliberately short visit.

Cadence never minded the family visit. She thought his parents were sweet and they always spent the whole time telling her how great she was. She lapped it up.

He parked outside the semi-detached house and they walked up the drive. He knocked on the door and they were greeted within seconds by a huge beaming smile.

'They're here!' his mum called, presumably to his dad. She gave Adam a huge hug and then she did the same to Cadence. His mum was quite small with naturally curly blonde hair and a very made-up face. She never set foot outside the house without her make-up done to perfection.

'I love what you're wearing,' she said to Cadence.

'Thank you,' Cadence replied, posing in a scarlet lacy

dress that left little to the imagination.

'You look stunning. But then, don't you always. I'm forever saying to Adam what a beautiful girlfriend he's got.'

'She's a model, mum,' Adam said rolling his eyes and stepping into the house. 'It's her job to be beautiful.'

'Oh, you two,' Cadence smiled. 'You'll have me the colour of this dress if you don't stop it. I'm just like any other girl, really.'

'Is that what you're wearing out tonight?' his mum asked as she led them into the kitchen. The kitchen was the largest room in the house and was always immaculate, despite the fact that the fittings were a little dated. It was the place where his mum could always be found, pottering around doing something.

'Yes, it's new,' Cadence replied. 'It was designed especially for me.'

'How lovely! It must be fabulous to have designers wanting to make you clothes.'

'She paid for it,' Adam interjected. 'It's not like we have designers queuing up at the door with tape measures around their necks.'

'Adam, don't be so mean,' his mum said. 'I'm sure you couldn't get Versace or Banana Man or whoever it is to design clothes for you. Whether she asked for it or not, that's beside the point. Well done, Cadence. You should be very proud.'

'Dolce and Gabbana,' Adam corrected. For someone who liked clothes and shoes, his mum was pretty useless when it came to designers.

'Thank you, Patricia,' Cadence said. 'Maybe for your birthday we could get you something designed. What do you think?'

His mum's face lit up with delight. 'Really? Could you arrange that? How amazing would that be!'

'It would be my pleasure. Leave it to me.'

'Did you hear that, Adam? You are lucky to have such

a kind girl in your life.'

'Yeah,' Adam said, pulling his phone out of his pocket to catch up on Twitter.

'So where are you off out to?' his mum asked Cadence as she filled the kettle with water. The kettle was rarely switched off in his parents' house.

'There's a Gala Ball tonight,' Cadence explained. 'I'm being picked up from our house at ten.'

'At ten? That seems quite late.'

'I don't need to be there until eleven. It's on Park Lane.'

'Ooh, very fancy. Did you hear that, Adam? Why aren't you going?'

'It's not my scene,' Adam replied.

'Could Adam not come?' his mum asked Cadence.

'Of course he could. He never wants to, though.'

'Don't you want to go to a Gala Ball, Adam? It sounds like so much fun.'

'It's not even a Gala Ball,' Adam stated, feeling his irritation levels rise. 'It's some fashion awards. But because Cadence isn't nominated for anything, she's skipping the awards and going straight to the after party.'

'Adam!' his mum snapped. 'I'm sure it's not as straight forward as that.'

'Adam's right that I'm skipping the awards dinner,' Cadence explained. 'But it's because of the food. They always give you so much potato and bread; you know, to fill up the plate. It really disagrees with me. Gives me terrible stomach pains.'

'I know exactly what you mean. All that stodge is awful. Especially when you're trying to look all elegant, like you always do.'

'I'm so glad you understand. Adam never gets it.'

'Men never do,' his mum stated, shaking her head.

'Have you heard from Lizzy?' Adam asked, trying to change the subject. He really hated the girly chit-chats that Cadence and his mother always had.

'Yes, just a few days ago. We did that online telephone thing.'

'You mean Skype, mum.'

'Yes, that's it. What about you? I hope you're still speaking with her?'

'You know I do. We Skyped last week,' Adam said.

Lizzy had been living in Australia for the last four years. She'd been given the opportunity to transfer there for work and she'd grabbed it with both hands.

Adam had been over to Sydney to visit her about two years ago and she'd made the trip back last Christmas, but other than that the only time he got to see her was via the webcam on his laptop.

He was very close to his younger sister and he spoke to her at least a couple of times a month.

'She's broken up with that boyfriend of hers. Did she tell you that?' his mum said.

'Yes, but I don't think she's bothered. She said he was boring.'

'I think she's just putting on a brave face.'

'No, I think he was actually boring, mum. She said he decorated his flat and then suggested that they stay in to watch the paint dry.'

'Don't make stuff up!'

'No, seriously. Apparently he said it's fascinating when the colour brightens up as it dries, or some crap like that. She said they had a bottle of wine and tequila shots and it still didn't make it more interesting. So she dumped him.'

'Wasn't he an artist, though? Maybe he was looking at it from a more artistic viewpoint?'

'He puts up shop signs, mum. I suppose someone might call that art. I don't know where she meets them. She's a good looking girl, I can't believe she's not been able to find anyone decent.'

'She is, Lizzy's very pretty,' Cadence said.

'Aww, so kind. Thank you, Cadence. I have very beautiful children... and soon to be daughter-in-law... I hope?'

Adam exhaled sharply. His mum was off with the wedding talk again. He grabbed his phone and headed into the small, cosy living room, leaving Cadence and his mum to bitch about the lack of a ring.

He could feel the anger raging inside of him again and he rubbed his hand through his hair with frustration. He was sure he never used to feel angry all the time, but it was now an everyday occurrence. In fact, over the past few years the moments where he was feeling calm and happy were the ones that stuck out in his mind, so infrequent were they.

His thoughts suddenly turned to Jenny. Most of the happy moments had been with her. She was his best friend and he couldn't imagine his life without her in it. She could always bring a smile to his face and it was their Sunday afternoon get togethers that kept him sane.

Most unusually, he'd barely heard from her all week and he felt the niggle of worry deep inside. She'd sent a quick response to him on Tuesday after he'd asked how the world record attempt had gone, but he'd heard nothing since. It was most unlike her.

He opened up his messages to send her a quick text.

How's your week been? Same old boring one for me. Hope you haven't been too upset after missing out on the world record on Monday.

'Do you want tea, Adam?' his mum called through from the kitchen.

'Nonsense, he'll have a beer with his dad,' his dad said appearing from the staircase. He was a tall man, like Adam, but he had thick grey hair and broad shoulders.

'Hi,' Adam said, standing up.

'How's it going, son?'

'Good. How are you?'

'My knee's been playing up, but otherwise I'm doing all

right. For my age.'

'Do you want tea or not?' his mum said poking her head into the living room.

'I told you, he's having a beer,' his dad replied.

'I've got to drive, dad,' Adam said.

'I'm only having green tea,' Cadence said, appearing at the doorway next to his mum. 'I can drive, baby. You have a beer with your dad. You know he'd love that.'

'Isn't she a sweetheart,' his mum said.

'Hello Cadence,' his dad said, going over to give her a hug. 'Don't you look beautiful. As always.'

'In the fridge?' Adam asked, very eager to get that beer.

'Yep, just grab whatever you can find,' his dad replied.

Adam went to the fridge at the back of the kitchen and pulled out two bottles of Peroni. He grabbed the fridge magnet bottle opener that Cadence had bought his parents from a photo shoot somewhere in Europe and he popped off the tops.

He handed his dad one of the beers and he took a seat at the table. He looked at his phone. Jenny still hadn't replied to his message. He hoped she was okay.

'Don't be so anti-social!' his mother called over. 'What's so important on your phone that can't wait until you're gone? We never get to see you.'

Adam stood up. 'It's Jenny. I was just checking to see if I'd had a text from her. I've barely heard from her all week.'

'I hope nothing's wrong,' his mum said. 'She's such a nice girl, isn't she Cadence?'

Cadence was too busy sipping at her hot green tea to reply. She just sort of nodded.

'I'll see her Sunday, anyway,' Adam said. 'I'm sure she's all right.'

'Has she found herself a nice young man yet?' his mum asked. 'There's no justice in the world if a girl like her can't find a nice man.'

'She's had a few dates but that's all,' Adam said. 'She

just keeps meeting these complete losers. I feel really bad for her.'

'I do hope she settles down soon. Is she coming to your gran's party next Saturday?'

'I don't know.'

'Oh, I'd love to see her. She's not been around in weeks.'

Jenny and his mum were very close. Having gone to school with Adam's sister, Jenny had always been a friend of the family's one way or another and his mum thought the world of her. They got on so well. Jenny would pop in for a cup of tea and a gossip whenever she could, deliberately just to see his parents.

Jenny really was like family to Adam. That was why he was so worried that he hadn't heard from her.

'Does she know about the party?' Adam asked.

'Have you told her?' his mum replied.

'No, have you?'

'No. Invite her now. Text her now before you forget. It wouldn't be the same without her joining us.'

'So now I'm allowed to use my phone?' Adam gibed.

'Don't be smart. Just get on with it.'

'Okay,' Adam said with a smirk.

He opened up his messages again and typed out a second one to Jenny.

My mum says do you want to come to my gran's party next Saturday? It's at the social club in town.

He pressed send and looked at the time. They had to stay until at least half nine. It already felt like they'd been there for a week.

'Tell me about your latest celebrity parties,' his mum said to Cadence and Adam knew it was time to head back to the living room. He found his dad flicking through the channels on the TV and he sat down on an armchair. Perhaps they could leave about nine. He was sure Cadence would need to reapply her make-up or something. Maybe he'd suggest that.

He looked at his phone again. Still no word from Jenny. He really hoped she was all right.

VISIONS OF EMMETT

Sunday afternoon soon came around and Jenny, Adam and Zack were all together in their favourite pub again. Their plates were being cleared away by a waitress after their scrumptious Sunday roast, and Zack was telling them all about his rather unusual week.

'And typically, it's been the busiest week we've had in ages,' Zack said.

'Surely they've got to close for a while. How are you meant to cope?' Adam asked him.

'You've got to be kidding! They enjoy making my life a misery. This is probably fun for them in a really backwards way.'

'How can every single person call in sick at exactly the same time?' Jenny asked.

'I don't know, but they did. I knew something was off straight away. I'm always the last to arrive at work - I refuse to spend a minute longer at that place than I have to - but when I got there on Thursday it was all shut up.'

'What did you do?'

'I finally got hold of Rachel and she said everyone had this sickness bug.'

'Who's Rachel?' Adam asked.

'Our Office Manager. She's one of the worst. Such a stirring little bitch. When she told me everyone had got this bug and no one could stop throwing up, I thought at first she was joking. I wouldn't put it past them locking me out to make a fool of me.'

'Have you felt ill at all?' Jenny asked.

'No. Not even slightly. I can't think how everyone in the office can be affected except for me. There are only like twenty of us.'

'You could be immune. It happens,' Adam suggested.

'Well, it's got to be something like that.'

'But they won't close the office?' Jenny asked.

'No. Rachel asked me to go to her house to pick up the keys so I could open up and man it all singlehandedly. I had to drive ten miles over there. She did look green though. Good. Serves her right.'

'How are you meant to man it all on your own?' Adam asked with sympathetic frustration for his friend.

'I've just been answering the phones and stuff. I've been telling everyone what the situation is, but a lot of customers aren't happy.'

'That's not your fault,' Jenny reasoned. 'You're doing the best you can.'

'It won't be good enough, though. Not for that bunch of bastards. They'll all come back in moaning about the things I haven't done. I certainly don't expect a thank you.'

'Adam, baby!' The conversation was interrupted as Cadence breezed into the pub, looking exceptionally glamorous in a black floating dress. 'Have you missed me?' she said, slipping herself onto Adam's lap.

'It's only been a day,' Adam remarked, leaning around her to place his drink down.

'Hi Cadence,' Zack grinned, doing his silly little wave.

'Hi!' she said, as if she'd only just noticed he was there.

'Where have you been?' Jenny asked.

'I was invited to the most amazing Gala Ball on Friday night,' Cadence replied, twisting herself on Adam's lap so she could face everyone. 'You would have loved it, Jenny.' Then she turned to Adam. 'You should have come. I missed you.'

'If that was Friday night, where have you been since?' Jenny asked.

'At the Gala Ball,' Cadence replied, as if it was the most obvious thing in the world. 'You don't get thrown out at three am at the events I go to. But I knew this morning it was time to go home as I was missing my Adam. I wish you'd been there. We could still be partying now.'

'As enticing as that sounds,' Adam said, 'I did want a more relaxing weekend.'

'You relaxed last weekend,' Cadence said, pulling her overdramatic sad face.

'If you ever need a plus one, you can count on me,' Zack said. 'I'd love to go to a Gala Ball. It sounds amazing.'

'Aww,' Cadence replied, momentarily looking in Zack's direction. 'Have you eaten?' she then said turning back to Adam.

'Yes, we just finished,' Adam said.

'Oh, sorry I missed it,' she said.

'There was a lot of potato,' Adam said.

'Oh my God, I've just been told about these amazing vitamin pills that give you everything you need with absolutely no calories,' Cadence said.

'What sort of pills?' Jenny asked.

'They sound fabulous,' Cadence said, turning to Jenny. 'You get all the nutrients you need in one pill. They're totally natural, none of this synthetic stuff. I can put you in touch with someone if you're interested.'

'Do you miss chocolate?' Jenny asked.

Cadence shook her head. 'I can't have lactose.'

'What about dark chocolate? You know, the proper chocolatey chocolate. I love it when it melts on my tongue.'

'No, I'm much happier with a strawberry. I'm lucky like

that. I never crave sweet stuff.'

'Oh yes, a whole bowl of strawberries,' Jenny said with enthusiasm.

'No, she just means one strawberry,' Adam replied. 'Just the one.'

'Not strawberries and chocolate?' Jenny queried. 'Or what about a huge bowl of strawberries and cream. Lashings of whipped cream.'

'As I said, I can't have lactose.'

'You know what, lads,' Jenny said with a brightness to her tone, 'shall we order dessert? We meet virtually every week but we never have dessert. They do the most gorgeous chocolate fudge cake.'

'Sounds good to me,' Zack said. 'I'll grab us some menus.'

As Zack headed off to the bar, Cadence turned to face Adam. 'Why don't we go? I've got the car waiting outside. We could be home in ten minutes and I could show you how much I've missed you.'

Adam sighed. 'Be fair, Cade, this is the only chance I get to see my mates.'

'But you haven't seen me in days!'

'It's been one day. Besides, I'll see you later, and tomorrow and all week. Let me have my afternoon with my mates.'

'Fine,' Cadence huffed, standing up.

'Are you off?' Zack asked, returning with four menus.

'Yes,' Cadence said, flashing her dazzling smile as if all was well with the world. 'I've barely slept in days. I'm going straight to bed.' She glanced at Adam as if her words might entice him, but he just grabbed his pint as if he hadn't heard.

'Nice to see you again,' Jenny said with a grin, but Cadence didn't reply. She just strutted out of the pub, grabbing the attention of virtually everyone in there.

Zack finished his wave goodbye and then he placed the menus on the table, but no one looked at them.

'Anyway, what have you been up to?' Adam asked Jenny. 'You never replied to my texts on Friday night. I was worried.'

'Didn't I?' Jenny replied with confusion. 'I thought I had, sorry. Count me in for your gran's party. It sounds great.'

'I'll let my mum know. She'll be thrilled. So what have you been doing? Have you had any more dates?'

'No,' Jenny replied, quite to the point. 'I'm thinking of giving the online world a rest for a while.'

'Was it really that bad with the world record bloke?' Adam asked with surprise.

'What world record bloke?' Zack asked.

'Oh, it was just a joke,' Jenny said. 'He actually went to the toilet, got soaked by the tap and decided to go home. I ended up having an early night.'

'You never told me that,' Adam said.

'Didn't I?'

'You don't have a lot of luck with dates, do you?' Zack said.

'It's got to change sometime,' Jenny shrugged.

There was a moment of contemplative silence before Zack announced, 'I've revised the illustrations, if you want to see?'

He grabbed his backpack and pulled out a few sheets of paper, all with Empathy Man on them. Some were just rough sketches but two had the man in full colour, sporting his blue Lycra but now without a cape. Everything else looked exactly the same, though.

'Do you see what I've done?' Zack asked, pointing to the face. 'I've emphasised his temples and forehead. I think as he's in touch with everything around him, his mind would be larger. Don't you?'

Adam and Jenny just glanced at one another blankly.

'I'm really proud of what we've created here,' Zack said, admiring his picture. 'Would you mind if I sent it off to some publishers? Maybe see if we can get some feedback?'

Adam screwed up his face. 'You really think someone's going to be interested in him?'

'I think he's brilliant,' Jenny stated. 'Go for it, Zack.'

'All right, I'll give it a go. Then I think I might take a little break from him. I've definitely spent far too much time working on him this week. I swear I've been seeing him everywhere I go.'

'Are you serious?' Jenny asked with urgency.

'Yeah, it's been really weird.'

'Me too! A couple of times I thought I saw him out of the corner of my eye, but then on Friday, I swear he was standing right in front of me. I thought I was going mad.'

'That's exactly what happened with me! What's that about?'

'What are you two talking about?' Adam queried, shaking his head. 'I think you both need more sleep.'

'So you've not seen him?' Jenny asked Adam.

'No, I can safely say I haven't been seeing visions of Empathy Man walking around.'

'Can we call him Emmett?' Zack asked.

'No,' Adam replied.

'It's far fewer syllables.'

'What about Em?' Jenny suggested with a sly grin.

'Or what about Pathy?' Adam added, as he joined Jenny in a snigger.

'You can laugh all you want, but it'll catch on,' Zack countered. 'I'm going to start calling him Emmett and before you know it you won't be able to think of him in any other way.'

'You do that,' Adam grinned. 'Then I'll call him Pathy and we'll see which name Jenny starts to say first.'

'Come on, let's be serious,' Jenny said. 'Zack's worked really hard on re-drawing Pathy following our chat last week.'

Adam and Jenny burst out laughing.

'We'll see,' Zack said with confidence.

'Do you like the name Pathy?' Jenny asked the illustration before her. 'See, he does. He's smiling.' She held up the picture for the others to see.

'Don't be stupid,' Zack said, and then he stopped. He grabbed the image from Jenny's hand. 'What did you do? How could you mess with my picture?'

'I haven't done anything,' Jenny said.

'What's the matter, mate?' Adam asked.

'I made him serious. I wanted him to be serious. He has serious work to do. But look.'

Zack turned the drawing around for Jenny and Adam to see and there, right across Empathy Man's face, was a huge beaming smile.

ADAM'S EARLY NIGHT

Adam propped his pillow up, then he pulled the duvet over him and he sat in bed with a sulk. It was Monday and Cadence had just announced that she wanted an early night. Adam had learnt long ago that when it came to Cadence's beauty sleep, nothing was going to stand in her way.

The first few times that Cadence had declared she needed an early night, Adam had tried to reason with her. He'd said that he wasn't tired; that she was free to go to bed but he wasn't going to go for at least another couple of hours. But Cadence had thrown back how the smallest noise would wake her and the safest option was for both of them to retire at the same time.

He'd tried all sorts to get her to see his side of things, but he could never win. She'd just reel off how her nutritionist, dermatologist, GP, or even once her hairdresser had stated that she should get more sleep due to the high demands of her daily life. He could hear her now: 'If you want your girlfriend to keep her model looks then you need to respect the fact that I need an early night every now and then.'

It used to be every now and then when they first

moved in together, but it was turning into a few times a month and Adam wasn't liking it.

He grabbed his Kindle next to him. He needed a distraction while he waited for his beauty queen to finish in the bathroom.

His favourite books normally featured the Avengers, but lately he'd been enjoying the bromance of Spider-Man and Deadpool. The story he was reading really made him laugh and it had proven to be a great vehicle for calming him down after Cadence had tensed him all up.

'Don't start reading now!' Cadence whined. Adam hadn't even noticed her standing over him, her toothbrush in hand. The en suite was opposite the bed and the immaculate, softly purple room was very big, but she'd somehow managed to sweep across without making a sound, just to irritate him.

'I'm just dipping into it until you've finished in the bathroom,' he said.

'Is it comic books again or something normal?' she asked, peering over at the Kindle.

He wanted to tell her the truth. She used to humour his love of comics. But ever since he'd asked her agent if he could get them complimentary tickets to the San Diego Comic-Con, she'd been a little prickly about his passion for the world of superheroes.

He knew that she could get them tickets. That was what hurt him the most. It was the biggest show on the Comic-Con calendar and incredibly difficult to get in to. It was on his, Jenny's and Zack's bucket lists, and his girlfriend had the ability to get them access. But she refused. She'd told her agent to ignore him as he was just being silly.

The problem wasn't that she disliked his love of comics per se, the problem was that if she was getting the tickets, then she'd have to go as well, and that was never going to happen. She'd rattled off something about her image and her reputation and how much she hated superheroes and

Star Trek Wars. She always had some excuse, much to Adam's disgust.

She'd once got them tickets to the Monaco Grand Prix, which Adam had loved. They'd walked on the grid and had enjoyed hospitality with McLaren. It had been amazing. But Cadence had left the event saying that Formula One was the most boring thing on the planet and that was that. They'd never visited another race.

'I'm just catching up on a bit of stuff about Spider-Man,' Adam said, trying not to go into too much detail about DeadPool and Spider-Man being tied up together.

'You don't even like spiders,' she tutted, strutting off to the bathroom again.

'Peter Parker wasn't a huge fan either,' Adam muttered under his breath.

He tried to focus on his book, but after reading the same section three times he gave up. He was riled and this time even DeadPool's smart comments weren't helping.

He wanted to go back downstairs. He'd just completed his fastest lap ever at the Circuit Gilles Villeneuve. He was desperate to keep up the momentum, but when Cadence said the PlayStation had to go off, it had to go off. She couldn't sleep with the PlayStation on. Even if he turned the volume down, apparently his expressions of joy or anger at the games kept her awake.

He'd tested the theory once by getting up in the middle of the night. He'd barely started his Marvel Pinball game when Cadence had appeared at the door with death in her eyes. He'd never turned off his PlayStation quicker. She knew. She always knew.

'I hope you've tidied up after yourself,' Cadence said, re-appearing from the en suite, now dressed in her silk chemise. 'The cleaner's coming tomorrow.'

Adam took a deep breath before replying. This was one of the most ridiculous things that Cadence insisted upon. They had to clean the house before the cleaner arrived as Cadence didn't want the cleaner thinking that they lived in a pig-sty.

Most often it was just tidying up, a bit of vacuuming and a quick dust around. There was just the once after their Christmas party when Adam had hit the roof. Cadence had actually cleaned the bathroom the morning before the cleaner was due as she said it was grimy from all the people that had used it. 'We can't have the cleaner thinking we're dirty,' she'd said.

That had caused a huge row. Until Adam, as always, backed down in the end. Cadence was so stubborn he knew he'd never be able to win.

'Yes, of course,' he said through gritted teeth.

'Thank you, baby,' she said before heading back into the en suite.

Adam looked at the clock next to him. It was only quarter to nine. He'd only been home from work for two hours.

Adam worked about ten miles closer to London for a global electronics company. He'd started there at eighteen on the phones, straight from school. Adam had never excelled academically. His grades were okay but his real gifts in life were his confidence, determination and ability to talk to people.

It was rare that a person didn't instantly like Adam. He had natural charisma and he was a very good listener. He'd found that just by properly listening to clients and letting them yammer on, he could quite easily ascertain exactly what sort of a person they were and exactly what it was they needed. Then all he had to do was meet or, even better, exceed their expectations. It was a simple formula that had led him to be a massively successful sales person who had easily built his way up to Head of Sales. He was now earning a very healthy salary and he was incredibly well respected.

It was through work that he'd met Cadence. Well, sort of. He'd been in Miami at one of the company's annual conferences and Cadence had been staying in the same hotel doing some sort of modelling job. They'd met in the bar one night and the rest was history.

He'd liked her back then. She was fun and would take him to all these amazing places. But he'd soon got bored of it, and six years on it was all still exactly the same.

After he'd been to ten exclusive parties, they all started blending into one. He was much happier meeting his mates down the local for a few pints. He wasn't the kind of man to mingle with so-called celebrities and knock back free champagne at events where all everyone really did anyway was pose.

In all honesty, Adam had got bored of Cadence about two years into their relationship, but by then she'd met all of his friends and family and everyone loved her. No one had a bad word to say about her.

Every single time he'd considered breaking up with her, one of his mates would tell him how he was the luckiest man alive, or his mother would say how she couldn't dream of a better future daughter-in-law, and it would confuse his thoughts.

On paper Cadence was great. She was absolutely stunning, incredibly wealthy, she owned her own place in London and was also quite intelligent. She could talk about anything and could mix with anyone. A person only had to meet her for five minutes and it would feel like they'd met a friend for life.

But that was all on the surface. Once Adam had started to dig a little deeper, there wasn't really anything else there. She didn't eat properly, she was obsessed with her looks, and she seemed to believe that going to parties was actually a good use of her time.

He used to excuse it all. She was a hugely successful model who travelled the world, of course she would diet and be conscious of her looks. But when he thought about it, that was only her job. Surely there had to be something else in her life on top of that?

Whinging about stuff. That was the only thing Adam

could think of.

'I hope you told the gardener to be more careful next time,' she said, poking her head around the bathroom door again.

Adam sighed. The gardener had not mowed the lawn in the straight lines that Cadence insisted upon. Adam hadn't been able to spot where he'd apparently been 'haphazardly throwing the lawn mower around', but if Cadence believed that the lawn was crooked, then the lawn was crooked.

'Of course,' Adam lied. He'd been far too embarrassed to tell the hard-working gardener that the enormous lawn he'd spent two hours mowing wasn't done to the ridiculously high standards of a woman who barely even set foot out there. 'He took it very seriously.'

'Good. Thank you, baby.'

She disappeared again and Adam could feel the rage flaring up inside of him. He used to be so chilled out; nothing ever used to bother him. Then a couple of years ago he started to feel himself getting irked by the simplest of things. Over time it had got worse and worse, and now there were days when the anger would enflame his whole body and he couldn't let it go. Half the time he didn't even know what he was angry about.

Despite his inner rage, Adam still always kept himself together, though. He had a great ability to handle pressure and he always remained professional at work. He'd just bite his lip or count to ten, or do anything to calm himself down and put things into perspective.

He turned to the clock. It was almost nine pm. He could be off to Europe now to complete the next stage of his Formula One season, probably smashing lap after lap based on his current form. Why the hell couldn't Cadence order him to bed when she was finished with her laborious beauty regime?

It was only when they'd moved in together two years before that Adam had first been confronted with the horror that was the early night. Before that they'd only spent a few nights a week together. Back then it was the nights that she wasn't with Adam that she'd go to bed early. But now it was the nights she spent away that she'd stay up all hours, and then she'd come home to get her beauty sleep.

Adam had been born in Miloworth and he'd lived with his parents until the age of twenty-one. It was at that age that he'd first moved in to his very own bachelor pad. They had been good days. He'd been young, free, single and unexpectedly wealthy. As a successful sales man who would regularly smash his targets, he would always maximise his commission meaning he was never short of disposable income. From his early twenties, he'd got all the latest gadgets, he could enjoy luxurious holidays and he was certainly always dressed to impress.

It was at the age of twenty-five that he'd moved out into the more affluent area that he now lived in, about four miles from Miloworth. He'd bought a beautiful three bedroom house and he'd loved every inch of it. Then Cadence had suggested that they move in together and everything went wrong. He'd hardly been happy with her suggestion, but hadn't been able to think of a reason to say no. Breaking up with her just didn't seem a sane option, and so progressing the relationship was all that was left.

So now, at the age of twenty-nine, he was sharing the mortgage of a six bedroom luxury home. Adam liked the house, it was quite spectacular, but his life in it was not a happy one.

He should just leave her. He really should.

His phone pinged a message and he grabbed it from the bedside table. It was his mother.

We're getting your gran a vase for her birthday, will you get her some flowers to put in it? Perhaps they could match the colour nail varnish that Cadence brings with her. Your gran will love having her nails done by such a glamorous girl. So kind of her. Love you. Keep in touch. xxxx

'Was that your phone?' Cadence asked as she appeared again, this time stripped of her make-up. She looked a lot paler.

'It was my mum.'

'Put it on silent. I don't want to be disturbed all night by your phone going off.'

Adam obediently did as he was told.

'What time do you want the alarm for?' he said, flicking to the clock settings on his mobile.

'It's fine,' she replied.

'What do you mean, fine?' Adam asked.

'I don't need an alarm tomorrow.'

'Why?' he asked, feeling the rage intensify.

'I don't have work now until Friday. Friday's going to be mental, I can't tell you. My agent said that going in and out of London is clearly taking its toll on me, so he's packed everything in to one day.'

So many issues were spinning around Adam's head, not least that it took just half an hour from where they lived to get into London. It was hardly taxing. But one issue was grinding at him more than anything.

'You're not working tomorrow?' he asked, rubbing his hands through his hair, the trademark sign that Adam was frustrated.

'No.'

'You're at home tomorrow? You have the whole day to do whatever you like?'

'Well, I'm going out when the cleaner's here. I can't bear to watch her battling with the Dyson.'

'Why the fuck are you making me go to bed at half eight if you have the rest of the week off?' Adam was livid.

'How dare you speak to me that way!' Cadence shouted back, coming over to the bed. 'You want it all, you do.'

'What's that supposed to mean?'

'My nail technician told me last week that my nails are looking weak and brittle and she suggested that a few early nights might be beneficial.'

'Why didn't you think of that before you went gallivanting around all weekend at your lavish party?'

'You know I need to attend those parties for my job. If I'm not there, people notice.'

'Bullshit. You love it.'

'Stop swearing at me. My audiologist said that foul language will affect my hearing. At this rate I'll need a hearing aid by the time I'm forty.'

Again, Adam was flummoxed as to which part of her statement to question first. 'You have an audiologist? Why do you have an audiologist?'

'So I don't go deaf. Those parties are very loud, you know. My agent is concerned about me.'

'It seems to me that the partying is actually your biggest enemy. Maybe you should stop going out?'

'I've just told you, I need to be out and about for my job. At first you disappear off the scene and then you stop getting the work. It's happened to loads of people.'

'Like who?'

'Maybe you'd know if you ever joined me.'

'I don't want to. I can't stand those parties.'

'Well I think more people would like to be a VIP at an exclusive A-Lister party than go to some stupid comic convention. You should be embarrassed.'

'At least it's an interest in my life. You're getting boring, Cadence, you know that.'

'How dare you!'

'I mean what the fuck is with those pills you're taking? We don't even eat proper meals together anymore.'

'You know what your problem is?' Cadence said, her voice firm and measured. 'You want your cake and you want to eat it.'

'Oh, I'd love a bit of cake right now.'

'You want the glamorous girlfriend with all the connections and the trophy to hang off your arm, but you also want me to drink pints, play darts and... you'll be wanting me to dye my hair a stupid colour next!'

'What the hell are you talking about?' Adam said, feeling his fist clenching.

'And another thing,' Cadence added. 'Why am I still your girlfriend? When are you going to propose? *Hello* has promised to feature our wedding, but I actually need a ring on my finger before I can discuss the arrangements. I mean, doesn't that excite you at all?'

Adam took a deep breath. His anger levels were off the scale and he knew he needed to calm down. He wanted to scream at her to get out. Or he wanted to leave himself. He didn't want her in his life anymore. But all he could hear were the praising comments from his friends and family and he could imagine their disgust if he was to announce their parting.

It confused him so much. There had been times when he'd questioned to himself whether he'd actually stopped liking her because everyone else liked her so much. But as she stood before him at that moment, he knew he wanted to punch her in the face. Not that he ever would.

'Look at the time!' Cadence said, after receiving no reply to her engagement probing. 'It's approaching ten now and I'm still not in bed. Are you trying to make me ugly?'

'It's nine fifteen,' Adam argued back, but Cadence had stormed back into the bathroom.

He couldn't break up with her. He knew he couldn't. It just seemed too hard. He also knew that she'd never leave him. There was something about her vice-like grip that left him so suffocated he knew she'd be there for life.

If only she'd disappear. If she'd just vanish and not come back, everything would be fine. Maybe she could have an affair with someone else and then Adam could play the broken hearted boyfriend and it would take her down a peg or two. He could scream at her and claim that his heart doctor said he may never recover and his toe doctor was concerned about how much she'd stamped on him. There really would be no going back.

Adam sighed. That was far too much like wishful thinking.

He knew she wouldn't be in there crying. She wasn't a crier. He'd actually started to believe that she was made of concrete inside with just a pretty exterior.

He waited patiently, hating this limbo he was stuck in. If he couldn't finish his game and she'd got him too riled to read, then all that was left was sleep. But if he turned the light off before she got into bed then all hell would break loose.

The 'I might fall over and break my leg, rummaging around in the dark' argument was classic Cadence. Even though she could certainly manage stumbling around night clubs in the dark.

Adam waited and waited and waited, and finally ten o'clock did come and go. What the hell was she doing?

Impatience got the better of him and he jumped out of bed. He opened the door to the en suite, expecting to see her rubbing some cream or other into some random part of her body, but instead he was faced with emptiness.

He checked all over the bathroom but she was nowhere to be found. She'd literally vanished into thin air.

Just then he saw a face in the mirror. It wasn't Cadence, though, it was a man. He turned around quickly to see a flash of blue. He raced back to the bedroom but no one was there.

He knew that face. He'd seen it before. He knew that smile.

Had he just seen Emmett?

ADAM ON THE HUNT

Adam sat on the edge of the bed, totally confused. Where could Cadence have gone? There must be a logical explanation. And what on earth was he doing seeing visions of Emmett the Empathy Man? In a matter of minutes, Adam's world had turned crazy.

Adam got back under the duvet. Perhaps this was some ploy to try and make him feel bad for not proposing. She'd never done anything like this before, but he knew she was getting desperate for a wedding.

Then Adam got out of bed again. If Cadence was gone, he didn't have to go to bed early. He could go back to his game and he wouldn't be disturbing anyone.

No. No, he couldn't. She'd know. She was most likely hiding somewhere in the house. Where else could she be? If he didn't look as if he was worried about her then she'd never forgive him.

Was he worried about her? He searched his mind. He was a little, he supposed. It was a strange disappearance. But the truth was he was more worried about how she was going to react when she reappeared. Even though he had no clue what to do for the best, he knew whatever he did would be wrong.

He got back under the duvet and decided to try and sleep. If he pretended he hadn't noticed that she'd disappeared then she would no doubt crawl back into bed during the night and this silliness would all be over with.

He shuffled down, got himself comfortable and then he tried to drift off.

But sleeping was very difficult. Even when he did drop off, he was haunted by weird dreams about Cadence shouting at him for not finding her sooner or not caring about the trouble she'd found herself in. He should have called the police because she'd been gone for half an hour!

He woke up with a terrible fear. What if this wasn't a game? What if she was stuck somewhere? People don't just disappear into thin air. The window wasn't open in the en suite so she had to be in the house somewhere. Nothing else made sense.

Then he became overwhelmed with worry that she'd become trapped around the side of the bath or in the shower curtain, or somewhere else ridiculously implausible. So strange was her disappearance, a peculiar scenario seemed the most likely outcome. Also, if she was stuck somewhere, there was no way she'd ever forgive him for not finding her.

He had a flash of her weak and feeble body being found in a few days' time in the cupboard under the sink. Her first reaction wouldn't be to thank him for rescuing her from the stiff door that she couldn't open. She'd more likely shout at him for not being clever enough to find her sooner. Even though, what the hell was she doing in the bathroom cupboard under the sink?

He flicked on the bathroom light and waited for his eyes to adjust. Then he started to look more closely in every nook and cranny he could find. He looked in any place that she could have slipped into, fallen behind or got stuck under. She was so incredibly thin, nothing at this stage seemed impossible.

He called her name and then waited in silence to hear if

her muffled cries for help could be heard. But there was nothing. He felt alone. He knew there was no one in there, and he could think of absolutely nowhere else she could be.

If she'd left the bedroom he would have noticed. The door was closed and he'd been sitting up in bed. He would have seen her run out. And she certainly wouldn't have done it quietly. That wasn't her way.

With no other options, though, he decided to search the house just in case. He made his way across the landing into each of the spare bedrooms, looking for any clues. Finding nothing, he then headed downstairs, but still Cadence was nowhere to be seen.

He went back to bed utterly confused. He knew there had to be a logical explanation and they'd probably be laughing about it (or rowing about it) in a few days' time, but for now he was stumped.

He tried to go back to sleep. He kept telling himself that all will be revealed with the light of morning. People don't just disappear with no explanation.

But by the time six o'clock arrived, Cadence was still missing and Adam was exhausted. He'd barely slept at all.

He got up and headed down to the kitchen. He needed coffee if he was going to think straight. He turned on the machine and waited for his caffeine.

Should he call the police, he pondered? What would they say? How could he explain what had happened? He didn't even believe it himself. And didn't someone have to be missing for forty-eight hours before you could raise the alarm?

He knew he needed to speak to someone, though. He was starting to go mad with confusion and worry.

There was only one person he could speak to at times like this. Jenny was his closest friend and someone he thought the world of. Zack had become a very good mate over the past couple of years, but Jenny was Adam's rock and he couldn't imagine his life without her.

It was only quarter past six, though. She'd never be up at that time. She didn't leave for work until eight forty-five and she definitely wasn't an early riser.

He'd learnt that when he'd suggested that they go to Boot Camp together in the local park. He'd got sick of going to the gym with Cadence. He'd wanted to try something different. But when he'd told Jenny about the six am start, she'd nearly fallen off her seat in shock. 'There's only one six o'clock in the day that matters,' she'd said, 'and it's the one right after work.'

Cadence wouldn't go to Boot Camp either, but for very different reasons. Apparently her stylist had said the fashion that season wouldn't allow for it. Whatever that meant. He admired Jenny's honesty more.

He decided to have some breakfast, shower, get ready for work and then head over to her flat to catch Jenny before she left for the office. He knew she wouldn't mind.

Dressed smartly in a tailored royal blue suit and stripy tie, Adam got in his expensive company car and he headed on the short journey to Jenny's flat. It was just before eight and he prayed that she'd be awake.

He made a quick call en route via his Bluetooth to his sales team to say he'd be late in. That was one of the perks of being the boss: he never had to explain himself. He was well-liked, certainly respected, and he worked very hard. If he ever did need to disappear for a while, no one would ever question it.

He arrived into Miloworth at about quarter past eight and it was heaving. He finally found a space on the street just down the road from Jenny's flat, and then he walked up to the front door.

She lived in a newly developed block of about twenty flats and he pressed the buzzer for number five. A few seconds went by, which felt like forever, before Jenny answered the intercom.

'Hello?' she said.

'Hi Jen, it's Adam. I know you're getting ready for

work, but have you got five minutes? I've got a problem.'

There was absolute silence on the other end. Then she finally said, 'Now?'

'I'm sorry to land this on you. You know I wouldn't just turn up like this if it wasn't urgent.'

'Erm... I'm not really ready at the minute. Could I meet you for lunch?'

Adam thought for a moment. That was a fair suggestion, but he needed to talk now. Cadence had been gone for nearly twelve hours and he needed help.

'You know I don't care what you look like. Please, Jen, I need to speak to someone.'

After another long pause, the buzzer for the door went and he was allowed in. He headed up the single flight of stairs to her front door where she opened it just a crack.

'What is it?' she asked.

'Can I come in?' he said with wariness. She was acting weirdly.

'Is everything all right, Jenny?' a male voice suddenly said from within.

'Yes, fine. It's just my friend.'

Jenny opened the door to reveal herself fully dressed and there, standing behind her, a man in nothing but a towel. A man that Adam had never seen before. He didn't know what to say.

'Adam, meet Nathan. Nathan, this is Adam. You know my friend who was texting me the other night, checking I was okay.'

'Oh yes, great to meet you,' this Nathan said, holding out his hand for Adam to shake.

Adam politely obliged but his senses had pricked up. He didn't like this one bit.

'Are you okay?' Adam said quietly, hoping that only Jenny would hear.

'I'm fine. What's so urgent?'

Adam was too flustered to think about Cadence anymore. Seeing Jenny with a man who had clearly not just popped around to discuss plumbing had almost knocked him off his feet.

'Nothing,' he replied.

'Well something's clearly wrong. What is it?'

'You know, it doesn't matter. It was a work issue, but you've obviously got a man on your plate. I mean a towel. I mean another man. Company! I mean company. I'll just text you.'

'You can come in if you want.'

'No, I'll leave you to it. Catch up with you Sunday.'

With that Adam left as quickly as he could. He stepped out into the courtyard of the flats utterly discombobulated.

What was going on? The last Adam had heard Jenny had been left by a wet world record holder. She'd not told him about any dates since. Why would she lie?

Unless she was in trouble. He had looked shifty. All those muscles in that tiny towel. He had to be on steroids or something. He clearly wasn't to be trusted. Adam would have to watch out for Jenny. She was obviously in some sort of danger.

But then she had seemed happy. So why hadn't she told Adam about him? It all seemed very suspicious, and it left Adam riddled with... nerves. Yes nerves. And anger. Anger that his friend had lied.

He walked back to his car with only thoughts of Jenny now spinning around his head. At that moment he'd forgotten that Cadence even existed.

Suddenly, though, all of his thoughts vanished. He looked to his car in the distance and he could see someone sitting in the passenger seat. He raced towards it, wondering what the hell was going on. Was it Cadence?

No. It was blue. It was that blue again. But just as he approached his car the figure disappeared. Disappeared into thin air, just like Cadence had.

Adam took a deep breath. He didn't want to think what he knew his brain was telling him. He didn't want to consciously acknowledge what couldn't possibly be true.

But he could have sworn the man sitting in his car was exactly like Emmett the Empathy Man.

Now he felt ridiculous. He was seeing things as well as losing things. And that was on top of fearing for the well-being of his closest friend who was keeping secrets and inviting strange men into her home.

But then she had looked happy. She'd seemed quite flustered but she'd also looked happy. So why was it bothering Adam so much?

He needed help. He needed to talk to someone. There was only one other person that could help him. He got in his car and drove straight over to the little industrial estate on the outskirts of Miloworth where he knew Zack worked.

ADAM'S ADMISSION

Adam arrived at Zack's work just after nine o'clock. It was a small building on a small industrial estate with a very empty car park at the front. He parked his car right outside the entrance and made his way to the reception. No one was there, just a sign that said to dial 123 for help. He did just that, immediately recognising the voice that answered.

'Zack? It's Adam. Have you got five minutes?'

'What are you doing here?'

'I know you're at work, but can you take a coffee break or something?'

'Come through. It's the door on the right.'

Adam followed Zack's instruction and he entered into an open plan office. Despite the fact that there were desks, computers, cabinets and paperwork everywhere, there wasn't a single person in sight except for Zack who looked exhausted.

The phone rang and Zack immediately picked it up. 'Good morning, Energy Biz, how can I help?'

Adam took a seat at the desk next to Zack. He was in utter disbelief that Zack was still having to manage things alone. It had been days.

'I'm really sorry, Arnold's off sick at the moment,' Zack

explained down the phone. 'In fact everyone but me has been struck down with a rather nasty bug. I'm just taking messages at the minute. That's the best I can do. Okay. Thanks for understanding.'

Zack placed the phone down and turned to Adam. 'What are you doing here?'

'Everyone's still off sick?' Adam asked.

'Apparently no one has even improved. Most of them have now been ordered into quarantine. It's going to be at least a week, they reckon.'

'Sorry mate, that's awful. Can't you just leave a recorded message or something and go home?'

'I wish.'

'What about faking the illness too?'

Zack considered this for a second. 'No. They'd find out. I'd get the sack knowing my luck. But I know you didn't come here to check up on me, so what's wrong?'

Adam leaned forward to speak to Zack more directly. 'Did you know that Jenny was seeing someone?'

Much to Adam's frustration, the phone rang again and Zack had to take the call. 'Good morning, Energy Biz, how can I help?'

Adam jangled his car keys in his hand. His heart was pounding, but he wasn't quite sure why.

'I'm really sorry, the sales team is off sick at the moment,' Zack said to the caller. 'As unlikely as it sounds, everyone in the office but me has been struck down with a rather nasty bug. I'm just taking messages at the minute. That's the best I can do.'

Zack looked increasingly stressed as he listened intently to the person on the other end of the line. 'We do want your business. Of course we do. We're just in a very difficult situation at the minute.'

Suddenly the phone rang again. Without hesitation, Adam picked up the line to help out. 'Good morning, Energy Biz, how can I help?'

He saw Zack mouth 'Thank you' as he listened.

'Can I speak to someone in customer service, please?' the female voice on the line said.

'I'm really sorry, I'm not going to be able to transfer you. The whole office has been struck down with a very unfortunate stomach bug and all we can do at the minute is take a message. Is there anything that I can pass on?'

'I'm sure you can help me, can't you?'

'I would love to, but I'm quite confident that you'll need to speak to one of the customer service team when they return to get the best support.'

'I've been overcharged on my bill. I want someone to look into it for me.'

'That's definitely not good. What I'm going to do is leave a message for one of the team to get back to you as soon as humanly possible. I'll make sure you're top of the list. If I can just take a name and number.'

'Can't you deal with this? I just want someone to look at my bill.'

'I'm really sorry, it's not my area. I wish I could.'

'Is it that you can't or you won't?' the lady replied with growing aggression, enflaming Adam's already unsettled state.

'I don't think you're quite understanding the grave situation we're in here,' he replied as calmly as he could. 'The truth is I don't even work for Energy Biz. I've just been called in to take a few calls to help out the only man who is holding the company together while all of his co-workers recover from their very nasty illness. I totally appreciate the terrible issues you're facing but there is literally no one here who can help you. I'm sure, however, when the customer service team returns they'll be full of sympathy. How dreadful to be so worried about your bill. It puts the whole mass illness thing into quite a different perspective.'

'What sort of ridiculous company is this?'

'One that has hit very sickly times. Very sickly times indeed. In fact, this is a particularly contagious virus. Surely you must have been warned that people have even been catching it down the telephone? Have you had your vaccination?'

'What vaccination? What are you talking about?'

'Oh dear, it may be too late already. If you start to feel unwell at any point over the next seventy-two hours, you must seek medical assistance immediately.'

'What?' The voice now seemed panicky.

'I think it's best we leave it there. You need to limit your chances of infection.'

'What?'

'I do hope you're not going to be violently sick as well as having all that worry about your bill. How will you cope?'

'But...'

'You'd better go, before it's too late.'

'Do you think I'll be okay?'

'So hard to tell. I'd better hang up now to save you. Bye.'

Adam hung up to see Zack glaring at him. 'Who was that?'

Adam shrugged. 'Some incredibly insensitive woman who had problems with her bill.'

'You shouldn't have said that to her. What's she going to say to customer services when she calls back?'

'They'll think she's crazy. Who gets infected down a phone line? Stupid woman.'

Zack shook his head. 'Well, thanks for taking the call anyway.'

Adam watched as Zack started nervously biting his finger nails. He knew he shouldn't have said what he did to that woman. He'd dealt with hundreds of difficult customers in his time without even batting an eyelid, but her complete lack of compassion had got right under Adam's skin. It was as if his anger and irritation had reached a whole new level of intensity. He must be more worried about Cadence than he'd realised. And maybe

Jenny too. But the last thing he wanted was to make life worse for his friend. 'How are you coping with this?' he asked Zack.

'As best I can,' Zack mumbled. 'I didn't even have a lunch break yesterday. The phones haven't stopped. Although I've now put an out of office on everyone's computers so at least I don't feel the need to answer everything immediately.'

'You're far too good for this place.'

'You got any jobs going?'

Adam shook his head and smiled. 'You'd be a lousy salesman, and you know it.'

The phone rang again. 'Good morning, Energy Biz, how can I help?'

Adam waited as patiently as he could while Zack once again reeled off his explanation about the sickness bug. This was a quick one though, and within seconds he'd placed down the receiver.

'Before the phone rings again,' Zack said quickly, 'you still haven't told me what you're doing here.'

Adam sighed. 'Cadence has disappeared.'

Zack looked genuinely shocked. 'What? What's happened?'

'She was in the bathroom and then she just didn't come out again. I don't know where she's gone. The window was shut and she didn't open the door. I don't know what to do. I don't know what to think.'

'Is there another door? Where could she have gone?'

Adam leaned forward and dropped his voice. Although no one else was around, he still didn't want to risk anyone hearing what he was about to say. 'It gets weirder. I've started seeing Emmett the Empathy Man everywhere.'

'Emmett! I knew you'd start calling him that.'

Adam rolled his eyes. This really wasn't the time for smugness. 'I saw him in the bathroom, I swear I did. Then he was in my car. It had to be him. But that's crazy, isn't it? He's just a drawing.'

'It can't be crazy, not if you, Jenny and I have all seen him. I keep catching him in the corner of my eye in the office. I know it's him.'

'It doesn't make any sense. Are we ill? Are we going mad?'

'I have a theory,' Zack said, just as the phone rang again.

As Zack answered it, Adam stood up. He looked out the window at the rather run down industrial estate around him. Although he should have been thinking far more about Cadence and his visions of Empathy Man, all that occupied his mind were thoughts of Jenny.

Who was this Nathan? Was it serious? How long had they been going out for? Was it the record holder who had appeared back in her life again after last Monday? Maybe she hadn't lied to Adam after all.

What if it was serious? What if she was now going to get married and have children? She might not even speak to him anymore. Would there still be room for Adam with this Nathan in her life?

What was bothering him? They were best friends. They were always going to be best friends, weren't they? Surely he should be happy for her.

But Adam couldn't shake the feeling that there was something shifty about this Nathan. Why was he in a towel? Who has a shower in someone else's home?

Before Adam could dwell on the very obvious answer to that question, Zack ended his call.

'Quickly, before the phone rings again,' Zack said as Adam returned to his seat. 'I think we've made Emmett real.'

Adam just glared at Zack. There was no possible response to such a ludicrous statement.

'Before you start telling me I've lost the plot,' Zack continued, 'you have to look at the facts. I'm not saying I know all the answers, but what's going on for me at the minute is exactly what I wished for. It's as if Empathy Man has empathised with my needs and desires and then he's made my wish come true. Which is exactly what we said he'd do.'

'Are you saying you wanted everyone in the office to fall seriously ill with some horrific bug?' Adam asked with disbelief.

'No, it wasn't like that. I just wished, prayed for, desperately hoped that everyone would disappear. I said to myself that I wanted to come into work one day to find all the bastards gone. Then I woke up one morning to find that very thing had happened.'

Suddenly Adam felt sick.

'I'm even more convinced now as you said before that Jenny was seeing someone. She's had so many bad dates and now she's seeing someone. Is that right?'

Adam could barely speak. He just nodded, and then managed, 'I think so.'

'But what about you?' Zack looked at him with suspicion. 'Cadence has disappeared and you have no clue how it could have possibly happened. What aren't you telling me?'

Adam gulped. It was time to tell the truth. It appeared that someone out there disguised as Empathy Man had been reading his mind, so he might as well tell his friend.

'I can't stand Cadence.'

'What?' Zack was utterly shocked.

'She's a whinging, whiney, shallow, boring, over-demanding, complete control freak of a woman and I've been desperate to leave her for years.'

'What?' Zack gasped again. He fumbled around for words, but all he could manage a third time was, 'What?'

'You lot all think the world of her, though. Every time I've thought about leaving her, someone has told me how great she is and it's made me question myself. But you don't know what she's really like. I think I might actually hate her.'

There was a long, stretched out silence as neither of

them knew what to say next.

Then Zack finally uttered, 'You wanted her to disappear?'

Adam nodded. 'Yes. It seemed like so much effort to break up with her, so I fantasised about her disappearing off the face of the planet. And then she did.'

Zack shook his head. 'I don't know what to say. At least my work lot are all still here. You've eradicated your girlfriend from existence.'

Adam stood up. 'Don't say that! I didn't want that! What am I going to do? This is all such bullshit.' Adam shook his head, refusing to believe any of this nonsense. 'There's no such thing as Emmett the fucking Empathy Man. He was a character we made up one drunk Sunday afternoon as none of us had anything better to do. I mean you're a good illustrator, Zack, but you're not that good.'

'I know it seems impossible, but all three of us have had the weirdest, most unexpected things happen to us in the past week. And they're all things we've desperately wished for. How else do you explain it?'

'Fate?' Adam blustered back. 'Coincidence? Certainly not the incredible emergence of a superhero who only exists on the papers in your backpack.'

'He doesn't just exist there,' Zack replied. Adam just looked at him, not sure what he was talking about. 'He's in our minds too. The power of thought is strong. All three of us wishing for something so much; that's not insignificant. You said it yourself, you hate Cadence - God knows why, but you hate her. I hated my colleagues, and Jenny was desperate for love. They're pretty strong emotions.'

'What a load of soppy crap,' Adam said.

Just then the phone rang again and Zack answered it, but Adam couldn't wait around anymore. His head was spinning. He refused to believe a single word that Zack was saying, but deep inside he was very afraid that it could be true.

Had Jenny really been wishing for love and had she finally met the man of her dreams? That terrified Adam more than anything.

'I've got to go,' Adam whispered to Zack who was listening to the caller. Zack nodded and put his thumb up. 'See you Sunday,' Adam added and then he headed back his car.

Adam knew he had to get to work. He really didn't need his job right now. His head was far too deep in other things. But his job had to take priority.

He started the engine and headed to his office. Who knows, maybe the distraction would do him good.

CAUGHT BETWEEN ZACK AND A HARD PLACE

The phone would not stop ringing!

Once again Zack had been forced to sacrifice his lunch, just managing to stuff his sandwiches in his mouth between the torrent of calls. He was having yet another day of endlessly reeling off the same statement over and over about how his colleagues had all been simultaneously struck down with a severe illness. Most people had been surprised or sensitive, but a few had been down right rude, especially the man that had demanded to speak to the Managing Director. He just couldn't seem to get his head around the fact that everyone – everyone – was off sick.

It was now five to five and Zack was desperately counting down the seconds to home time. Just five more minutes of hell.

Zack had been working for Energy Biz for four years. It had been his first and only job since leaving university, where he'd studied animation. He'd chosen quite a specialised course as he knew it was his dream to bring pictures to life. He'd only taken the administration position at Energy Biz, apparently the UK's freshest Energy

Management Consultants, to bring the money in while he waited for his big break. But that big break was still yet to come.

From day one at Energy Biz, Zack had hated it. The people were unfriendly, the work was incredibly boring, and even the atmosphere was likely to stab you in the back. The freshest thing about it was how good it felt to leave at the end of the day.

Zack wasn't originally from Miloworth. He was from the south coast and he'd only moved to the area for university. Not long before finishing his degree he'd started dating a local girl so he'd decided to stay in the area to give their relationship a chance. But she broke up with him a couple of months after he'd started working at Energy Biz and he quickly found himself very alone.

He'd been incredibly miserable in that first year. He wasn't exactly heartbroken about the break-up. She wasn't the nicest girl that Zack had ever met. He didn't make friends easily thanks to his lack of confidence, so when she'd asked him out on a date one day after a lecture, he'd felt flattered. They'd been together for six months before she announced that she was in love with someone else, leaving Zack to feel even more alone than he had before.

He'd thought many times about moving back home, but just the idea of it made him feel like a failure. Therefore, he'd made the decision that his next move would be the life changing one and he stayed put in Miloworth. He applied for any job he could that might offer him his first step on the ladder to his dream and he patiently waited.

Zack always had big dreams. The only problem was he lacked the drive to make them come true, no matter what he might tell himself. He just didn't believe in his talent. His humility was his greatest barrier, and working at Energy Biz had just amplified his lack of confidence even more.

After living in Miloworth for a year, he'd not even had

so much as an interview and he'd begun to sink into quite a depression.

It was just at that time when he'd made the trip to London for Comic Con and, finally, something good happened to him.

It had been his third year of going to the convention, and his third year of doing it in secret, all on his own. He had an obsession with Star Wars, but he'd never told anyone up to that point. He knew other people loved the film, but to Zack it was an overwhelming passion that he'd had ever since he was a kid. Luke Skywalker was like a God to Zack and he'd always thoroughly enjoyed his secret escapes to Comic Con. He thought no one else could ever understand.

But three years ago he'd stopped being alone. By pure coincidence he'd sat opposite Adam and Jenny on the train. Adam always liked to chat to people and before long they were all sharing their stories of Comic Con visits of the past.

They spent the rest of the day together and Zack learnt so much about comics, and he taught Jenny and Adam many of the secrets behind Star Wars. Then they got the train back together and became instant friends for life.

Zack had gone to the same university as Jenny and, being just a year younger than her, he'd been there at the same time as her. But their paths had never crossed until that day on the train.

Meeting Adam and Jenny for their Sunday afternoon get togethers was always the highlight of Zack's week. He might hate every second of his Monday to Friday, but come the weekend he always had something to look forward to.

Things had got even better a few weeks ago when they'd started joking about coming up with their own comic book. They'd stayed in the pub for hours that day, debating character traits and special powers, and then Zack had offered to come up with some concepts.

He'd loved it so much. Being able to spend every night working on a project that actually meant something was amazing. He'd even found the confidence to send samples of his work off to three comic book publishers, after Jenny and Adam had agreed to it. After his run of bad luck, he hadn't got his hopes up, but it was still nice to feel like he was doing something positive.

Zack watched the seconds on the clock tick through the agonising final minute. As soon as the second hand hit twelve, with no hesitation at all, he flicked the phone system to night mode and he stood up. He'd never spent a second longer in the place than he had to, and it wasn't about to start now.

He secured the building properly and then headed to his little, run down car. He spluttered the engine into gear and he made the journey home.

As he sat in traffic he cast his mind back to seeing Adam that morning. He'd been so shocked to learn that Adam didn't like Cadence.

To Zack, Cadence was magnificent. He couldn't deny he was a little bit in love with her. He remembered the first time he met her. It was at a party at Adam's house and she lit up the garden. Literally. She was trying to help Adam light the chiminea when a match suddenly sprung out of her fingers and into a bush. Jenny had thought quickly and she'd grabbed the hose nearby to put the small fire out, but it had been a close call.

Cadence's reaction had been wonderful, though. She'd made so many jokes about 'burning desires' and 'what a flaming good party it was.' How everyone did chuckle. She was so witty and charming and beautiful, and she made the best of what could have been a disaster with such grace. She really was the most remarkable woman that Zack had ever met.

He'd always been jealous of Adam, but if Cadence had to be with anyone other than himself, he couldn't think of a better man. Adam was the closest friend that Zack had ever had and he would never begrudge such a friend happiness.

But it had transpired that Adam wasn't happy. Why? He was the luckiest man alive yet he'd wished for Cadence to disappear off the face of the planet. Why would he do that?

For a moment Zack conceded that perhaps he didn't know Cadence that well. But then he couldn't think of a single instance in all the years that he had known her that he'd ever doubted her greatness. Nor, for that matter, her and Adam's love for one another.

She'd always been the perfect hostess at their parties. And what about when she popped by on a Sunday to check Adam was okay, or say hello or goodbye to him? She never had an issue with how much he was drinking or how long he was spending with his friends. She always seemed to encourage him to be his own man. She'd always come across as the ideal woman.

Zack found himself shaking his head as he pulled up into the car park. Zack lived in a one bedroom flat above a carpet shop and the available parking directly related to how busy the little row of shops were. All in all, it was far from a glamorous abode, but it was the best he could afford.

He unlocked the stiff door on the side of the pavement and then walked up the musty staircase to his brown, battered front door.

As he opened it up, he saw that he had a couple of letters waiting for him. He picked them up before quickly deciding that they were of no interest, and then he headed to his tiny bedroom to get changed into something more comfortable.

Just then he thought he heard a squeak. He stopped moving to listen more carefully, but there was nothing. It must have been his imagination. He took his shirt and trousers off and started rummaging through his drawers for his jogging suit bottoms and a comfy T-shirt.

There it was again. It was more like a shriek or a gasp, and it seemed to be coming from the living room.

Warily, he stepped out of the bedroom. His living room door was shut. He never shut his living room door. What was the point? It was only him in the flat. He knew something was wrong.

He needed a weapon. This could be bad. He dashed into the kitchen across the other side of the hallway and grabbed a saucepan from the cupboard, then he slowly made his way back to the living room door.

Carefully, he pushed the handle down. His heart was racing. When the door was released, he quickly pushed it open to surprise the unexpected guest, when suddenly he dropped the saucepan on the floor, barely missing his toe.

Sitting on his tatty brown sofa was Cadence.

'What are you doing?' he asked with shock.

It didn't look like the Cadence he was used to, though. This Cadence looked terrified. Terrified but still breathtaking in her striking red nightdress. Well, what there was of it.

Zack found himself having to take a deep breath. Then suddenly he was very aware that he was dressed in only his boxer shorts. He needed to keep a hold of himself.

At least he'd chosen his new black pants that day and he wasn't wearing one of his scruffy, trusty favourites. That was something to be grateful for.

'Is this your flat?' Cadence replied, very meekly.

'Yes. What are you doing here? Adam's been worried sick about you.'

'Has he?' she asked with hope. Then Zack felt awful. Should he have said that?

'He came to see me earlier. He said you'd just disappeared.'

'I have no clue what happened. I was in the bathroom moisturising and then the next thing I knew I woke up here, on this sofa. I've been stuck here for hours.'

'But Adam said you disappeared last night. You weren't

here when I left this morning. Where were you all night?'

'I don't know.'

'Why haven't you gone home?' Zack asked, although he had to admit he was quite glad that she was sitting in his living room looking all needy.

'I can't. I've tried.'

'What do you mean you can't?'

'I'll show you,' Cadence said standing up.

She raced to the front door and Zack followed her. She opened it up and tried to take a step out, but she stopped. It was like she was hitting an invisible force field that was trapping her in his flat.

'Come here,' Zack said, not quite able to believe what he was seeing. He touched her back to try and push her forward, but the second any of her body tried to cross the threshold it stopped. It was as if the door was still shut and she was walking into it.

'See!' she said with panic and worry.

'What the hell is going on?'

'I've been so scared, Zack,' she said. She looked down at him with deep sincerity. Zack only came up to her nose. It wasn't that he was short, of course, just that she was very tall. 'I'm so glad you live here. I'm so glad it's you who's come to rescue me.'

She threw her arms around him and his head became buried in her bosom. Suddenly he was more aware than ever that he was only in his boxer shorts.

'Zack,' she said, looking down at him. 'You're my hero.' Then she took his cheeks in her hands and she kissed him passionately on the lips.

ZACK'S PREDICAMENT

'What are you doing?' Zack said, fumbling away from Cadence. He scampered back to his bedroom where he quickly threw his dressing gown around him to hide any further embarrassment.

'What are you doing to me, Zack?' she said breathlessly, standing in the doorway.

'What do you mean?' he mumbled.

'It's like I've suddenly seen you in a whole different light.'

Zack didn't know what to say. He sat down on his bed fearful that he may collapse.

'I've had my suspicions that you may like me. Am I right?' she asked, sitting very closely next to him.

What was he supposed to say? It was his best mate's girlfriend. They were practically engaged. But no, hang on, they weren't. Adam didn't want to be with her.

'What about Adam?' Zack said, trying to see how things lay from her perspective.

'What about Adam?' she replied. 'I don't see him here.'

'He's your boyfriend.'

She looked to the floor. 'It's true,' she said. 'We love each other.' Then she looked across at Zack again, 'But the lust I'm feeling for you at this moment is like nothing I've ever experienced before.'

Zack stood up. He didn't know what to do with himself. On the one hand, his friend had admitted to him only hours before that he didn't want to be with this woman and he'd been trying to break up with her for years. Thinking about it, it was actually all Adam's fault that she was now sitting on his bed.

Then Zack also had to consider how he saw Cadence as a Goddess. He'd fantasised about a moment like this on many, many occasions. Talk about a dream coming true.

No. As it stood at that moment, she was still his best mate's girlfriend, and she'd just admitted herself that she was in love with Adam. It wasn't right.

'Have you eaten?' Zack said, trying to change the subject.

'Not since last night,' she said. 'But at the moment I'm only hungry for you.'

She stood up to throw her arms around Zack again when he made a quick dash for the kitchen, calling back, 'I'll whip us up a sandwich, shall I?'

He headed straight to his bread bin to pull out a loaf and he grabbed a few slices. 'Will corned beef be okay?' he asked as Cadence appeared next to him.

She pulled at his dressing gown. 'I never knew what a gorgeous body you had,' she said, rubbing her hand across his chest.

Zack stopped still. Was she joking? Adam had a six pack. He trained three times a week and ran half marathons. Zack didn't even know what the inside of a gym looked like. This had to be some sort of a wind up.

'I know what you're thinking,' Cadence said, as if she was reading Zack's mind. 'But I'm surrounded all the time with these seemingly perfect people. It's all so fake. I've yearned for a real man for so long; someone who isn't afraid of a bit of hair on his chest or a slight podge around his stomach. It's grittier, I love it. If I have to see another toned set of abs I might die. I want a real man who isn't afraid to be himself.'

She yanked Zack's dressing gown off him and threw it to the floor. He suddenly felt incredibly shy. Then she backed him against the wall and she kissed him again.

She was a very good kisser. She knew just how to touch him.

'You really like me?' Zack asked, pushing her away for a second.

'I don't understand how I've not noticed before,' she breathed back. 'It's like suddenly I'm seeing the man of my dreams. Oh Zacky!' She kissed him again and this time Zack didn't hesitate in kissing her back.

Adam didn't want to be with her and it would appear the feeling was now mutual. She wanted to be with Zack. Everything was just as it should be. What did he possibly have to feel guilty about?

Cadence stepped away, grabbing Zack's hand. She silently led him to the bedroom where she lay down on the bed and waited for him to join her.

He paused for a second, thinking through what he should do. But there really was only one option. The most perfect woman in the world was lying on his bed, waiting for him to make love to her. How could he not oblige?

He leapt on top of her and before he knew it they were kissing and caressing one another with such urgency, he was worried he might actually explode.

'Zack?' he suddenly heard from the hallway. He knew that voice. It was Adam!

They'd left the front door open!

Before Zack had time to react, Adam was standing in the bedroom doorway agape.

'What the fuck are you doing?' he said.

Zack wanted to say something like 'It's not what you think,' or 'There's a really simple explanation,' but it was quite obvious what was going on. There was really no denying how aroused he was and, when he looked across at Cadence, her breasts were popping out of her nightdress. It actually couldn't have looked much worse.

'Why is Cadence here?' Adam demanded to know.

She sat up straight and tidied herself. 'What are you doing here?' she demanded to know in reply, as if somehow Adam was in the wrong.

'Foolishly, I was worried about you. I was coming to talk to my friend about it. Some friend he turned out to be.'

'I'm sorry, mate,' Zack said. He scurried to his feet and quickly grabbed the T-shirt and jogging suit bottoms that he'd been looking for earlier.

'Why were you two in bed together?' Adam said.

Cadence elegantly got to her feet. 'Someone was finally showing me some attention. It was hard to resist.'

Adam shook his head. 'Well, good. You two can have each other. It's over, Cadence.'

'What?' she said, seemingly far more angry than upset. 'How dare you! Nothing really happened here. You don't get to treat me like this.'

'You were about to have sex with my mate. I think I have every right to say it's over.'

'No!' she screamed.

'How could you do this?' Adam asked, now glaring at Zack who was finally relieved to be dressed.

'I didn't do anything,' Zack replied, not even convincing himself.

'She's my girlfriend.'

Zack felt the scratch of indignation. 'You told me this morning you didn't want to be with her.'

'You said what?' Cadence shrieked.

'Oh shut up!' Adam shouted back at her. 'You have no right to comment. You ran off in the middle of the night to sleep with my mate.'

'That's not what happened!' she yelled in reply, for the first time looking upset.

'It was Emmett, I tell you,' Zack whispered in Adam's

direction.

'One minute I was in our bathroom, the next minute I woke up on his horrible sofa,' Cadence explained.

'Hey!' Zack said.

'I'm not judging,' Cadence replied to Zack. 'But it is covered in food stains.'

'So you woke up here and then you decided that Zack was the man for you and you jumped straight into bed with him?' Adam asked, incredulously.

'No! I couldn't leave. I can't leave.'

'It's true, Ad,' Zack said. 'She's stuck in here. There's like an invisible barrier that won't let her out. It's Emmett, I know it is.'

'Will you stop all this crap!' Adam said, getting visibly irate.

'I suppose I was just taken over by how much Zack looked after me,' Cadence said to Adam. 'When was the last time you acted like my knight in shining armour?'

Zack nodded along before questioning to himself exactly how heroic he'd been. He had offered to make her a corned beef sandwich, he supposed.

Adam exhaled sharply. 'It really is time we call it a day, Cade. This hasn't worked for a long time, and we both know it.'

'No, Adam baby. No.' She raced over to hug him but he pushed her away. He stormed off into the living room and Cadence looked heartbroken.

'Let me go and have a word with him,' Zack said to her. She nodded meekly.

Zack closed the bedroom door behind him and he walked into the living room to find Adam pacing the carpet.

'What the hell were you doing with her?' Adam said as he rubbed his hands through his hair with exasperation.

'I don't know. She came on to me. She kept telling me she wanted me.'

'Don't make me laugh,' Adam scoffed. His words had

such a sharp edge to them, Zack actually felt quite hurt.

'Why can't she fancy a man like me?'

'Because it's Cadence. She's obsessed with hair and clothes and fitness.'

'And what? I'm an unfashionable slob with bad hair?'

Adam shrugged. 'You said it.'

'You bastard.'

'You slept with my girlfriend!'

'You told me you couldn't stand her! I thought that opened up a green light for another man.'

'You were supposed to be my mate.'

'You know what your problem is,' Zack said, feeling such hatred towards Adam all of a sudden. 'You want your cake and you want to eat it.'

'What!' This seemed to flare up a new level of anger in Adam and he swung out to punch Zack.

By nothing but pure luck, Zack managed to edge out of the way. His heart was pounding.

Adam lurched forward a second time, this time catching the top of Zack's ear. Zack tried to back away, but before he knew it Adam had grabbed him in a head lock.

Zack didn't know what to do. It hurt. It really hurt. He'd never been in a fight before and he really wanted it to end quickly.

He tried to struggle free but Adam's grip was tight. Then he had the bright idea of swinging his arm back. In his mind he imagined that he'd knock Adam over, but as he thrust his arm backwards, it had such little momentum, all he did was lightly tap Adam on the leg. It was hardly threatening.

Suddenly Adam let go. Zack gasped for breath, expecting Adam to be ready to apologise, but as soon as he turned around he was gobsmacked.

Standing directly between them, like an exact replica of Zack's imagination, was Emmett the Empathy Man. He was really there, in the flesh.

'Can't you see you're both getting what you want?' Emmett said in a deep and meaningful voice. 'Why are you fighting?'

Zack and Adam just glared at one another, then their eyes simultaneously turned back to Emmett.

'You're supposed to be friends. There's no need for this fighting.'

'He had no right to sleep with Cadence behind my back,' Adam justified. 'No matter what I said, she was still my girlfriend.'

For the first time, Zack felt awful. He'd betrayed his friend, there was no denying it. His groin had taken over when his head should have been in charge.

'I'm sorry, mate,' Zack said.

'Why aren't you happy if this is what you both wanted?' Emmett asked. Then he shook his head before walking off into the wall and disappearing.

For what seemed like hours, Zack and Adam said nothing. Zack didn't even know what to think.

Then finally Adam shook his head and said, 'I can't handle this. I'm out of here.'

He walked straight out of the living room and Zack heard the front door slam shut just seconds later.

Zack took a few deep breaths. The past week had most definitely been the weirdest of his life. He had to take a moment just to be sure he wasn't dreaming. What was going on?

He headed back into the bedroom to find Cadence sobbing on the edge of the bed.

'Come here,' he said, putting an arm around her. 'It's going to be all right.'

'How?' she sniffled.

'Because it has to be,' Zack replied, but deep inside he knew there was no real answer to her question. Had he just lost the best friend he'd ever had?

JENNY'S BOYFRIEND

The smile was stretched across Jenny's face as she read the text again.

How have we only known each other a week? It feels like forever (in a good way) xxxxxx

Jenny and Nathan had been texting non-stop since he'd left her flat that morning. After seeing him twice over the weekend, she'd joined him at the pub for last orders the night before and then, for the first time, he'd come back to her place.

She'd told him that they couldn't stay up too late as she had work the next day, but then they'd barely slept all night. They were like loved up teenagers who couldn't take their hands off each other, and it was making her tingle all over just thinking about it.

She texted him back.

I know. So glad you have dodgy taps at your pub otherwise we may never have met. xxxxxx

She was still grinning inanely as she checked her fridge

to find something for dinner. She'd finally met a really nice man. Her time had come.

Her phone beeped again and she grabbed it from the kitchen side.

Be honest if it's too soon, but would it be OK with you if I called you my girlfriend? xxxxxx

Jenny felt delight flutter through her. She was a girlfriend. She had a boyfriend! She'd not had the pleasure of calling anyone her boyfriend for years. Not since her second year at university with that lad who'd ended up cheating on her after eight months.

She knew Nathan was different, though. She knew Nathan was a keeper. She didn't hesitate in texting him back.

You've just made me even happier :-) I have the best boyfriend ever! xxxxxx

She went to open her fridge again, but she knew there was no way she could eat. She was jittery with excitement.

Her phone started to ring and she picked it up expecting it to be Nathan wanting to discuss the good news. But it was Adam.

Just for a moment, the butterflies in Jenny's stomach flourished, but she refused to acknowledge it.

'Hi!' she said. She recalled how he'd turned up at her flat in a fluster that morning. That had been a bit weird.

'Hi,' he said. He sounded awful.

'Are you okay?'

'Are you home?' he asked. 'I mean home alone?'

'Yes.'

'Can I come up?'

'Yeah, of course.'

'I'm actually right outside your front door. Buzz me in?'

Jenny couldn't believe it. In all the years she'd known

Adam he'd never made a surprise visit, yet this was his second unannounced visit that day. Something was clearly very wrong.

Jenny jogged over to the intercom in the hallway. 'Come in,' she said, pressing the buzzer.

She hung up the line and opened her front door.

Her one bedroom flat was large and newly refurbished, but Jenny was not the neatest of people. It was a bit cluttered. She kicked her shoes out of the way as she waited for Adam to appear.

She'd been living there for the past two years, after moving out of the home she grew up in. Her parents and younger brother only lived about a mile away, but as Jenny's confidence had grown her need for independence had grown with it. With very little help from her friends and family, she'd dealt with estate agents, located her flat and had set up a home for herself. It ate up most of her wages paying the rent and bills all on her own, but she loved having her own space.

Adam appeared at the top of the stairs looking haggard. He was in the same suit he'd been wearing earlier, but he seemed to be half the man. It really wasn't like him. He was normally so sharply dressed, with exceptionally polished shoes and perfectly ironed shirts. But at that moment he was bordering on scruffy.

He hugged her the second he stepped foot in her flat and she felt her heart quiver. He may have lost the smart edge to his appearance, but he never failed to smell good.

'Do you have any whiskey?' he muttered.

'Since when have I been a whiskey drinker?' she smirked. 'It's beer, or I might have some wine in one of my cupboards. I'm not sure.'

'Beer would be great.'

'No problem. Make yourself at home.'

Jenny dashed into the kitchen to grab two cans of Budweiser, then she paced through to the living room to find Adam slumped on the sofa.

She placed the two beers on the coffee table and she looked down at him with concern.

'What's happened?' she said, the worry in her voice quite evident.

Adam sighed. He leaned forward, not able to look at her. Then he shook his head. 'Where I do start?'

'Anywhere you like.'

'Well... Emmett is real, and I've just broken up with Cadence.'

Jenny's mouth dropped open. As soon as he'd finished his sentence the first part of it vanished from existence in her mind. There was only one thing she was willing to register at that moment: he'd broken up with Cadence.

Jenny couldn't move. He'd broken up with Cadence!

Suddenly Jenny's phone beeped a message. She grabbed it from her jeans pocket and glanced at it. It was Nathan.

Nathan!

Adam was single and she was with Nathan. How had that happened?

This was all wrong. She'd been keeping herself free for Adam for years. She'd wanted to be the one to pick up the pieces. She'd imagined this moment for five years, and now it had finally, inexplicably happened, she was someone else's girlfriend. It just couldn't possibly be true.

She quickly read the message.

I've just managed to get Saturday off. Fancy spending the whole day together? I'm going to spoil you rotten. xxxxxx

Jenny felt sick. What a mess.

'Is everything all right?' Adam asked. Then he looked at her more seriously. 'Is that your new bloke?'

Jenny breathed in deeply to try and control the nausea. 'It's not important,' she said. 'Just give me a sec.'

She knew she had to text back. She had to try and put Nathan off texting her again that night. They were now on what must be text eight hundred for that day, but suddenly Jenny wasn't so keen on the exchange anymore.

Great, can't wait. Adam's just turned up. He's broken up with his girlfriend. Am going to be a shoulder to cry on for a few hours. Call you later?

She threw her phone down on the chair behind her, but she was still unable to move her legs. What was she going to do? Adam was single.

No, it couldn't possibly be true. They'd just had a fight. There was no way Adam was going to leave Cadence. Jenny didn't even know any of the details, she had to stop panicking. They were probably going to be back together, happier than ever, by the weekend.

'Have you two had a fight?' she asked, realising that getting the facts was going to be the only way to stop her mind overthinking it.

'Who?' Adam said.

'You and Cadence,' Jenny stated, not sure who else she could have meant.

Adam shook his head. 'You could say that.'

'It might not be so bad. Just take a little time out,' she said, not really able to believe that she was actually encouraging him to sort it out with the bitch.

'I don't think so. I caught her in bed with Zack.'

Jenny automatically sat down. Of all the things she'd expected Adam to say, that wasn't even in the same galaxy. Words really had failed her.

Suddenly her bum vibrated. She realised that she was sitting on her phone. She grabbed it to see another text from Nathan, but she couldn't face dealing with him at that moment. She threw her phone on the coffee table and totally ignored it.

She had so many questions, she didn't even know where to begin.

Adam opened his can and took a gulp before slamming

it back down quickly. 'I can't. What am I thinking? I drove here.'

'Stay the night!' Jenny blustered out before her brain could catch up.

Adam turned to her and for a moment he looked relieved. 'Would that be okay? I really don't fancy going home tonight.'

'Of course. You know I'm always here for you.' *I'm picking up the pieces just like I'd always planned,* she thought to herself. Although the reality was now not at all as she'd expected.

'Thanks.' He bounced up and down. 'You have a very comfy sofa, this will be perfect.'

'Or you could top and tail with me?' she said, again without any thought at all for the words that were coming out of her mouth.

Adam smirked. 'Share your bed? What would your new bloke have to say about that?'

Jenny felt the surge of sickness again. 'What could he think?' she said, trying to grin. 'We've known each other for years. If something was going to happen between us, I think it would have done by now.' As soon as the words left her lips, her heart sank. That was the truth of it. All the fantasies aside, Adam was in love with Cadence and always had been. He was bound to get back together with her, or at the very least this was going to take him years to get over. He must be utterly heartbroken. He'd found his girlfriend in bed with another man; and not just any man, but a close friend.

An image of Cadence and Zack together flashed through Jenny's mind. That seemed far too odd. It was like the world had turned completely upside down.

'Shall we go to the pub?' she said. Fresh air and a fresh pint suddenly seemed desperately appealing.

'That's the best suggestion I've heard all day,' Adam declared, pulling off his tie. 'I'm having a triple whiskey the second we get there.'

'I'll just get my shoes on,' Jenny said, searching around for her pumps.

'And I'll just down this,' Adam added, grabbing the can of beer firmly in his hand.

By the time Jenny had hunted down her favourite shoes, Adam had gulped down his drink and they were ready to go.

JENNY'S NAUGHTY THOUGHTS

They walked mostly in silence to their favourite pub, The Red Lion, just five minutes away from Jenny's flat. It was where they met every Sunday and there was nowhere else they'd considered going.

'Triple Glenfiddich and a pint of Amstel, mate,' Adam ordered as they reached the bar.

Jenny scanned to see what Glenfiddich looked like. She'd never known anyone drink it before. Then her eyes caught the Courvoisier and she felt very silly.

'What's Courvoisier?' she asked.

Adam looked at her curiously. 'It's brandy,' he said. 'Why? Do you want some?'

'No,' she said, shaking her head. 'I had some recently. Would you ever have it with blackcurrant juice?'

Adam smirked. 'Are you joking?'

Jenny frowned. 'Never mind.'

She was saved as their drinks were presented in front of them.

They took a seat towards the back of the room where they could find the only free table. For a Tuesday night, the pub was crowded.

They sat quietly for a moment, sipping at their drinks.

Jenny had so many questions swirling around her head but she didn't know where to begin. Maybe it might help if she knew more about what had happened with Zack.

'So, were Zack and Cadence actually having…?'

Adam shook his head. 'No, not quite.' He sighed and she could tell he didn't want to think about.

'She made a mistake. If you love her then I'm sure you can find it within yourself to forgive her.' Jenny couldn't believe she was encouraging him again. When she'd imagined herself as the girl who was going to pick up the pieces, she'd never seen herself as being quite so pro-Cadence.

Adam shook his head again. 'I haven't exactly been honest with you, Jen,' he said. He couldn't look at her and she felt her heart pound. What was he going to say? Had he cheated on Cadence too? Had he slept with Zack? No, that was ridiculous. She really needed to stop panicking so much.

'I've wanted to break up with Cadence for years.'

Once again, as if it were weighed down by an anchor, Jenny's jaw dropped open. 'What?' she managed after a few seconds. She was riddled with so much shock and anger that she virtually spat at him.

'I know. I know! This is the exact reason why I've not told you. Every single time I've thought about breaking up with her, someone tells me how great she is and how lucky I am. I've been so confused. I can't stand the woman but everyone else seems to think she's the best thing since sliced bread.'

Jenny gasped. He hadn't wanted to be with Cadence for years. He can't stand the woman! If she'd just said something. If she'd just commented on the many faults of the bitch, then Adam might have walked away years ago.

But there lay the problem. Jenny couldn't really think of many faults. Other than the fact that she was living with the love of Jenny's life, generally Cadence had always been nothing but lovely. It made it very hard to hate her.

'Why can't you stand her?' Jenny asked, utterly desperate to know.

'Because she's the most annoying woman on the planet!' Adam replied and Jenny could see how irate he'd become just talking about it. 'You don't know what it's like living with her. She drives me up the wall.'

'Give me an example,' Jenny said, trying to sound vaguely curious but actually soaking up the gossip.

'You mean besides the fact that she's obsessed with her appearance, tells me how to live my life and thinks that a cleaner should enter an already clean home? I mean what's the fucking point!' Adam said.

Jenny tried hard to stifle her giggle. This was great! 'Anything else?'

Adam thought for a second. 'How about the fact that she's always lying to people about stuff?'

'Okay,' Jenny said, eager to see where this was going.

'She always tells people that she's allergic to things, or certain foods disagree with her. Remember when she told you she was lactose intolerant?'

'Yeah.'

'Well, she's not. It's bullshit. I'll admit she only ever touches skimmed milk, but nothing stops Cadence and her morning coffee. And she does eat chocolate, you know, on her birthday and at Christmas.'

'Maybe she's just embarrassed about dieting all the time.'

'No, she's just weird. She's told the postman that she's allergic to paper. She says he has dirty hands and she doesn't want to touch the envelopes that he's been pawing, but she also doesn't want to offend him. She leaves these little gloves by the front door so she can pick up the letters as they arrive, and the postman completely falls for it. He told me how much he felt for her being allergic to something so fundamental in life. He loves giving her sympathy and she laps it up. I've never known anything like it. It's ridiculous!'

'That does sound-'

'Then take our love of comics,' Adam continued. Jenny could see he was on a roll and she had no desire to stop him. This was so much fun! 'I never told you, but she could have got us those tickets for San Diego.'

'You said her agent had tried every lead and they were impossible to get.'

'No, he could have got them easily; she just refused to help. She's never supported me. Empathy Man's another prime example. I wasn't keeping our comic a secret from her because I wanted it to be a surprise, I was doing it because she'd make fun of us.'

'She'd make fun of us? What a bitch!'

'Shit, Empathy Man!' Adam said, taking a large gulp of his whiskey.

Suddenly Jenny remembered something that Adam had mentioned earlier. Something about Empathy Man being real. Or had she imagined that? There was a lot going on at that moment.

'It's all my fault, you know,' he said, shaking his head and staring at his whiskey like it was telling his fortune.

'What's your fault?'

'I can't really be mad at Zack. Nor Cadence. I mean it's over between us, that hasn't changed, but I might be completely to blame.'

Jenny felt a mixture of delight and confusion as she pushed Adam to elaborate.

'Zack's got this theory,' Adam said, then he sipped at his whiskey again.

'I'm sure Zack's got a lot of theories,' Jenny said, impatient to find out what was all Adam's fault.

'He told me this morning that he thought Empathy Man was real. Zack reckons Emmett's working his powers on us. He's making our wishes come true.'

Jenny snorted with laughter. 'You've got to love Zack's imagination.'

'It turns out he's right. We saw him. We saw Empathy

Man. Zack and I were fighting in his living room and Empathy Man broke us up. I mean he actually touched me.'

'What? What are you talking about?'

'Zack thinks it's to do with how powerful our desires are. He hated all of his colleagues and every single one of them is now off sick. Look at the facts. What is the chance of that happening? Then I wished for Cadence to disappear.'

'You did what?' Jenny was at first surprised and then she couldn't help the spasms of delight that shot through her.

'That's why I came around this morning. I was totally confused. Last night Cadence went into the bathroom and then she never came back out. She just disappeared into thin air. Puff. Just like that. Then she turned up later today at Zack's place.'

'Why had she gone to Zack's?'

'I don't think she had. I think Empathy Man had sent her there.'

'Why would he do that? Or, more accurately, how could a fictional character do that?'

'I didn't just wish that Cadence would disappear,' Adam said before glaring at his drink like it was the most important thing in the room. 'I thought maybe she might turn up again and I didn't want that. I actually wished that she'd have an affair so then she wouldn't be so perfect and I could finally break up with her without feeling bad.'

This was a hell of a lot for Jenny to take on board. The mixture of confusion, delight and slight nausea every time she remembered Nathan was getting hard to manage.

She took a deep breath. 'That still doesn't explain why Cadence turned up at Zack's flat.'

'I think he has a bit of a soft spot for her.'

Realisation dawned on Jenny. 'It was a wish of his to be with Cadence?'

Adam just shrugged. Then he finally looked across at

Jenny. 'You've got your wish too, haven't you?'

Jenny kept her mouth shut. How did he know? Did he feel the same way?

'After all those crappy dates, you seemed quite smitten with that Nathan this morning. You must have wished to find a decent man after all this time.'

Jenny couldn't speak. She could almost hear her heart cracking inside her chest.

'How come you never told me about him?' Adam asked.

She looked into Adam's eyes. He was the only man she wanted. This was all such a cruel joke.

She searched her mind. What had she really wished for?

The night she met Nathan popped into her head. She'd been crazy with jealousy at the thought of Adam having sex with Cadence and that had been a sobering lesson in the morning. It had forced her to make the decision to move on. Just at the moment that a fictional character was in their lives making all their wishes comes true, she'd wished to move on.

How unfair was that!

'Jen?' Adam nudged. 'Are you okay?'

Jenny snapped out of her self-pity mode and she forced a smile. 'Of course.'

'Tell me about this Nathan. Where did you meet him?'

'Not before I get us another round in. Triple whiskey was it?'

'I'm not asking you to pay for that,' Adam said. He had such kindness in his voice.

'My best mate has hit a real low, I'll buy him whatever I like.'

'Then you can buy me an Amstel, same as you.'

'Are you sure? You can have anything you want.'

Adam stared at her silently for a moment. Then he said, 'A pint of Amstel will do just nicely.'

It was two pints later when Jenny and Adam staggered

back to her flat. With each sip of alcohol, the conversation had lightened greatly, and as they were walking home they were full of smiles and laughter.

Adam had tried several times through the night to throw in the odd question about Nathan, but Jenny had replied with as little information as possible. Part of her really wanted to forget that Nathan even existed.

'I've got a cleaner anyway,' Adam smirked as he walked on the pavement next to Jenny. 'I'm looking for something better than that if I'm going to pay for you and Zack to go to San Diego.'

Jenny's head was spinning with all the things that she'd like to do for Adam in return for tickets to San Diego Comic-Con, but most of them she could never say out loud.

'What about cooking? I could cook your dinners for you,' she said.

'Be honest, you know you're not the best in the kitchen,' he replied.

'But Zack is! Do you remember those homemade burgers he brought to your barbecue last year?'

'Yeah, they were really good. Okay Zack can cook for me, but I want something extra special from you.'

Jenny's head spun into naughty mode again. She didn't know whether it was the fact that Adam was now single or perhaps that they were spending time together just the two of them - which they hadn't done in ages - but something about that night was making her fantasies spiral out of control.

'I could be your slave,' she said. Then she giggled quickly with slight embarrassment.

'My slave?'

'Yeah. Not permanently. Just for say a month.'

'And what would you do for me as my slave?'

'Anything you'd like me to,' Jenny replied, her words a little more serious. She couldn't help it. She bit her lip, excited at the thought.

'I'm interested.'

'I could be at your beck and call.'

'I'm liking the sound of this. Perhaps when I want a beer from the fridge while I'm watching TV or playing on my PS4, you could get it for me. Or you could go to the door to collect my pizza.'

They reached Jenny's front door and she felt deflated. That wasn't exactly what she had in mind. But it would have to do, she supposed.

'Sounds like a plan,' she said.

It was after midnight when they got into her flat.

'Are you sure it's okay for me to share your bed?' Adam asked. 'I'm all right on the sofa.'

'Don't be silly,' Jenny replied, trying to calm the panic in her voice. 'I've shared my bed with lots of friends.' She knew that was a complete and utter lie. Why would she be sleeping all the time with her friends? It didn't even make sense. But at that moment she was willing to say anything to ensure that Adam slept with her. Erm... next to her.

'If you're sure, then thank you.'

Jenny's whole body wanted to dance and punch the air but she kept herself composed. 'Great.' Even though she'd barely slept the night before, the adrenaline that was racing through her made her believe that she may never sleep again.

Then suddenly the thought of Nathan and how he'd been in bed with her just twenty-four hours before sent jitters through her. She couldn't sleep next to Adam in a bed that still had essence of Nathan in it. That was far too much for her mind to process.

'I'm just going to change the sheets!' she said.

'What? Now?' Adam asked.

Jenny glared at Adam. She didn't want to say why. Then his face seemed to click.

'Nathan stayed over last night,' he said, his face void of emotion.

'Yes.'

'I'll help.'

'No, it's fine. You just get ready for bed. There's a spare toothbrush in the bathroom cabinet if you want.'

'I don't mind helping you.'

'It will only take me a second.'

Jenny opened the cupboard behind her to grab some new bed sheets. She turned around again with her arms full to suddenly find Adam removing his clothes.

In her mind, at that moment, she believed that she was only glancing surreptitiously, just from the corner of her eye. But the truth was that she was standing agape, watching his perfect body appear from under his shirt and trousers as if it was the most beautiful unveiling a girl could ever witness. Luckily it seemed Adam was too drunk to notice.

When he was down to just his boxers, Jenny found herself praying that he wouldn't stop. But he did.

'Is everything all right?' he asked, turning to her and seeing her mouth wide open.

'I didn't think I had any clean sheets,' she said, thinking fast. 'Phew, I just found some.'

She quickly started rummaging around with her duvet, trying to look busy, pretending not to notice that the man of her dreams was now standing in her bedroom virtually naked.

He smiled and then headed off to the bathroom and Jenny had to take a second to compose herself.

Now she really knew she wouldn't be sleeping. He was the most gorgeous man that Jenny had ever seen. How was she meant to not look overwhelmed?

She'd never made her bed quicker. She yanked at the duvet cover and pillowcases like the world depended on it, and it was all done (although far from tidy) by the time Adam returned, and she sat on the bed smiling like it had all been a piece of cake.

Placing his glass of water down on the bedside table, Adam looked at her. 'Which is your side?' he asked.

Jenny had no clue what to say. She really didn't care where he slept as long as it was next to her.

Then she quickly stopped the naughty thoughts that popped into her mind again.

'You choose,' she said. 'I'm just going to get my pyjamas on.'

He nodded and then tucked himself under the pink stripy duvet on the side closest to him. Jenny grabbed her pyjamas that were strewn on her floor, but she quickly decided against them. They were her old ones. She needed to look her best tonight. Adam certainly did.

She opened her drawer to find her lacy ones that she'd treated herself to in the sales. She took them to the bathroom to get changed and then appeared back minutes later in sexy looking shorts and a vest top.

She snuggled under the duvet and Adam immediately put his arm out so she could cuddle up next to him.

Her breath extinguished as she nestled in against his chest. She'd never felt his body before like this and it was even more amazing than she'd imagined.

'I don't know what your boyfriend would say if he could see us now,' Adam sniggered.

Jenny's heart sank. Why did he keep reminding her about Nathan? Just when she was lost in the fantasy that she and Adam were together and this was any other night in their bed, he had to talk about her actual boyfriend and bring her hurtling back to reality.

'You and I are just friends,' she said. 'What does he have to worry about?'

Adam rolled over to look at her. They were now lying face to face and she could feel his breath against her skin.

'I don't know what I'd do without you, Jen,' Adam said, stroking her cheek.

Jenny could feel her heart pounding. *Kiss me, kiss me, kiss me,* she prayed over and over.

But Adam just slowly closed his eyes and within seconds he was asleep.

SURPRISING JENNY

For the second night in a row, Jenny barely slept. Both she and Adam had dozed for a bit, then they'd woken up and chatted, then they'd dozed for a bit. Or at least she'd told Adam that she was dozing. In truth, she'd spent most of the time just watching him sleep. She was desperate to log the image into her long term memory so she could flick back to it whenever she wanted. A moment of perfect happiness.

But she wasn't really happy. The reality of the situation actually broke her heart. After all, this was just pretend.

The truth of the matter was that Adam had been upset and all he'd done was turn to his friend for comfort. He would have been happy on the sofa but she'd pushed to get him into her bed. The second that morning came, it would all be over, never to be repeated again; and there was absolutely nothing Jenny could do about it.

Jenny's phone alarm played its silly tune at eight o'clock sharp and she sighed.

'What time is it?' Adam said, sitting up straight.

'Eight.'

'Fuck! I'll be late for work.'

'How are you feeling?' Jenny asked, noting that she felt

pretty awful herself. The hangover was wretched, but she also felt drained from the lack of sleep. It had been worth it, though.

'Like utter crap.'

'Why don't you call in sick?'

Adam looked at her like she'd just come out with the most unacceptable idea on the planet. 'I can't do that.'

'Well, it's not exactly a lie. You feel like crap, and I think you might be able to justify not being in the right frame of mind for work considering the fact that you've just broken up with your girlfriend.'

Adam sighed. 'Maybe you're right. I can't remember the last time I was off sick. It's not like I make a habit of it.'

'It will give you a chance to sort your head out.'

Jenny didn't move for a moment. She couldn't help but hope that he might suggest that she take the day off with him. It wouldn't be easy pulling a sicky considering her work was just a five minute walk away. But they could stay in her flat all day. They could stay in bed all day.

'I'd better get in the shower,' Jenny said, cutting her own fantasy short. She had to stop it. It was getting too painful. Even though Adam was now single, she didn't want to be the rebound girl. That would totally ruin their friendship and then she'd have nothing.

After a swift bowl of cornflakes, Jenny left Adam in her bed and she reluctantly made her way to work. He'd promised to be gone before lunch and there was nothing Jenny was able to say to change his mind. She wanted him to stay forever, but that was never going to happen.

At just before nine she reached her office block. "Heart Attack Marketing" was on the first floor and Jenny slowly clambered up the steps trying to think away her hangover.

After leaving university, Jenny had been lucky enough to get an interview at a large marketing agency in London for a junior Graphic Design role. It would have been a huge opportunity for her. But after visiting there for her first interview, she knew that city life wasn't for her. Instead she secured herself a job at an agency about ten miles away. But after six months she discovered that a commute wasn't right for her either. Therefore, when an opening had come up at Heart Attack Marketing, she'd jumped on it, and she'd been very happily working there since.

She made her way into the small, open plan office. There was a team of eight that sat together and then one isolated office to the side that housed the two owners of the company.

The whole place was blood red with images of hearts and heart monitors scattered all around the walls. It wasn't exactly a calm environment but the owners were incredibly passionate about what the brand stood for.

Fundamentally, their idea was that their marketing was so good, clients were in danger of getting a heart attack upon seeing it. As soon as the owners spoke about it, it made perfect sense. Their enthusiasm for it was so contagious that everyone who left the office was reeling about the breathlessness that they were inevitably going to suffer from when the first marketing pieces were laid before them.

On just one occasion had Jenny found herself presenting the introduction piece. One of the owners had been off sick and it was a new client that they couldn't put off. They'd all sat through the PowerPoint presentation so many times, everyone thought she'd be able to do it effortlessly. But it was a disaster. When she spoke about it, she managed to make it sound like they were sadists who were angling to bring about the suffering, pain and perhaps even death of their clients. No matter how hard she tried to save it, it just got worse and worse. She could have sworn one of the men had tears in his eyes.

That client never signed with them. And Jenny had not been asked to present since.

Jenny turned her computer on, said her hellos to her colleagues, and then she headed straight to the little kitchen where she was in dire need of a coffee.

She came back out a few minutes later to find an enormous bunch of flowers on her desk and all her colleagues staring at her.

'Where did they come from?' she asked.

'They were just delivered,' Jodie said from the adjacent desk.

With a flutter to her heart, Jenny opened the card that was taped to the box. She'd never had flowers before.

To my darling Jenny
Just a little gift to celebrate us in an official relationship. I couldn't ask for a better girlfriend.
Nathan xxxxxx

Jenny froze. She didn't know how to feel. Something about it deeply unnerved her. Long gone were the tingles of excitement she'd had yesterday.

Then she remembered she still had a text from him that she hadn't read. She'd deliberately avoided looking at her messages all night after Adam had turned up.

She grabbed her phone from her bag to find that she actually had five texts from him. Was that too much?

19:03
Oh dear, sorry to hear that. Send Adam my best. There's nothing worse than a broken heart. I look forward to speaking to you later. xxxxxx

Of course, that was after she'd told Nathan that she was acting as a shoulder to cry on. Well, she had been. Sort of. Then there were four more.

21:11
Thinking of you and missing your texts. Hope Adam is okay.

Do let me know. xxxxxx

23:38
*I've just finished work so I'm free to speak whenever you are.
Call me whenever Adam has left. No rush. xxxxxx*

00:43
Hope you're okay? Worried as I've not heard from you. xxxxxx

02:14
*I have to go to bed now. Sorry if you wanted to talk. But please
still try if you want, if I can't sleep I'll answer. Missing you.
xxxxxx*

His last text was after two in the morning! She didn't
know whether to feel flattered or scared. She shook her
head. She had to remember that she'd been on top of the
world twelve hours before. Just yesterday they'd texted
each other more times in half an hour than he had all
night. She couldn't think anything badly of it.

She smelt the enormous bouquet. It was full of all
different colours. A rainbow, just as she liked. That was
sweet.

Had she ever told him that?

'Who are they from?' Jodie asked, full of enthusiasm.

Jenny didn't know what to say. Then she supposed she
should just tell the truth. She had to stop hoping that
something would happen with Adam. 'My new boyfriend.'

'Ooh, do tell! Who is he? Where did you meet him?'
Jenny could feel all the eyes in the office staring at her,
waiting for her to elaborate.

Jenny didn't talk much about her personal life. She'd
not mentioned to anyone that she'd been online dating,
and she was always sketchy about how she'd spent her
weekends. The only people she ever really opened up to
were Adam and Zack.

But now Nathan too. She'd felt so comfortable with

him, she'd told him things that she would never normally talk about. He really was a nice man and they did get on very well. Maybe he actually was the one who was going to make her happy after all.

'He's the manager of a pub in town,' Jenny said. 'We just got talking one night and then... the rest is history.' A flash of Jenny demanding that they have sex after she'd only known him for half an hour sparked in her mind. She wouldn't be telling that version of events, that was for sure.

'What's his name?' Jodie asked. She was bubbling with excitement. Jodie was slightly older than Jenny with a husband and a toddler, so they led very different lives. They never socialised outside of work (except for work parties, of course), but they got on very well and always had a giggle in the office.

'Nathan. He's a sweet man.'

'How long has it been? Why are we only just hearing about this?'

'It's only been a week. It's early days, but all good so far.' As soon as Jenny said that she felt sick. If Jodie had asked her yesterday, Jenny might have bounced around the room with elation. But today she just felt confused. Nathan was nice but Adam was still the love of her life. What a mess that made.

Jodie's phone rang and Jenny was given a lucky escape. She sat down, very happy to throw herself into her work. What she needed now more than anything was a distraction. She didn't want to think about the complicated state of her love life, let alone talk about it.

She buried her head into her work and refused to make eye contact with anyone else. If she didn't look at them then they might forget she was there.

She'd been working on some new direct mail concepts for a client that had recently rebranded and she dived straight into finalising them, ready to show her bosses.

Her morning flew by and luckily all talk of her new boyfriend had been forgotten about. At just before midday she pressed print and she grabbed the four A3 sheets of paper, ready to present her work to the owners of the company.

She knocked on their office door and Sebastian and Charlie welcomed her in.

'Are you happy with these for the presentation tomorrow?' she asked, laying out her four concepts on the table in the middle of the room.

'These are for the Grabfield account?' Sebastian checked and Jenny nodded.

Both Sebastian and Charlie were tall and lanky, and about the same age, perhaps late thirties. They were so alike they could have been brothers, and they certainly loved and hated each other like family. Jenny had always admired them as bosses, with their passion, caring nature and wealth of experience. She'd learnt a great deal from them and they'd always been very encouraging. She counted herself as very lucky to be working there.

The pair studied the detail on the paperwork before them for a moment and then they looked at each other seriously.

'Let's take one at a time, shall we?' Sebastian said. 'Concept one is definitely heart attack material. I can feel my blood pressure rising just looking at it. I love what you've done with the brand colours, Jenny, how you've blended them with the coldness of winter. Just as we talked about. Amazing work.'

'I agree. Heart attack city that one,' Charlie said.

'But two and three are lacking something,' Sebastian continued.

'Maybe slight tingles,' Charlie said, 'but a long way off a heart attack. It's the stock image on three, I don't like it. Do we have to use a stock image?'

'We wanted one with a different slant. A simpler proposal,' Jenny reasoned.

'I don't like it, scrap it,' Charlie said. 'Let's try and make two bolder, but ditch three. It's never going to cause a heart attack and that's definitely not what we want.'

'But four,' Sebastian said, clasping his hands together. 'My, my Jenny, you have surpassed yourself.' Suddenly Sebastian grabbed his chest, pretending to be in pain. She'd learnt over the years that this was a time to feel proud. This was him acting like he was having a heart attack and it was because she'd smashed her work.

'I agree,' Charlie said. 'If they don't have to be stretchered out after seeing four, then we may as well shut down.'

'Great work, Jenny. Fabulous work. If you can just give two a bit more pizazz then we'll be good to go.'

Jenny tried to downplay her excitement as she gathered up her papers. Her last project had been a bit of a flop so she'd needed to hear that she'd smashed it this time.

She headed back to her desk when suddenly she was grounded to a halt. She grasped the papers tightly in her hand, double checking that she was really seeing what she thought she was, because it definitely looked like Nathan was sitting at her desk.

She took a deep breath and walked over to him. He had a beaming smile. 'What are you doing here?' she asked in a low voice.

'I thought I'd surprise you and take you out for lunch. Your colleague buzzed me up.'

'So romantic!' Jodie grinned.

'I've got a lot of work to do,' Jenny said. She'd only considered popping to the sandwich shop in town. She wanted to focus on getting the concepts ready for the big meeting.

'It's not healthy to not have a break,' Nathan said.

Jenny sighed. Maybe half an hour wouldn't be so bad. 'All right. But we've got to be quick.'

She placed the papers on her desk and then grabbed her bag.

'Bye you two,' Jodie smiled. 'Have fun!'

JENNY'S MESSAGES

It took all afternoon for Jenny to get concept two right and she didn't get home until half past six that night. But she'd been happy with the end result so it had all been worth it. She just really could have done without the half hour wait for food at lunchtime. Why had Nathan insisted on taking her out for a proper meal? She would have been happy with just a sandwich.

She had to remember that it was very sweet of Nathan to surprise her like that. It had also been a useful hour as spending that time with him had reminded her of how much she did like him. They'd chatted away like they'd known each other for years and she'd felt happy to call him her boyfriend.

She popped her flowers in the sink and ran water over the stems. Having never had flowers before, she wasn't the owner of a vase, but she didn't want to see the flowers die. She told herself she'd pop into town during her lunch hour the next day and buy one.

Suddenly her phone beeped in her pocket. It was a WhatsApp message from Lizzy.

Hi, how are you? Major news — I lost my job yesterday :-(My company has gone into liquidation. Don't know what I'm going to do. I've barely slept all night worrying about it. Haven't told the family yet, so please keep it to yourself. Hope things are good with you. xx

Jenny couldn't believe it. Poor Lizzy. Jenny knew that Lizzy had never really loved her job but it's still not nice to lose it.

She didn't know how to respond. What could she say? After a few moments of contemplation, Jenny decided that Lizzy just needed a friend rather than someone to counsel her.

Oh no! I'm so sorry to hear that. I'm sure you'll get a new job really soon. You're the best IT Manager I know! Stay positive. xx

Jenny headed out of the kitchen and into her bedroom where she was immediately halted by the sight of her bed all neatly made. It never looked like that. She always went to bed with her duvet in the same mess as when she'd woken up that morning. It was Adam who was all neat and tidy.

She couldn't resist smelling her pillow. It smelt of his musk and it sent tingles through her. She pondered to herself as to what time he must have left.

There was only one way to know. Why couldn't she text him?

Hi, how are you feeling now? Any better? What time did you get up in the end? xx

She sat on the bed. She didn't know what to do with herself. All she wanted was the reply. After a few minutes of silence though, she realised how silly she was being. She pulled herself together and moved into the living room. She plonked herself down on the sofa and flicked the telly on.

Finally her phone beeped. She grabbed it so quickly from the coffee table that she nearly fell on the floor. She sighed. It was just another Whatsapp from Lizzy.

To be honest, I've been thinking all night about coming home. Maybe this is the universe telling me that my time in Oz is up. xx

Jenny sat up straight and smiled. She would love to have Lizzy home again. And she certainly knew how much Adam had missed his sister.

I definitely think you should listen to the universe. We've all missed you so much, it would be great if you moved back home. Obviously you need to do what's best for you, but I vote for you to come back :-)

Jenny placed her phone back on the coffee table and then mulled over what she could have for dinner. After having a big lunch and still feeling nauseous from the madness of events that had taken place in the last twenty-four hours, she didn't feel even remotely hungry.

Her thoughts were cut short when her phone beeped again. It was another message from Lizzy.

So sweet! Moving home is seeming like a good option at the minute but I need to think some more. Just please don't tell my family yet. I want to decide what to do first. They'll only worry. Anyway, how are you? Any gossip? xx

Jenny thought for a second. She certainly had tons of gossip but she wasn't really sure whether she wanted to share it or not. Jenny had told Lizzy about a year ago that she was in love with a man who had a girlfriend, but she'd been otherwise vague with the details. Lizzy really liked Cadence and Jenny felt somehow wrong in admitting the truth to Lizzy. Were there rules about whether you could date a friend's brother or not? Jenny had never been sure about the etiquette so she'd always been light on the details. Besides, with Lizzy not really knowing the facts, it had allowed them total freedom to have fun thinking up ways to get rid of the horrible girlfriend.

Jenny decided that she wanted to share the exciting news that her Mr Dream-Man was now single, but she couldn't bring herself to mention anything about Nathan. It was too complicated to detail in a message. But that was the only reason, of course.

My main news is that my Mr Wonderful is now single. He broke up with his crappy girlfriend yesterday. Don't know what to do. Can't tell him how I feel. xx

Jenny sat back and flicked through the channels, but she wasn't really watching any of them. She was now eagerly awaiting two responses.

Her phone beeped and it was Lizzy.

You really should tell him. What do you have to lose? x

Jenny felt sick. That was ludicrous. How was she supposed to be honest?

He's a good friend. I'm worried that if I tell him and he doesn't feel the same way then it will change our relationship. I'd rather have him as just a friend than nothing at all. x

Jenny stood up. She needed something to do. She looked out the window, down to the street below. There were kids playing with a football, making the most of the beautiful weather. It was nice to see.

At last her phone beeped again. She scurried back over to pick it up and she saw that it was a reply from Lizzy

You know what you should do — make him jealous! You need to flirt with another man in his presence. I bet as soon as you show

someone else more attention than him, you'll have him wrapped around your little finger. It's only when you're not available that men seem to notice. xx

Jenny shook her head. That was all very well in theory, but she'd got a boyfriend and Adam wasn't even remotely jealous. In fact all he ever seemed to do was talk about Nathan, like he wanted to get to know him better. It made him a lovely friend and it was so disappointing.

Jenny had never been able to work out why men were always so difficult.

She sat back down when suddenly a thought came to her. Adam wasn't jealous, but he had only seen Nathan once; very briefly. Other than that, Nathan was nothing but a name and Adam was still very much the centre of her world.

She thought about inviting Nathan to their next Sunday get together. She could spend the whole afternoon flirting with him and holding his hand. She could pretend that she'd completely forgotten Adam was even there.

She quickly decided against that idea. It wasn't that she didn't want Nathan there, of course. It was just that it would upset the balance. It had always been just the three of them and it was always the highlight of Jenny's week.

Besides, she didn't know if she could flirt with Nathan when Adam was around. It was too messy.

If it was going to work then she needed to flirt with someone that she didn't fancy and who definitely didn't fancy her in return. She needed to duck in and duck out with only Adam noticing. Just enough to get him riled.

Of course! What about if she was to flirt with Zack? Perhaps on their next Sunday get together she could hang off Zack's every word and act as if Adam didn't exist? That would surely make him jealous. It was worth a try. As Lizzy had said, it's only when they can't have you that men seem to sit up and take notice.

Suddenly her door buzzed. Someone had come to see

her. It must be Adam!

All thoughts of flirting and game playing vanished from her mind as she leapt to her feet and raced to the intercom. 'Hello?'

'Hi! It's Nathan!'

Jenny's whole body slumped down with deflation. What did he want? Again?

'Are you okay?' she asked.

'I'm on a break and I thought I'd pop over quickly to see how you are. You seemed a bit stressed at lunch.'

Yes, I was, she thought to herself, *because I had work to do and some man turned up out of the blue to take me away from it.*

But she knew she couldn't say that. 'I'm fine,' she replied instead. 'No need to worry.'

'Can I come up?' he asked. 'I only have half an hour.'

Jenny sighed. She was watching the telly. This was hugely inconvenient.

'Sure,' she said, buzzing him in.

She opened the door to immediately find his beaming smile heading up the stairs.

'Hi,' he said as he entered, and then he kissed her straight away, knocking the door shut with his foot behind him.

He pinned her against the wall and kissed her deeply, and for a second she gave in and it was quite enjoyable. But then she knew it had to stop. She pushed him back gently.

'Sorry, it's been a long day. I'm not in a good place right now,' she said.

'Oh no, darling. I'm so sorry. Work troubles?'

'Yes. I only got home a short while ago.'

'Still working on that big presentation?'

'We got there in the end.'

'I knew you would. You're so clever.'

'You want a cup of coffee or anything?' she asked.

'That would be lovely. You make the best coffee I've ever had. Then we could cuddle up on the sofa together if you want? We could also have a nibble on these?' He presented a huge box of chocolates from behind his back

'Oh, how nice,' Jenny said, although the gesture just left her cold. None of what he was saying had any appeal at all. She just wanted to be alone.

She sighed. It was only for half an hour and he was her boyfriend. She should make some effort.

'I'll pop the kettle on,' she said.

She heard her phone beep from the living room and her heart fluttered. What if that was Adam?

She filled the kettle with water at break neck speed and then raced to the living room to pick up her phone, leaving Nathan in the kitchen to sort out the mugs.

It was! It was finally a reply from Adam. Yippee!

I'm doing OK. I left yours late morning. Thanks for last night. You're the best.

Jenny read the message three times. It felt so cold.

'Shall I go ahead and pour the water?' Nathan called from the kitchen.

Jenny shuddered. For a moment she'd forgotten he was there.

'Yes, thanks,' she called back before looking at the message again and sighing with disappointment.

She'd been hoping that after their wonderful night together Adam might be a bit more chatty and it might bring them closer together, but this was a message that left no opening for a reply.

He was going through a break-up, she had to remember that. Or maybe he was distracted and he'd texted her back quickly?

Then she considered another option. What if he'd only been talking with a bitter tongue the night before and, in fact, he didn't really dislike Cadence as much as he'd said? What if he was on his way to see her and they were going to patch it up?

'Here you go,' Nathan said, bringing the two mugs into the living room.

'Thanks,' Jenny said. Then she realised that maybe she should stop obsessing over a man that was nothing more than a friend and focus on a man that clearly really liked her. Maybe that would just be the better thing all round.

If she kept up this behaviour then she might lose Nathan too and then where would she be?

Nathan grabbed the box of chocolates and they curled up on the sofa together.

This was Jenny's new life now and it really wasn't that bad. She chose a coffee crème from the box and she nestled into Nathan's arms.

Life really could be a lot worse, she told herself, and she tried to finally relax.

ADAM'S FRESH START

That morning, Adam had lay in Jenny's bed feeling full of confusion. He'd wanted to kiss her so much the night before.

He knew that Jenny had always been the centre of his world. There had been so many times that he'd put Jenny first, ahead of Cadence, but he'd never questioned why before. Not until he'd seen her with that man. Suddenly it was like jealousy had woken him up to the truth.

But she had a boyfriend. She was gone. He was single for the first time since he'd met her and now she was off the market. Why couldn't he have realised his feelings sooner?

None of it mattered, though. Jenny was just his friend. Adam was never going to be her type. She clearly preferred more edgy men. This Nathan had tattoos across his chest and his hair was long and straggly. He couldn't be more different to Adam's clean-cut business look. Jenny was never going to want more than friendship.

As much as he'd wanted to spend the day in Jenny's flat and be there, cooking dinner for her when she arrived home, he hadn't wanted to outstay his welcome. He'd pulled himself together around midday and he'd headed straight home.

However, when he got there it didn't feel like home. Looking at it with a fresh perspective, he'd realised how much of the house had Cadence's influence on it. None of it had been what he'd wanted. She'd chosen the furniture, the colour scheme, the layout; even in his games room she'd insisted that only artistic pictures of his superheroes be placed on the walls. He'd been permitted to display his expensive canvas of an old Spider-Man comic book cover but he hadn't been allowed to put up his free Avengers poster.

Not that it mattered now. He'd already made the decision that morning to give the tenants in his old house notice and move back in. This had never really been his home and he couldn't wait to get his own space again.

It had never occurred to him once to sell his old house. He'd had a gut instinct from the start that he'd need it again one day. He actually couldn't understand why he'd moved in with Cadence in the first place. Now he'd finally ended it, he felt a huge weight had lifted. The only thing he regretted was all the time he'd lost.

After making himself a quick sandwich for lunch, he'd spent the afternoon trying to complete his F1 season on his PlayStation, but his lap times were appalling.

He'd wasted hour after hour playing his games, enjoying the fact that no one was about to walk in and stop him. Cadence was still trapped in Zack's flat and that was the best news he'd had all year.

He'd completely lost track of time, shut away in his games room, when suddenly he heard a text message buzz on his phone. He gazed over at it lying on the arm of his chair and his heart instantly skipped a beat. It was from Jenny.

Hi, how are you feeling now? Any better? What time did you get up in the end? xx

He sighed. Jenny was lovely. Look at her worrying about him.

For a small second, he considered telling her the truth. Should he tell her that he'd got feelings for her? No, he quickly decided against it. She'd said herself the night before, if anything was going to happen between them then it would have happened already. All his honesty could do was ruin their friendship.

He tried to think of a suitable response.

You are the best friend a man could ever want. I don't know what I'd do without you.

No, that was such sloppy rubbish. He tried again.

Thanks for last night. I'll remember it forever. I loved waking up next to you.

No, far too much. It was true, he had loved the night before and he'd certainly loved waking up next to her. It used to be just Jenny and him all the time until they'd met Zack that day. Adam really liked Zack, and the three of them always had a good time together, but the night before Adam had been reminded of how much he enjoyed having Jenny all to himself. He wanted that again. He wanted that more. He wanted that forever.

I think I'm in love with you. You just need to know.

He definitely couldn't say that!

Adam had never felt so despondent. He was finally free from Cadence, he should be happy. But he'd just realised, far too late, that there was something he wanted more than being rid of Cadence. Although it was never going to be within his grasp.

The more he thought about it, the more he felt like he'd just about lost everything. He wanted to always be friends with Jenny, but he didn't know if he could see her with a new man. What if they got married? It would be just like Jenny to ask him and Zack to be male bridesmaids or something. How could he watch her slip through his fingers like that?

Adam lay down on the soft, cream carpet. Never before had a girl broken his heart. He'd been blissfully unaware of what it even felt like until that moment. It wasn't pleasant.

He thought back to the first time that he'd met Jenny. She'd been the only person to laugh at his "with great power comes great responsibility" quip and she'd captured his attention straight away. She had such an infectious smile and she could talk about anything. He also couldn't believe she had a passion for comic books. How he'd always longed to meet a girl who shared his passion for comics.

They had so much in common and he hadn't been able to leave her side all night. Maybe he'd had feelings for her straight away? But they were the days when he was happy with Cadence. Cadence used to be his world. Or so he thought.

Then he remembered the first time that he'd seen Jenny's new look. She used to be such a quiet, mousey girl when he first met her. But the day she walked into the pub with her new blonde hair and that skimpy denim dress was the day that Adam really sat up and took notice. That was the day that Jenny had morphed from a nice friend that he thought the world of into a woman he couldn't stop thinking about. That was the day that lust came into the mix.

Her new appearance brought with it a new confidence. Her blonde hair suited her so much and then, when she started getting streaks in her hair, Adam had nearly fallen of his chair. She was so striking. She was stunning.

Her skirts had got shorter, her clothes had got tighter and her whole essence began to ooze sex appeal. She wasn't afraid to be an individual and he absolutely loved her for it.

But he still hadn't realised quite how he'd felt. Adam sat up, frustrated with himself. Why had he left it so late to realise his feelings? He'd had loads of sexual fantasies about Jenny. Why hadn't he put two and two together? Why had he been so fixated on his tragic relationship with Cadence rather than putting his energies into the one woman he actually wanted to spend all his time with?

It didn't matter anyway, it was all too late. She was with someone else and this new man would now get to enjoy her in a way that Adam could only dream about.

He closed his eyes and wished that it would all go away. He didn't want the pain. He didn't want to see Jenny with her new man and he didn't want to have to face Zack or Cadence any time soon. Maybe he could just hide in bed for a week or two? Or go away on holiday on his own?

He got up and perched himself on the armchair. He needed to text Jenny back and then he would order a calorie-crazed, self-pity pizza, and eat and drink himself into a coma. That would make it all better.

I'm doing OK. I left yours late morning. Thanks for last night. You're the best.

That would do. It was nice and to the point but gave nothing away. She was probably only asking because she was bored, waiting for Mr Tattooed-and-Muscly to show up.

He sent the message and then opened up the Pizza Hut website. It was going to have to be extra large.

The next morning Adam woke up feeling rough, but not because of the food and drink. He'd managed two slices of his enormous pizza and just one beer. He'd been far too depressed to eat and drink in the end, and he'd been buried under his duvet by half past nine, wishing the world away.

He felt rough because he'd had a restless night, mourning the loss of, what he now believed to be, his soulmate. He felt a huge gaping hole within himself and he knew he only had himself to blame.

As much as every inch of him wanted to stay hidden in bed all day, he knew he had to go to work. At least there were only two days until the weekend.

He'd decided in the middle of the night that he was going to excuse himself from Sunday's get together down the pub. He couldn't face Zack and he was worried that Jenny would invite Nathan along. He couldn't bear the thought of that.

Reluctantly, he clambered out of bed and got ready. He couldn't eat breakfast, and he was in his car for quarter past seven.

He was one of the first to arrive in the office at just before eight o'clock and he didn't hesitate in getting straight down to work. He was desperate to focus on something other than the mess he'd made of his love-life.

By ten he was caught up on everything that he'd missed from the day before, and then he started to plan for the sales meeting that was scheduled for the next week. He always liked to be well prepared for everything.

'Adam, you got a second?' Terence, the Managing Director, said, appearing at Adam's office door.

'Of course,' Adam said.

Terence took a seat before pressing his fingers to his lips, clearly looking for the right place to start.

'We have good news,' he said.

'Yes?'

'We've just had the go ahead to open the Hamburg office.'

Adam smiled. 'At last.' The global company, headquartered in the USA, had been looking to open up new offices across Europe, but the decision making process had seemed to take forever. 'I was starting to think it would never get signed off.'

'Quite. But as these things go, you wait for what feels like a decade and then they want everything yesterday.'

'Tell me about it!' Adam nodded with a smirk.

'They've already chosen the premises and they're looking to start the recruitment process immediately.'

'That's great news.'

'And they want you to lead it.'

Adam didn't respond for a moment. He wasn't quite sure what to make of that statement. 'What do you mean, lead it?'

'I've been on the phone to Detroit and we all agree you're the best man for the job. We want to promote you from Head of Sales to European Head of Sales, and we're looking for you to spend six months over in Hamburg finding the right people and then training up the team. What do you say?'

Adam was gobsmacked. That was the last thing he'd expected. It was totally out of the blue.

'Don't worry, we'll pay all your expenses out there, and Cadence's too. And this promotion will come with a very generous pay rise,' Terence added.

Adam shifted in his seat. Did he want to move to Hamburg?

Then he thought about the current mess of his life. Maybe it was perfect timing. It would get him away from Jenny, Zack and Cadence. It was only six months, and it would allow him a bit of space so he could come back a refreshed, happy man and be ready to be a friend again.

Besides, who knows, maybe he might meet a nice German girl and he could be happy for Jenny and her future husband.

'I'm interested,' Adam said, playing it cool. 'Although I should tell you that Cadence and I are no longer together. It would just be me that would make the move.'

'Oh dear, I'm sorry to hear that.'

'It's fine. It's for the best. If we can just go over the

finer details - maybe negotiate terms - but in principle I think this is a huge opportunity for me. I also think it's come just at the right time.'

A large grin wrapped itself across Terence's face. 'Great news, Adam. You were the only man we thought of. Hamburg won't know what's hit it.' Terence stood up and shook Adam's hand. 'I'll get the contract drawn up today and hopefully we can get you on a plane tomorrow afternoon.'

'Tomorrow?' Adam asked with surprise.

'I know it's short notice, but they're already paying rent on the office. We need you there ASAP to get the ball rolling.'

Adam sighed. What did he really have to wait for? 'I'll look over the contract as soon as you have it, and let's see if we can get this sorted.'

It was after seven o'clock when Adam got home that night. There had been a bit of going back and forth on the details, but in the end he was satisfied with the offer. He was going to be earning a six figure salary, which had nearly knocked him over, plus all of his expenses were going to be taken care of. How was he supposed to say no?

From tomorrow, for a few weeks he was going to be staying in a hotel in the heart of Hamburg, and then they were going to find him more suitable accommodation for the rest of his time there. The USA team was going to meet him next week, and interviews to fill up the Hamburg office were already being discussed with potential candidates.

It was all happening so fast, but Adam was loving it. He needed this escape. The timing couldn't be better. He'd also never been to Germany so he was looking forward to that.

He grabbed his suitcase from the top of the wardrobe and started to pack. He knew it wasn't so far that he couldn't pop home in a few weeks, just for the weekend, to grab a few extra things should he need them. He'd just focus on the essentials for now.

Then he stopped. He had to say his goodbyes. It was his gran's birthday on Saturday. His mum would go mad, but what could he do?

He sat on his bed and dialled his parents' home number.

'Adam, I was just thinking about you,' his mother answered. 'We need decorations for Saturday. Your dad said we should look on Amazon. He's obsessed with Amazon and this instant delivery thing they do. Do you think that's the best place to look?'

'I don't know mum, I'm actually calling about something else. I have news.'

'A proposal?' she asked, and Adam could hear the anticipation in her voice. Then Adam realised that the moment had come. He was going to have to tell her that Cadence was no longer in his life. Still, one thing at a time.

'I've just been offered a huge promotion,' he said.

'That's incredible. Congratulations!'

'But it means I have to go to Hamburg for six months.'

'Hamburg? Why Hamburg?'

'We're opening a new office there and they want me to take the lead in heading up the sales team.'

'Well, that's exciting. What an amazing opportunity.'

'I have to fly out tomorrow.'

'What? They can't do that.'

'I have to, mum. It's part of the contract. They need me there straight away.'

'But your gran's birthday!'

'I'm really sorry. If there was anything I could do.'

'Is Cadence going to Germany with you?'

Adam paused. This was it. 'Erm... no. Actually, there's news there too. Cadence and I have broken up.'

'What?!' his mum screamed. She sounded traumatised. 'What happened? What did you do? You two are made for each other.'

'It's a long story, mum, but trust me it's for the best. Things have been rocky for a while. I'm much happier now.'

'It might not be over forever. Maybe you going to Germany will give you some space. Absence makes the heart grow fonder, you know.'

Adam sighed. 'We're not getting back together. It's over.'

'But Adam-'

'Mum, leave it. It's time for me to move on.'

'Oh dear, I'm so worried about you. Is that why you're running away, to deal with the heartbreak?'

'Don't be silly,' he replied, but he knew there was an element of truth in what she was saying. Although he certainly wasn't heartbroken over Cadence. 'This is a huge opportunity for me. I really wasn't in a position to say no.'

There was a long pause. Adam knew his mum was dying to probe more about his break-up, but he wasn't going to make it easy for her. He just remained silent too, waiting for her to continue.

'I'm always here if you want to talk,' she finally said. 'And you know you can come home at any time, don't you. Just leave. Your dad and I can help you with money.'

Adam smirked. 'Thanks, but I think I'll be fine.'

'What about Jenny? Will she still come to the party?'

It was Adam's turn to pause this time. He shivered for a second imagining Jenny with Mr "I only need a small towel because there's not much to hide" and his face cringed.

Would she bring him to the party? What if Adam's family all liked him and then he got invited to everything? Adam would come back from Germany to find him sitting in his mum's living room sipping a cup of tea, telling her about his latest tattoo. He couldn't have that!

'She can't make it any more. Sorry, mum. She would have loved to have been there.'

'Oh no! None of you are coming? I don't suppose Cadence-'

'We've broken up, mum. I think she might have even met someone else.'

'What?'

'But I don't want to talk about it.'

His mum was struggling for words again. He knew that somewhere in her mind she'd be blaming him. Even though Cadence had cheated on him, his mother would want to find fault with her son as Cadence was just so bloody perfect.

'Okay, I can see you're not ready to talk about it. Tell Jenny to drop by soon, won't you? It would be good to see her.'

'I'll let her know,' Adam replied.

'And you'd better keep in touch. Let us know you get there safely.'

'I will do. I'll be back for weekends and things, don't worry. It's not like Lizzy. I'm still in Europe.'

'I know. Not far at all. Your dad sends his love.'

Adam sighed with relief as he ended the call. Just two more messages to send out. He needed to tell Jenny and Zack. As it still stood at that moment, they were all meeting on Sunday and Jenny was expecting to go to his gran's birthday party on Saturday. He needed to rectify that, and fast.

He typed out a quick message, firstly to Zack.

I'm being sent to Hamburg for work for 6 months. Flying out tomorrow. A big promotion and huge opportunity for me. Won't be there on Sunday now but I'll keep in touch when I can.

He pressed send and then thought about his message to Jenny. This one was much harder to write.

Amazing news, I'm being sent to Hamburg for work for 6 months. Flying out tomorrow but it's a huge opportunity for me. My mum said don't worry about the party on Saturday, plans have changed. I'll keep in touch when I can. Take care. x

He pressed send with a heavy heart. That had been really difficult. He took a moment to compose himself and then he focused again on his packing. His next stop was Heathrow first thing tomorrow morning and it couldn't come fast enough.

ZACK'S IMPROVED FLAT

A week later, on the Friday evening, Zack sat in his car in the car park by his flat and he rested his head against the steering wheel. The last thing he wanted to do was go into his own home.

Adam's text saying he was going to live abroad for six months had given Zack a reason to escalate his relationship with Cadence. It had felt like Adam was giving them his blessing and so that night they both slept together for the first time.

Zack hadn't been able to believe it. He was a complete nobody who'd never really done anything, yet he was having a sexual relationship with a model who had achieved global status. He felt at the time that all of his dreams had come true.

Cadence was very much still stuck in his flat, but he'd promised to try and find a way to set her free. She'd said she was glad of the time anyway, to deal with her break-up and to get used to a new man in her life. She'd told her agent that she was having some time out due to a change in her circumstances and everything had seemed wonderful. They'd barely got out of bed last weekend.

Then Monday came and it all went wrong.

Zack had arrived home from work on Monday night to find a cleaner tidying everything and the furniture in his flat rearranged. Apparently Cadence had invited her Feng Shui Guru over to help balance the yin and yang energies to create a more calming atmosphere. It had been essential for Cadence - so she'd said - during her time of evolvement. Or something like that.

Zack wasn't so keen on the changes but he'd consoled himself with the notion that if it kept Cadence happy then it was all worth it.

It had got worse on Tuesday, though. He'd arrived home to find a brand new leather suite in his living room, a new sideboard, and a rather sophisticated bookshelf with hidden compartments. Apparently the ugly furniture was negating the power of the Feng Shui and it all had to go; although she wasn't being very open about where "go" actually was. He'd loved that sofa, even if it was a bit stained. It had been a hand-me-down from his grandfather.

Feeling a bit miffed, he'd gone to the fridge for some comfort food only to find that had been messed with as well. All of his beers, cheeses and full fat milk had been pushed to one tiny corner to make room for fruit, yoghurts and health food snacks. He'd supposed that wasn't all bad, but it would have been nice to have been asked.

Wednesday had brought cushions, a 'more pure magnolia' painted living room wall and new artwork. Gone were Zack's Star Wars posters and in their places were city landscapes and a couple of half-naked women elegantly photographed. He didn't know whether to like them or not, but he knew that none of them were to his taste and his own home was starting to feel a bit alien to him. She'd promised that his posters were safely put away in the cupboard at the back of the kitchen and she'd pleaded that the new look of the place was more "them". Whatever that meant.

Thursday had brought a fresh challenge when the Yoga

instructor knocked on the door at six o'clock in the morning. Zack had nearly fallen out of bed it had shocked him so much. Then it got even worse when Cadence somehow managed to convince him to join in with her. 'It will revive you ready for the day,' she'd said, but all it did was make him even more tired before having to face yet another day of handling the office all on his own.

His colleagues were still all off sick, and a few had even now been hospitalised. The ones who were feeling a little better had started to work from home to help him out and to try and keep the business afloat, but it was still pretty much a one-man show when it came to Energy Biz.

So it was now Friday night and Zack was dreading going upstairs. He had no clue what new changes were awaiting him but he was sure that Cadence would have been up to something trapped in those walls all day.

Even the sex wasn't that good, if he was honest. She had this way of looking completely disinterested, just saying a few mildly appropriate things without any sort of enthusiasm. She had an incredible body, yes, but he'd quite like her spirit to be present as well.

He bravely made the walk from his car to his front door and he took a deep breath as he pressed the key in the lock. He opened the door to hear cheesy pop music blasting from within; songs that would never normally be played in any home of his.

He slowly walked along his hallway to find Cadence sitting on a chair in the living room and a very glitzy man styling her hair.

'Zacky, is that you?' Cadence said with her back to him. She sounded full of life as always. At least she'd had a good week.

He placed his keys down on his brand new mirrored coffee table and he shuddered as he saw his unwanted reflection. He hated that coffee table. It now meant that no matter where he sat in the room he could always see himself. It wasn't exactly relaxing.

'Yes,' he said, finding himself waving back at the skinny man behind her.

'Go and get changed and then come back and get yourself ready.' She sounded like an overexcited school girl.

'Get ready for what?'

'We're having a make-over!'

'A what?' He desperately hoped that he'd misheard.

'A make-over! I thought it was high time I refreshed my look and I then thought even better if we did it together. Carlo here has some amazing ideas.'

Carlo stopped massaging Cadence's hair and he took a step back to examine Zack properly.

'I'm thinking more spike, more pizazz,' he said. 'Do you ever wear pink? You could so get away with pink. Yes!' He came over and started to rub Zack's cheeks. 'A bit more colour and a bit more showman, and you'll be transformed.'

Zack didn't want to be transformed. He quite liked the way he looked. He'd grown comfortable with it.

He took a deep breath. This really was the final straw. She might be trapped in his home, but he certainly wasn't.

'Back in a sec,' he said, then he grabbed his keys and made his way directly back to his car.

He couldn't believe it. Cadence was unbearable. No wonder Adam had wanted to leave her. She was ruining Zack's life. Not only was she changing absolutely everything, but he hadn't seen Adam nor Jenny since she'd appeared in his flat and he knew that wasn't right.

Not thinking anymore, Zack turned his engine on and he made the short drive over to Jenny's flat. He found a parking space with no problem and he quickly walked up to her front door, buzzing for number five.

'Hello?' she asked with what sounded like trepidation in her voice.

'Hi Jenny, it's Zack.'

'Zack!' He was relieved that she sounded pleased to

hear from him. 'Come on up.'

The door buzzed open and he made his way to her front door where she was waiting for him. The first thing she did was give him a massive hug and Zack felt a huge weight disappear. He really needed a friend.

'Come in, come in,' she said.

They sat in her living room and he declined her offer of a drink. He was far too edgy to drink anything.

'It's all gone to crap,' he said.

'What has?' she asked.

'Have you spoken to Adam? Do you know that I've been living with Cadence?'

Jenny's phone suddenly beeped a message. She checked it quickly and then threw her phone aside. 'Sorry,' she said. 'Yes, Adam, he's told me everything.'

'She's a bloody nightmare!'

'Really?' Jenny responded, clearly trying not to smile.

'She's changed my flat around, she's got rid of all my furniture and she's replaced all my Star Wars stuff. You know I love my Star Wars stuff.'

'I know you do. Too right you do!'

'Then when I got home tonight she wanted me to have a make over. A bloody make-over! Do I need a make-over?'

'Not in the slightest. You're perfect just the way you are. She's a bitch, I tell you. Such a bitch.'

'Well, lesson learnt for me. Never judge a book by its cover.'

'It's what's under the bonnet that counts,' Jenny nodded. Then they both chuckled.

Jenny's phone beeped again. She glanced at it quickly and then threw it back on the coffee table.

'Is everything all right?' Zack asked.

'It's fine. Just app notifications.'

'Oh right.'

Zack exhaled. He felt instantly more comfortable in the company of a true friend. What another awful week he'd had.

'Does Adam hate me?' he asked meekly.

'Of course not. He said he blames himself.'

'Blames himself? What did he do? I'm the one that slept with his girlfriend. I should never have done that.'

Jenny paused for a second. Then she said, 'He told me your Emmett theory. How he's been making our wishes come true.'

Zack nodded. 'Did Adam tell you that Emmett turned up out of the blue and stopped our fight?'

'It doesn't make any sense. How can that even happen?'

'I think our desire for change must be strong.'

'Well, Adam certainly seemed keen to get rid of Cadence. I mean I think he did. Do you think he did?'

'To get rid of her, yes. To shag his best friend, no.'

'I think it might be more complicated than that,' Jenny started and this caught Zack's attention. 'He admitted that he actually wished that Cadence would have an affair so he'd have a good reason to dump her. If Emmett really is controlling everything then it makes sense that he'd push her into your arms.'

'Why my arms?'

Jenny hesitated. 'Adam suggested that you might have a bit of a crush on Cadence. Maybe you'd wished to be with her?'

Zack went to argue but he stopped himself. He shrugged. 'It was just as a fantasy. She's a model, of course I thought about her. I bet most blokes on the planet have fantasised about her.'

'If that's what floats your boat,' Jenny said folding her arms.

'So he's not angry with me?'

Jenny shook her head. 'He was very confused, but he didn't say anything bad about you. I don't think he's angry with anyone.'

'Have you heard from him?'

Suddenly Jenny's phone beeped again and she visibly tensed as she glanced at the notification.

'Are you sure everything's all right?' Zack asked. He wasn't used to seeing Jenny appear so uncomfortable.

'Yes, I'm fine,' she said in a voice that told him she was anything but fine. 'And yes, I have heard from Adam. I texted him to make sure he got there okay and he texted me back to say he'd arrived at the hotel. And then I texted him a couple of days ago just to say hi. He seems happy enough.'

'I've not heard from him at all. I wish I could speak to him. I want to sort all this out. I want to tell him he was right to dump Cadence and agree that she's unbearable. I want to apologise.'

Jenny's phone beeped again and this time she studied it hard. Zack assumed it was a message from someone. After a few moments, she slowly placed it down on her lap and she glanced at Zack in deep thought.

'Do you think men always want what they can't have?' she asked. It was such a random question, Zack didn't know quite how to answer it.

'I don't know,' he shrugged.

'Like take Cadence. Did the fact that she had a boyfriend make her more alluring?'

Zack shrugged again. 'I don't know. It wasn't that I wanted to take her off Adam, if that's what you mean.'

'No! No, of course not. I just mean, do you take more notice of what you can't have than what is sitting there right in front of your face?'

Zack hadn't got a clue what Jenny was wittering on about and all he could think about was whether Adam might have believed that he'd been after Cadence for a while. 'Yeah, I suppose,' Zack replied, although he wasn't really sure what he was agreeing to. It just seemed easier to say yes.

'How about we go to Hamburg?' Jenny suddenly said.

'What?'

'It's the weekend, why not? You and me.'

'Just show up out of the blue and surprise Adam?'

'Great idea. I know what hotel he's staying at and he knows nobody in Germany. I bet he'd be thrilled to see us. The two of us together.'

'I don't know. I can't really afford to get a sudden flight out. Where would we stay?'

'I'll pay for everything. I've just had a bonus. Let's go and see Adam.'

'I can't ask you to pay.'

'You're not asking. I'm telling you.'

All of a sudden the Superman theme tune started to play out from Jenny's phone. It looked as if she was actually holding her breath as she glared at it in horror. She waited for it to stop ringing and then she threw it on to the coffee table.

'Let's leave right now,' she said.

'Now?'

'Yes, why wait?' She picked her tablet up from the table and she threw it at Zack. 'You find us the first flight we can get and I'll make sure we're on it. Doesn't matter what the cost.'

'From where? Luton?'

'Anywhere, I don't care. I think it will be really good for you and Adam to talk. Don't you?'

'I suppose,' Zack shrugged.

'Right, I'm going to pack.'

Jenny almost ran to her bedroom while Zack loaded up Skyscanner. He looked through all the options and then he stood up to talk to Jenny.

He poked his head around her bedroom doorway. 'There's a flight tomorrow morning just before eight from Stansted. We could get that.'

'Sounds perfect. We'll leave now.'

'The flight's not for like twelve hours. It'll only take an hour or so to get to Stansted.'

'Nonsense. Have you not heard about all those

motorway closures? They're all over the place. It's best we get there now and then we can stay in one of the airport hotels overnight.'

'I haven't got that sort of money, Jenny.'

'Good, cause you're not paying for it. We can stop at your place on the way to get your stuff.'

Zack hesitated. 'Do we have to go to mine? Cadence won't like it. What am I supposed to tell her?'

Jenny looked at him directly, for the first time not flustering around. 'Is she really that bad?'

Zack just nodded.

'Okay, then we can just buy you some underwear and stuff, you won't need a lot. What, just jeans and a couple of T-shirts, and perhaps a razor and toothbrush? You can use my shampoo and toothpaste, I don't mind. No, hang on, you'll need your passport.'

'That's not a problem,' Zack said, feeling a pinch of relief. 'Remember when I met with that recruitment agency a few months ago?'

'Yeah. What happened with that?'

'Not a lot. They never called me again. Anyway, I had to take my passport with me to show I was eligible to work in the UK, and I've just sort of left it in my car since. I know it's bad, but...'

'At this moment, it's great! So we don't have to go back to yours for anything?'

Zack bit his fingernail. This was a tricky situation. He really couldn't afford to buy new clothes; his money was tight at the best of times. But the other option was to go home where he'd have to tell Cadence that he was off for the weekend to see her ex-boyfriend. That wasn't going to be an easy conversation. Even if it was his best mate, she'd never see it like that.

Stuff it! He'd worked exceptionally hard all week and it was finally the weekend - and his weekend was always about seeing his mates. He was going to do this. He couldn't remember the last time he'd been abroad. This was going to be brilliant.

'There's no reason to go back to my flat,' Zack said. 'Next stop is Stansted!'

For the first time in days Zack actually started to smile.

ZACK'S APOLOGY

They landed at Hamburg International Airport at about half past ten on Saturday morning. They left the airport with minimal delay and got straight on a train to Hamburg Hauptbahnhof, the main city centre station.

From there they hopped in a taxi and Jenny asked to be taken to the "Hotel Sehrklein". It was the first time that either Zack or Jenny had ever seen a German city and they marvelled at how tall and grand the buildings were.

The journey only took a few minutes and they arrived down a very quiet street. The taxi dropped them off outside the rather humble building and they headed for the entrance.

With Zack not really having much in the way of clothes, they'd only brought one suitcase between them, and Zack had taken charge of carrying it. He approached the tiny doorway of the hotel and struggled to get both himself and the multi-coloured suitcase through. He finally won the battle though, to be immediately faced with what seemed like the world's smallest reception.

'Hallo, willkommen. Kann ich Dir helfen?' a blond man with glasses said. He was standing behind a tiny podium that was posing as the reception desk. He looked very young, almost like he could be a student doing work experience.

Zack glared at Jenny. He had no clue what the man had just asked them. The only German he knew was "Möge die Macht mit Dir sein," but he didn't think that was going to be helpful. He'd met a German man at Comic Con once who had taught him "May the force be with you", but it had yet to become a useful piece of trivia.

'Do you speak English?' Jenny asked.

'Of course. How can I help?'

'Our friend is staying at your hotel and we're here to surprise him.'

'Very good. What's his name?'

'Adam Valentine.'

The man took a second to look on his computer, then he nodded. 'Yes, let me call him. What are your names?'

'Tell him it's Jenny and Zack,' Jenny said. 'We're his best friends, he'll know who we are.'

'Very good. Please, wait in the bar.'

This felt like an instruction not a suggestion, and Zack and Jenny did as requested. They turned left, following his finger, to find a very small ledge with one beer pump and two metal chairs at a little metal table. They shuffled in and took the seats, the coldness of the metal sending shivers through Zack.

Even though it was the middle of summer, it was a rather grey day and not exactly warm.

They waited for a few minutes when suddenly they heard, 'What the hell are you doing here?'

'Adam!' Jenny leapt to her feet to hug Adam but Zack stood back. He wasn't quite sure how to act. After Jenny's elongated hug and a kiss on the cheek, Adam and Zack stood awkwardly before one another.

'Good to see you, mate,' Adam said, shaking Zack's hand.

'You too.'

'What are you doing here?' Adam asked, looking

between Zack and Jenny with astonishment. He did look happy, though.

'I wanted to tell you how sorry I am,' Zack said.

Adam shook his head. 'It's all right, mate.'

'You were right,' Zack added.

'About what?'

'Cadence is a nightmare. You did the right thing. I can't believe we didn't see it before.'

For a moment Adam didn't react, and then he chuckled. 'Well, it serves you right. I hope she's made your life a misery.'

'You can rest assured that she has.'

'Good.' Then Adam gestured back behind him. 'You'd better come on up.'

Zack and Jenny followed Adam as he led them down a very small corridor to an even smaller spiral staircase. They walked up a few steps to find what appeared to be no more than a thin line that had three doors on either side of it.

In single file, they shuffled along to door four, right at the end, and Adam let them in with his contactless key card.

They entered into another cramped space that was made even smaller by the sloping ceiling. It all felt terribly claustrophobic.

'It's only for a couple of weeks,' Adam said, sitting on the modest double bed. There was nowhere else to sit.

'It's clean,' Jenny offered.

It was white, that was all Zack could think. Apart from the metal chairs and table in the bar, everything else he'd seen had been a stark white colour.

'So, what have you been up to?' Jenny asked, making herself comfortable on the tiny carpeted area between the bed and the wall.

Adam smiled, but it didn't last long. He hung his head. 'It's been awful,' he said. 'What am I doing here? I'm really glad you came.'

'What's happened?' Zack asked, crouching down, trying to work out the best way to sit on the floor opposite Jenny. Jenny had her legs crossed, but that wasn't going to work for Zack. Instead he kneeled, but he knew he wouldn't be able to sit like that for long.

'I landed here last Friday, thinking at least I'd have a couple of days to settle in, but everyone else was already here. There's four Americans, one Austrian and one man from the Berlin office, and they're all work obsessed. From the moment I stepped foot on German soil, I've been pulled from meeting to meeting. I mean literally. They've had me meeting them for breakfast at six every morning, where by seven I'm in a car being taken to the office, or a factory, or some other place for an interview. They even decide what we're going to eat and when we're going to eat it. I've been dropped back off every night with about half an hour to spare before I have to meet them all over again for dinner plans. And then everyone speaks German all night. Well, actually, everyone's been speaking German all week. I've barely been able to contribute to anything. Apart for "Danke" at the end and a good firm handshake, I've been good for nothing.'

'Why did they send you here?' Jenny asked with concern in her voice.

'I was promoted to European Head of Sales and they said they wanted me to take the lead in opening up the new Hamburg office. But so far all I've led is the line to the toilets.'

There was a knock at the door and Zack scrambled to his feet. He felt silly sitting on the floor. Adam clambered over Jenny who had to shift herself onto the bed so he could answer the door.

'Hi, how's the presentation coming along?' a firm, female American voice asked.

'Hi Courtney. I'd like you to meet my friends. They've just surprised me out of the blue.' Adam opened the door to reveal a very tall lady with broad shoulders and a large grin.

'Hi gang!' she said. 'How nice of you to show up like that. Have you just come for the weekend?'

'Yes,' Jenny said standing up. 'We were missing Adam so much, we thought it might be a nice surprise.'

'That's so great. You guys are so cute. But you know Adam has a lot of work to do. We've got a lot on.'

'I've finished the presentation,' Adam stated quite to the point. 'I can email it over to you. Then, if it's all right with you, I'll dip out of tonight's meal. I need to spend some time with my friends. They have travelled all this way.'

Courtney sighed. 'It's an important networking night, Adam. I know you want to be with your friends-'

'You all speak German anyway!' Adam argued. 'I don't understand a word you're saying. I'm sure no one is going to miss me for one night.'

Courtney glanced at Zack and Jenny. 'If head office were to find out.'

'Find out what? That after working all week solidly, I want to spend Saturday night with my friends who have kindly travelled hundreds of miles to see me? I think the company has a duty of care to look after me. Don't you?'

Courtney glared firmly at Adam and there was a tense moment when she didn't say anything. Finally she said, 'How about I tell the guys you're sick and you're staying put for the night? That way no one needs to get upset, do they.'

Zack could tell that Adam was on the verge of snapping her head off, but he bit his lip right at the last second. All he did was mutter, 'Fine. Great.'

'But don't you dare be late for breakfast! I'll see you at six sharp.'

'It's Sunday tomorrow! They don't start serving breakfast until seven.' Adam was clearly trying very hard to stay calm.

'Oh right,' Courtney smirked. 'That would be a long

wait for some bratwurst, wouldn't it! Seven it is. See you then.'

Adam exhaled sharply as he shut the door and then he rubbed his hands through his hair. Zack was sure that he was ready to explode inside, but he kept his composure very well.

'You're working seven days a week?' Jenny asked. 'Who networks on a Saturday night?'

'I have no clue,' Adam said. 'I don't even know who we're meeting. Everything is constantly discussed in German and I've become too fed up to ask for it to be translated. You know, even when it's just me and the Americans, they still speak in German. They say it's good practice. I think they hate me.'

'I think they're threatened by you,' Jenny said.

Zack nodded in agreement. 'She may have a point. You are the superstar of the UK office.'

'I've never said that.'

'You got that award for the best ever salesman,' Zack argued. He recalled how Adam had brought in more sales in one month all on his own than the rest of the sales team put together. Then he managed it again for the next four months consecutively.

'I just work hard. I'm not a superstar.'

'You are,' Jenny insisted. 'You're the Superman of the sales world and we all know it. I bet that US team was quaking in its boots before meeting you.'

'That's very kind of you to say, but I'm not so sure.' Adam sat down on the bed again. He buried his head in his hands. Zack had never seen him so distressed.

A few minutes went by where no one spoke. Zack just didn't know what to say. This was a very different man before him.

Adam exhaled sharply again, breaking the uncomfortable silence. 'I need to be honest with you both,' he said.

Jenny shifted along the bed to get closer to him. 'What

is it?'

Zack felt like three on the bed was far too cosy and he didn't want to try the floor again, so he propped himself up against the wall.

'I think I might have wished to come here,' Adam admitted.

'You wanted to come to Germany?' Zack asked.

'No. Not quite. I was really pissed off after Cadence and...'

'I'm really sorry, mate,' Zack said. 'I didn't mean to do anything. I just got-'

'It's okay, Zack. I pushed you two together anyway. I can see that now. I really think you might have been right all along. I think Emmett is making our wishes come true.'

There was a moment of awkward silence before Jenny asked, 'If you didn't wish to come to Germany then what did you wish for?'

'To get away from it all,' Adam said. 'To get away from everyone. One minute these thoughts were going through my mind, the next minute I was being offered a huge promotion and the chance to move to Hamburg for six months.'

Jenny stood up. She took a step to the door and for a moment she looked at neither of them.

'I know it seems crazy,' Zack said, 'but we saw him, didn't we. That wasn't my imagination.'

'He was definitely there,' Adam said, now also standing up. 'He pulled me off you. I felt him. He's strong. Stronger than I gave him credit for.'

'You wished to get away from me?' Jenny asked, now staring very directly at Adam. Her graveness instantly extinguished Zack's fleeting moment of smugness. He'd always known that Emmett was strong.

'I was just messed up,' Adam replied. 'I regret it deeply. I'm really pleased you're here. I can't tell you how much it means to me that you came.'

For a moment Jenny didn't say anything. She just stared

at Adam like she was trying to work something out. Then finally she smiled, broadly. 'It was our pleasure to come. Wasn't it, Zack?' Jenny stepped over towards Zack and held his hand.

Zack was quite taken aback. They'd never held hands before.

'We enjoyed our little trip together, didn't we?' Jenny said, her eyes now intently focused on Zack.

Zack shrugged. 'It was a smooth flight.'

'Are you a member of the mile high club, Zack?' Jenny asked, quite out of the blue. 'I never thought to ask.'

Zack just shook his head. He couldn't keep up with Jenny's random questions.

'Me neither. We should discuss it on the way home. Maybe we could join together?' As soon as she'd said it she started giggling and nudging him, and it left Zack gobsmacked. He wasn't quite sure, but it sounded very much like Jenny had just proposed that they have sex.

No, surely not. He must have misunderstood. Maybe the mile high club meant something else entirely and Zack had just got it wrong. He made a mental note to Google it later, just to be sure.

'What's going on with you two?' Adam asked.

Zack wanted to answer but he wasn't quite sure himself.

'We've just been getting on really well lately, haven't we Zack?' Jenny said, still holding Zack's hand. 'I think this little trip together has been good for our friendship. It's like I've seen Zack in a whole new light.'

Zack couldn't believe it. He had to admit, it had been a really good weekend so far. They'd had a laugh and had learnt far more about each other. They'd never spent so much time together just the two of them. Had Jenny really started to see Zack differently?

Then Zack questioned to himself whether he fancied Jenny in return. He'd never considered if before. He'd always wondered whether she might secretly have a soft spot for Adam. They were very close.

But Jenny and Zack?

She was certainly attractive and they had loads in common. Maybe this was going to be the start of something amazing.

Maybe that's what she'd been talking about the night before! Hearing about him with Cadence had made Jenny realise what she was missing out on. Of course!

'I'm a member of the mile high club,' Adam announced. 'Back in the days when Cadence was enjoyable to be around.'

Jenny grabbed Zack's hand tighter. 'You've had sex on an aeroplane?' she asked. 'With Cadence?'

'Sort of. Believe me, it's not anywhere near as much fun as it sounds.'

'I don't think we should just take his word for it,' Zack said to Jenny with a glint in his eye. 'I'm always a fan of first hand experiences.'

Jenny let go of his hand. 'Yeah, maybe. Whatever.'

Zack glanced at Adam. The man before him was trapped across the channel in a country where he only knew one word of the language. Zack had always been a little bit jealous of Adam's seemingly perfect life, but he was now verging on rock bottom whereas things were definitely on the up for Zack. It was all turning around.

All he needed to do now was get Cadence out of his flat. How he wished she'd just leave his flat.

'That's it!' Zack suddenly announced. He felt a surge of determination.

'What?' Adam asked.

'We all believe that Emmett is real and he's making our wishes come true, right?'

Jenny and Adam looked at one another before they both nodded in agreement.

'Then why don't we just wish for change? I don't think we'd be able to wish our wishes away. Nothing could work like that. That would be far too easy and convenient. But I bet we could all wish for something new; something that would change our current circumstances and make things better. What do you think?'

All three of them contemplated the idea for a moment. Then Adam said, 'I don't know. This wishing thing hasn't worked out well for us so far.'

'But we've not really thought about it properly so far, have we?' Zack argued. 'We've flippantly said to ourselves things that we wish would happen, but none of us have been thinking it through. For example,' he continued, focusing on Adam, 'Jenny told me that you wanted Cadence to have an affair so you could dump her without feeling bad.'

Adam paused before mumbling, 'I guess.'

'But if you'd really known that your wishes could come true, would you still have made that wish?'

Adam shrugged. 'I guess not. I guess I would have just wished that Cadence would dump me, to save me the hassle.'

'Well, there you go.'

'But I know for a fact that I've been wishing to leave Germany ever since I got here and that's not come true.'

'But that's trying to unwish a wish. Things can't work like that. You need to think of something different; something new. I've been wishing all week that Cadence would leave my flat and it hasn't worked. But then why would it? Between us we both wished her there one way or another, so I've just had to live with the consequences. But I bet if I wish that Cadence gets a new decade-long modelling job then that might work. It's a new way of thinking. A brand new wish.'

'You've thought a lot about this, haven't you?' Jenny noted.

'I've been spending a lot of time on my own over the past couple of weeks,' Zack admitted. 'It gives you time to ponder on things.'

'I suppose it can't hurt to give it a go,' Adam said.

'Great. Let's do it now. Why don't we all take a second to think and then say out loud what we really want, to see if it comes true?'

'No!' Jenny suddenly shrieked. Both Zack and Adam glared at her with confusion. She shook her head. 'If we say it out loud then we may rush it. What if we get flummoxed and say the wrong thing? How about instead we write it down? You know, make a secret wish, like you do with birthday candles. That way we can consider it properly and take our time over it.'

Zack mulled over the idea for a second, but it seemed to make sense. 'Okay, let's do it now. You got any paper?'

Adam grabbed his notebook and he tore off a few sheets for Jenny and a few sheets for Zack and then they all moved to a space in the room where they could concentrate.

LETTERS TO EMMETT

Zack had chosen to lean on the tiny window sill towards the back of the room. He was deep in thought, biting his finger nails.

'Does anyone need a pen?' Jenny asked.

Zack looked across. Jenny was sitting on the floor leaning against the end of the bed and Adam was sitting up against the headboard with his laptop.

'Yes, please,' Zack replied. He watched as Jenny searched her bag and then she pulled out two black biros.

'I'm electronic,' Adam smiled, holding up his laptop to demonstrate his point. 'But thanks.'

Zack grabbed one of the pens and then he made himself comfortable again in his spot by the window. He glanced out at the rain lashing down but he seemed a million miles away.

After a few moments he started to write.

I wish for Cadence to get offered an amazing job that will last her for a decade. Because of that I then wish that she feels the need to start a new life and move back to her apartment in London. I also wish that she decides to take a break from men for a while as she strives to get over her break-up.

She won't need the new furniture though, I can keep that. Except for the mirrored coffee table. Cadence can take that with her.

In addition, can I also wish that a sudden cure is found to heal all my colleagues so they're back in work on Monday. Except maybe Rachel who can still have bouts of sickness for the next week or two following a bad reaction to the cure. Then I wish for them to make me redundant with a huge pay out so I don't have to work there anymore but I'm still financially stable.

Zack looked around to see Jenny and Adam still working away. He took a minute to read over his letter, and then he folded it over a few times and he shoved it in his pocket.

Jenny looked terribly serious. She was chewing the end of her pen with real bite. She kept putting the tip to paper, but then she'd back away again, shaking her head.

She started to mutter to herself. It wasn't audible what she was saying, but her whispers were noticeable as the only sound in the room.

She took a deep breath, as if everything rested on the words she was about to write, and then she finally began to commit her thoughts to paper.

Dear Emmett the Empathy Man

Thank you for all the effort you've gone to so far. I can see why you've done what you've done and we all appreciate the help you've tried to give us. You seem like a really good man. However, we'd now like to take the time to be more prescriptive and we're all sharing with you the things that we wish for most in the world. I hope that's okay? If you don't mind, there are two things that I'd like to wish for. I hope I'm not being greedy. Please find below the details:

*1.	I wish for Nathan Langley to disappear from my life. He's a nice man but he is not the one for me. I'd feel bad breaking up with him after all he's done. He's been very kind and affectionate, and I'm sure he'd make another girl incredibly happy. He did save me from two disastrous dates and I'll never forget that he was the first* *man to buy me a bouquet of flowers. But ultimately he's far too needy and I just don't want him. Please, Emmett, don't have him break up with me. That would be far too embarrassing. I'd hate that. I'd much prefer it if I didn't hear from him again and he'd just vanish from my world. Maybe I could just say hello to him when I see him in the pub and that would be it. Thank you.*

2.   For my second wish, I need to give you some background. You need to know, Emmett, that I'm in love with Adam Valentine and have been for quite a long time. Being that you're Empathy Man, you probably already know this, but it's only occurred to me recently that I haven't wished for him to love me in return. I've wished for Cadence's untimely death, as I'm sure you know (thank God you didn't make that come true), but I guess I've never really wished for more as I couldn't believe that he could ever love me back. You see he's been with Cadence for as long as I've known him and so I've always assumed that we'd never be more than friends. But now things have changed. He's left the bitch and I have the chance of a wish coming true. That's a pretty good combination! So here's my wish, Emmett: I wish that Adam Valentine would be my new boyfriend and I wish that he'd fall in love with me just as I love him.

Thanks Emmett, I appreciate your help so much. I don't know how you've managed to come to life, but I'm glad you're here, and it's amazing that you're making our wishes come true. Please feel free to pop round for dinner one night, or join us in the pub on a Sunday. It would be great to get to know you better.

Love from Jenny Orwell xxxx

PS. If you're only able to grant me one of these wishes, please make it number 2. Please.

Jenny read it back a few times and then bit her lip. She looked overwhelmed with worry. She chewed the pen again before finally folding the paper neatly and placing it in the side pocket of her handbag.

Adam rested his laptop against his thighs. He had a determined look on his face. It took him a while before he started typing, but once he did he completed his wish list quite quickly.

I wish for Jenny and I to get together and I wish for something urgent to come up in the UK office that means I have to return there ASAP. I then do not want to leave again. Except for attending international conferences.

Adam saved his word document into his personal folder, calling it "Personal_1", and then he emailed it to himself just to be sure. Job done.

All three of them looked around at one another. They'd all finished making their secret wishes and then it seemed nobody knew what to do. There was a long silence as if they were waiting for something magical to happen, but nothing did.

'Do you want to get out of here?' Adam asked, turning his laptop off.

'We need to find somewhere to stay. It might be a bit cosy in here,' Jenny said.

Adam scanned the room. 'You know what, sod it. This room is a joke. There's a five star hotel about two streets away. I'm checking us in for the night.'

'We can't ask you to do that,' Zack said.

'You'd be doing me the favour. I need a night away from these tiny little walls, or I swear I'll be punching a hole in them. Besides, I'm apparently ill so I can't take the risk of anyone seeing me. It would be better if we just disappeared.'

'Are you sure?' Jenny asked, getting to her feet. 'I mean, Zack and I could share a room to save you some trouble. I wouldn't mind. Would you be okay with that, Zack?'

Zack just nodded his head with a big smile.

'It's fine,' Adam said. 'It would be my pleasure to treat

you. I wouldn't feel right expecting you to bunk up.'

'If you're sure,' Jenny shrugged.

'I've never been surer of anything. Let me just grab a few things and then we're heading over there. Just don't let me sleep in! I have to be back here for breakfast at seven.'

'Adam, that's insane,' Jenny argued. 'Do you really have to be back here that early? What on earth are you going to be doing all day that requires such an early start?'

'They've got me doing sports tomorrow. Don't ask.'

'Then we'd better make tonight count!' Zack smiled.

As soon as Adam had thrown a few things into a bag, they all made their way to the deluxe "Hotel Riesig" that was just a few minutes' walk away.

They stared around the enormous lobby in awe as they made their way to the reception desk. Adam checked them in to three double rooms and they didn't hesitate in finding their way to them. They were all on different floors but their rooms all had the same large floor space, with queen sized beds and luxurious bathrooms.

After enjoying a delicious lunch, they headed to the spa to relax before getting ready for the evening. It was Adam's first free night in Hamburg and they were all equally excited.

'Just be warned, the beer's strong,' Adam said as three large beers were placed down before them in the clean and stylish bar. 'But it's always good.'

'At least you've managed to enjoy something while you're here,' Zack said.

'The food's been good too,' Adam replied.

'To friends,' Jenny said, picking up her glass.

'To friends,' Zack and Adam replied, clinking their glasses against hers.

'To really good friends,' Jenny said, clinking her glass a second time against Zack's.

'I've got one,' Adam said. 'I can't believe we've never discussed this before.'

'Go on,' Zack encouraged.

'If you could have any super power, what would it be?'

'Oh, yes!' Jenny said with a smile. 'How have we not already had this conversation?'

'I know the answer straight away,' Zack said. 'I've thought about this a lot.'

'Yeah? What would it be?' Adam asked.

'I bet it's going to be a really good idea,' Jenny said.

'Well, you tell me,' Zack replied.

'What is it?' Adam pushed.

'You know how Doctor Who has a sonic screwdriver.'

'Or sonic sunglasses,' Adam interjected.

'Don't!' Zack replied with disgust, but Adam couldn't resist a little snigger. 'He has a sonic screwdriver and that's it as far as I'm concerned.'

'I remember nothing else,' Adam agreed.

'Yeah, I hated those glasses,' Jenny added.

'Why would you want to replace the screwdriver?' Zack asked.

'I totally agree. You're very wise,' Jenny said, touching Zack's hand for emphasis.

'What about the screwdriver?' Adam pushed again.

'Oh right, yeah. Well, it's a great little tool, isn't it? I was thinking how amazing would it be if I had that same power, but in my fingers.'

'So, when you want to open doors or shoot at Daleks, you just point and that's all you need to do?' Jenny asked.

'Exactly! It's quite a versatile little thing if you think about it. I'd love to have that power, but if it was in my hands, even better.'

'Great thinking,' Adam said.

'What an amazing idea!' Jenny gushed. 'It's such a unique twist on the whole super power debate. I think many of us have overlooked the multiple assets of the sonic screwdriver. But not you, Zack. Not my clever Zack.'

'Thank you, Jenny. I thought it was a good idea.' Jenny

and Zack held each other's gaze for a moment before Zack asked her, 'What about you? What power would you have?'

She sat back and took a sip of her drink. Then she nodded. 'Super strength, super speed.'

'You can only have one,' Adam argued.

'It is one, really. They go hand in hand. With super strength you have the ability to build up amazing speed, so one goes with the other.'

'What a load of rubbish!' Adam said. 'You just want to be like Superman.'

'Or Supergirl,' Zack suggested.

'No, it's always Superman with her.' Adam rolled his eyes and shook his head.

'It could be like Supergirl!' Jenny protested. 'Yes, Zack, just like Supergirl. That's the power I want, and so that's what I'm going to have. You can't stop me.'

'I bloody can. This is my game, my rules,' Adam stated. 'You can only have one, so what's it going to be? Strength or speed?'

Jenny sighed. 'Strength then.'

'Fine.'

'Because with strength I can build up super speed as well,' she followed with really quickly.

'Until I get my hands on Kryptonite,' Adam said. 'You've chosen a super power that has an ultimate weakness. Very silly choice. One bit of green rock and you'll be a quivering wreck on the floor. What a waste.'

'I think I'll be all right. You don't have the contacts for Kryptonite and we both know it.'

'I have a few leads, believe me.'

'What would your super power be?' Zack asked Adam, bringing the Superman argument once again to a close.

'Right,' Adam said, taking a sip of his beer to properly consider his answer. 'I'd have to have teleportation.'

'Like it,' Zack said. 'How would it work? You'd just close your eyes and appear somewhere else?'

'Or you could click your fingers,' Jenny suggested.

Adam thought for a second. 'I like the idea-'

'Oh, I've got it!' Jenny interrupted with excitement. 'What about spinning around? You throw your hands out and spin around and then vanish to another place.'

'That sounds fun,' Zack said.

'That sounds like Wonder Woman,' Adam tutted.

'What's wrong with Wonder Woman?' Jenny asked.

'For starters, she didn't teleport!'

'Or what about like Firestar?' Jenny said. 'She just sticks out her arms without the spinning.'

'What is it with you and arms?' Zack asked.

'At least that's Marvel for a change,' Adam acknowledged. 'But I wasn't thinking of using my arms at all.'

'How's your teleportation power going to work, then?' Jenny asked.

'Well... I was thinking I could just put my hands to my temples and concentrate really hard, envisaging my destination. As it becomes clear in my mind where I want to go, I go there.'

'Sounds easy,' Zack said.

'How does that not involve your arms?' Jenny asked, raising her eyebrows for added effect.

Adam opened his mouth to argue, but he quickly backed down. Then all three of them laughed.

Over the next few hours they drank and laughed, danced and reminisced and had one of the best nights out they'd ever spent together.

They ended up with a final nightcap in the hotel bar and then they staggered to bed at around two o'clock in the morning.

If only for one night, they'd certainly managed to put their troubles aside. All three of them fell to sleep with smiles on their faces, and all three of them dreamt about the things they wanted most in the world.

ADAM'S WIN

Adam's alarm blasted out at six thirty the next morning and the first thing he noted was how rough he felt. He immediately rolled out of bed, hitting the luxurious carpet with a thud.

He rubbed his eyes as he staggered to the bathroom. The German beer was definitely strong. He felt dreadful.

He poured himself a glass of water before turning the shower on and praying the power of it would spring him into life.

Well, it definitely helped, so that was something.

He dried himself, brushed his teeth, threw his jeans and a T-shirt on and then packed up his stuff. He hated that he was having to leave the place. It made the hotel his company was paying for look like some sort of clinical holiday spot for small people. As Adam was six foot tall, the new bed for the night had made him realise that he hadn't properly stretched out since leaving the UK. But it wouldn't be for long, he had to remember that.

At six forty-five he sat on the edge of the bed. He knew he was going to be ferried around all day as usual, and he'd have no chance for any more time on his own, therefore he knew he'd not be able to see Jenny again. Or Zack.

That was devastating. What had he been thinking saying he'd come to Hamburg for six months?

He picked up the landline and dialled for Jenny's room.

'What? Hello?' she answered with shock.

'It's Adam,' he said. 'Sorry to wake you.'

'What time is it?'

'Nearly time I was going for breakfast.'

'What? No! That's awful. We've only been in bed for a few hours.'

'Tell me about it. Look, can I just pop down? I want to say goodbye.'

'What do you mean goodbye?'

'I've got a full schedule today, Jen. I won't be able to spend any time with you.'

'That's crap! They can't treat you like this.'

'They can. What can I do? Please can I pop down?'

'Of course. See you in a sec.'

Adam hung up. He checked his room one more time and then he made his way to the floor below where he knew Jenny's room was.

He knocked gently, very aware that it was early Sunday morning and there were loads of other rooms around him. She answered with a squint in her eyes.

'Hello,' she smiled. The new green streak in her hair was sticking up, as if independent from everything else, and she was clearly barely awake. She was wrapped up in a giant hotel dressing gown and Adam couldn't help but think how absolutely adorable she looked.

'Sorry to do this so early,' Adam said, stepping in to her room. It looked exactly like his room, only messier.

'When will I see you again?' she asked.

Adam looked at his fingers. He wanted to say later that day. He wanted to be able to say that he was flying home that evening and he would be coming straight round to her flat; and could he stay the night. But he was stuck in Hamburg and he would be for months.

'Soon. Really soon,' he lied. 'Let's keep in touch. Talk

daily?'

'We'd better do! I'm coming back if you don't come home to visit,' she warned, pointing at him for added emphasis.

He smiled and nodded. Then he said, 'Come here,' and he wrapped his arms around her.

She nuzzled her head in against his chest and it felt amazing. They'd hugged hundreds of times as friends, saying hello or goodbye, or to celebrate or commiserate, but there was something new about this hug. It was close and tender and Adam didn't want to let go.

He wanted time to stop as they stood there in each other's arms, but he knew the seconds were ticking by. 'I've got to go, Jen,' he said, trying to pull himself away. 'I'm sorry. Courtney will go mental.'

'Do you have to be there bang on seven?' Jenny asked.

Adam shrugged. 'It's just easier. I turned up at ten past six on Tuesday morning and it was all I heard about all day. They kept calling me "tardy Adam". And when I yawned at one point – because it's really boring listening to German all day long – I got a comment about how I couldn't possibly be tired after my lie in. That they could say in English.'

'They sound horrible. Are you going to be okay?'

'I've dealt with worse. Besides, it's not for long. I'll be home before we know it, meeting you for our Sunday lunches again.'

'I miss you.'

Adam didn't know what to say. He'd taken her for granted for so much time. How could he have not seen before how perfect she was?

'See you soon,' he said, kissing her on the cheek. 'Tell Zack I said goodbye, will you?'

'Of course.'

'You two seem to have grown close since I've left,' he said.

Jenny smiled. 'Yes. We've grown *very* close recently.'

'Well, I'm glad,' Adam replied. 'He's a good bloke and he could do with a friend like you. Make sure Cadence doesn't eat him alive.'

As soon as he'd said those words, Adam watched Jenny physically tense up before him. She seemed really annoyed all of a sudden. All he could assume was that he'd said the wrong thing about Cadence.

'I know you've always liked Cadence, but trust me she can be a right bitch. Even though a small part of me is glad that Zack's suffered, I don't want Cadence to ruin him.'

Jenny's frame stiffened even more and there was definitely a look of death in her eyes. It was quite unexpected. Jenny must have liked Cadence more than Adam had thought.

Adam glanced at the clock at the bottom of the TV. It was now approaching seven and he knew he'd have to dash.

'I really have to go, Jen. Take care.'

Jenny sighed and relaxed a little. 'Don't let the bastards grind you down too much, all right.'

'I won't.'

He kissed her again on the cheek and then he left the room. She waved goodbye to him from the doorway and he made a run for the stairs, not wanting to risk waiting for the lift.

He raced back to his hotel and legged it straight into breakfast to find all of his colleagues already tucking in to some toast.

'Nice of you to finally join us,' Courtney said. Adam looked at his watch. It wasn't even five past.

'Are you out of breath?' Kyle, another member of the US team asked, as he walked to the coffee machine.

Then Adam had a stroke of genius. 'Yeah, I've just been out for a morning run. Clear the cobwebs, you know. I wanted to be ready for the activities ahead.'

'In your jeans?' Courtney asked.

Adam addressed her quite directly. 'It's a British thing,

did you not know? It helps to burn off more calories. Jeans are obviously harder to run in, and they're thicker than Lycra so you sweat more. A great way to keep in shape.'

Courtney nodded, looking impressed. 'That makes so much sense.'

Adam grinned with satisfaction as he queued up behind Kyle for a mug of coffee. At least that was one win for him. Finally.

By eight o'clock, Adam was sitting in the back of an Audi being driven to the local badminton club about fifteen minutes away. They were apparently due to meet a couple of amazing sales people that they were hoping to persuade to leave the competition.

Adam hated badminton. He much preferred squash. It was faster paced and used a ball. But, as usual, Courtney was making all the decisions.

Adam followed his colleagues into the club where they greeted their guests in German. Then they talked a lot more in German before Courtney finally turned around to acknowledge Adam's existence.

'We've all decided to try and be British today,' she said with a grin.

Adam felt relief pour over him. At last they were going to talk in English. At last he would be able to show them what he was made of.

'We're all going to play in our jeans!' Courtney said. 'I can't wait to see the benefits.'

Adam nearly collapsed. Had she really just said that? Then they all went back to speaking German again.

After a hot and uncomfortable couple of hours on the badminton court, Adam couldn't wait to get out of his jeans. He was dropped off back at the hotel for fifteen minutes where he was allowed to freshen up before being shipped over to a golf course about half an hour away. This time he made the decision to wear his chinos.

Golf, Adam could do though, and he finally felt a bit happier. He'd learnt early on in his career that golf could open doors for him, so he'd dedicated hours and hours on the driving range and to lessons, and now he had a very proud handicap of fourteen.

Before the golf started, they all sat at a table where they were presented with some potatoes and meat. Adam still felt quite hungover and a fry up at that moment would have been far more appealing, but he politely and silently worked his way through the meal, banished from the conversation as usual due to the language barrier. It ended up being another hour of utter boredom before they finally made their way to the golf course.

Adam was given a rather shabby looking set of clubs, which he was sure was deliberate. As they were all away from home, some rented clubs had been arranged for them, but Adam could see his set were in the worst state by far. He suddenly felt more determined than ever.

And that determination certainly paid off. He'd never played better. Although he did think to himself that it probably helped that he was at no point distracted since he wasn't able to understand a single word of the people around him.

Two more potential candidates had joined them and he could see how much Courtney was trying to butter them up. Her pathetic efforts were visibly being played out in front of him and it was embarrassing. If only he could talk to them. He really wanted to be able to talk to them. Surely that was why he'd been sent over to Germany in the first place?

They weren't having much success so far in finding suitable candidates and Adam was incredibly frustrated. If only he could join in more then he knew he'd be of use. He had to acknowledge that the candidates were all German natives and he couldn't speak a word of the language, but he knew the issues he was having ran deeper than that. He couldn't help but suspect that the reason for them never speaking English was to actually prevent his involvement.

Maybe Jenny and Zack had been right. Maybe Courtney was a bit threatened by him. She certainly wasn't good at banter; that had been blatantly obvious. She could organise their day down to the last second, but when it came to conversing with potential candidates, she seemed to actually discourage them. Her verbal communication skills were pretty dire really. Adam didn't need to speak the language to understand that.

Still, he might be losing one battle to a German speaking control freak, but she couldn't beat him at golf. When he came in nine below everyone else, he had no desire to hide his smug grin.

He was dropped off back at the hotel at half past six and he felt absolutely exhausted.

He headed in with only thoughts of his bed, when Courtney halted the whole group in the lobby and announced something in German. She then turned to Adam to translate. 'We'll be meeting promptly at seven in the bar before heading out for dinner.'

In his tired state, he couldn't help the irritation that was itching away at his entire body. 'Everybody here speaks English!' he almost yelled. 'Yet not everyone speaks German. Wouldn't it be easier to say things once in English rather than having to say them twice? Especially when English is your own language!'

Courtney folded her arms and the atmosphere thickened with tension.

'I guess I'm not disrespectful like you,' Courtney replied, sourly.

'How am I disrespectful?'

'I think, as we're in Germany, it's only polite to speak the language.'

He knew there was no way for him to win this argument. If he was to learn German overnight, she'd have them all speaking Spanish.

'Count me out of tonight,' he said. 'I'm shattered. I'm just going to head straight to bed.'

'No, you're not,' Courtney immediately replied.

'I beg your pardon?'

'We're having a casual dinner tonight and you will join us.'

'I'm not hungry.'

'That's not the point.'

'Surely that is the point of dinner?'

'You quite rightly said yesterday that, as Vice President of Operations from HQ in Detroit, USA, I have a duty of care to look after you as my employee.'

Adam was pretty sure that he'd said nothing of the sort, but he was curious to see where she was going with her bold statement.

'And that duty of care is to ensure that all my workers are properly fed and watered. So I insist that you join us for dinner, for your own good.'

Adam couldn't believe it. She was such a crafty little bitch.

'Surely that duty of care is to also make sure that your workers are well rested?' he responded.

'Absolutely,' she nodded with enthusiasm. 'That's why, after our meal, which will be an easy going, causal affair, we'll get you straight to bed. You'll be tucked up before you know it.'

Adam sighed. She couldn't literally force him to go out. But he'd lied, he was hungry. He also knew that she would never give in, so if he didn't agree then they'd just spend forever arguing about it and he was far too tired for that. He hated it, but it was going to be much easier for him to capitulate.

'All right, Courtney. As my employer, who always has my best interests at heart, I'll join you for dinner. It's good to know that you're so caring. I'll be sure to let you know how else you can look after my interests in the coming months.'

There was a moment of strained silence as Courtney interpreted Adam's statement in her own way. Then all she said was, 'See you at seven, guys.'

Consoling himself with the fact that he'd had the night before off, and noting that there were only twenty-five weeks of this nightmare left, Adam reluctantly made his way back to his room to get refreshed ready for dinner.

He sat down on his bed and rested his head in his hands. He sighed heavily, trying to gear himself up for what would no doubt be another boring evening, but the lack of sleep from the night before was taking its toll.

As he went to stand up, a folded piece of paper on the floor caught his attention. He picked it up, wondering what it was. He opened the white sheet and his eyes widened with fascination.

It started *Dear Emmett the Empathy Man*. He knew that handwriting. It was Jenny's wish!

□

ADAM'S UPS AND DOWNS

Adam folded the paper back up. He couldn't look at it. Jenny had said they should all make their wishes in secret, like when you blow out birthday candles. If he looked then maybe her wish wouldn't come true.

Then he shook his head. This wasn't a birthday wish. This was a wish being granted by a fictional superhero from the depths of their mutual imaginations that they'd somehow, miraculously brought to life for reasons that none of them could fathom. The rules were clearly different. He was sure Emmett wouldn't mind if he just took a quick, sneaky look.

Adam opened the letter again. He didn't feel comfortable reading it all, so he just scanned to get the general gist.

Thank you for all the effort you've gone to so far... take the time to be more prescriptive... two things that I'd like to wish for... I wish for Nathan Langley to disappear from my life.

Adam stopped reading. She wanted to get rid of Nathan. She wanted to get rid of her new boyfriend. Maybe she didn't like him after all. Now he had to read on!

He's a nice man but he is not the one for me.

Adam couldn't help the little dance that he did around

the room. She'd wished for things to end with Nathan. Woo hoo! Suddenly Adam really hoped that reading the letter wouldn't negate the power of it.

So that was wish number one. What was number two? Adam scanned on.

For my second wish, I need to give you some background. You need to know, Emmett, that I'm in love with Adam Valentine and have been for quite a long time.

Adam froze. Had he really just read that? He read it again just to check, but it was definitely there in black and white.

Jenny was in love with him. Jenny had been in love with him for a while.

He read on, just to make sure it wasn't a joke. Could this really be true? His heart was pounding.

He scanned the next couple of lines, but she really had waffled on. He needed to get to the actual wish. So far this was just a long story. What was she actually wishing for?

Then he saw it.

So here's my wish, Emmett: I wish that Adam Valentine would be my new boyfriend and I wish that he'd fall in love with me just as I love him.

Adam couldn't believe it. She'd wished for exactly what he'd wished for: that they'd somehow get together.

Adam sat down on the bed again. They weren't wishing for a miracle, they just needed to bloody well talk. They didn't need Emmett at all. All Adam had to do was tell Jenny how he felt and they'd both get their wish come true. It was as simple as that.

Jenny loved him!

He threw his hands into the air and found himself dancing again. This lwas the happiest day of his life.

Then he stopped. It actually wasn't that great. He was in Germany. If only he'd told her last week. They'd been in bed together last week. In fact Jenny had insisted that they go to bed together. Now that made more sense.

He should have kissed her. As he was looking at her,

he'd been so tempted to kiss her. He should have done it.

Adam suddenly heard Courtney outside his door chatting to someone. He looked at his watch. It was ten to seven. He needed to get a move on.

Although not one part of him wanted to go to that dinner and every pore in his body was telling him to call Jenny and speak to her, he knew he had to get ready.

Besides, what was he supposed to say on the phone? Telling his closest friend that he was in love with her was not a telephone conversation. It needed to be done in person. As much as it pained him to think it, maybe his declaration of love was just going to have to wait.

He'd planned on having a shower, but now there was no time. He threw on a shirt and changed into some jeans and he was back ready for pre-dinner drinks with one minute to spare.

The night ended up being worse than Adam had expected. Just when he'd been hoping to have some alone time to think, banished away from the conversation as usual, his international colleagues had all decided that it was time to speak in English. His outburst earlier had caught their attention and they'd all agreed that they should speak English more.

Adam could see how much this riled Courtney, but he was too pre-occupied to feel any joy about it. Instead he just felt annoyed that they'd made this momentous decision on the one night that he'd wanted some time to think.

The night dragged even more than normal. He had to endure hours of listening to mind-numbing stories about growing up in Austria and the differences between America and Germany. Then every now and then someone would throw a question his way, asking what the English man thought.

It was well after eleven when he finally made it back to his room. He flopped on the bed and immediately grabbed his phone from his pocket. He scanned through pictures of Jenny and a smile lit up his face. She was so pretty. He'd never met anyone like her and he couldn't imagine anyone else ever completing his life like she did.

He decided to text her.

Hope you got back OK? I won the golf! But other than that it's been a crap day. Wish I could be at home with you. Really want to see you soon. x

He waited eagerly for a reply but one didn't come through. He was fidgety with nerves, desperately wanting to hear from her.

He went to the bathroom and brushed his teeth, all the time with his phone in his pocket. Then he lay his phone on the bed while he stripped down to his boxers.

As he climbed under the duvet, he was willing his phone to bleep. Then finally it did.

Got home at about 8.30. Was a smooth flight but Sundays are crap without us meeting up. Missing you loads. Glad you won the golf. Maybe we could Skype tomorrow? And don't be late for breakfast! xx

Adam couldn't wipe the smile off his face. That wasn't just words; she loved him. She really must be missing him loads. He cherished the thought deeply.

He loved her idea of Skyping. He couldn't wait to see her face again. He texted back immediately.

We should definitely Skype. I'll let you know when I have some free time between the planned meetings. Missing you too. x

As soon as he'd sent it he wondered if she was going to be happy to know that he was missing her too. If only she knew the truth. He wanted to tell her really badly but it needed to be a face to face conversation. His instinct was still right.

Within a minute, Jenny had replied.

Surely they should give you some time off for good behaviour? You weren't late for breakfast this morning, were you? xx

Adam was smiling from ear to ear as he typed his reply.

How can I be good if I never have a clue what's going on? I was ever so slightly late for breakfast but I covered it well. They now think Brits do sports in their jeans. Don't ask! Are you in bed? x

As happy and excited as Adam was about texting Jenny, his eyes were starting to droop. After incredibly boring and intensive back to back meetings, day after day after day, and then a late night out with his friends, Adam didn't stand a chance against his tiredness.

As he heard Jenny's reply come through, he had to fight to look at the screen on his phone.

No I'm watching a film. Are you in bed? xx

He shook his head with a smirk. Jenny didn't watch just anything on the telly. More often than not she was happier with a book or playing on her computer. He knew it would have to be some sort of action film to grab her interest.

Superman by any chance? Yes I'm tucked up now, feeling quite tired. It's been a long day. x

His eyes were winning the battle and he was fighting to stay awake. He really wanted to see if he was right, though. This was the happiest he'd been all day.

No actually I'm watching The Avengers. Made me think of you. xx

They were the last words that Adam was able to think about before sleep grabbed a hold of him once and for all. But they were words that ensured he went to sleep with an even bigger smile on his face, and he had very sweet dreams indeed.

His alarm blasted loudly in his ear the next morning. He'd still been holding his phone when he'd fallen to sleep and it was now tucked up right next to his cheek.

With very sore eyes, he turned it off. Then he noticed a message notification.

Hope you sleep well. Can't wait to talk to you tomorrow. I'm going to learn some German phrases to help you out. That'll surprise them! Night night, sweet dreams. xx

Adam felt a warm glow as he read it. She really was the nicest person he'd ever met and he felt lucky just to have her as a friend, let alone to know that she loved him. What more could a man ever possibly want?

But that part of his life would have to wait. He'd wished himself into this nightmare and now he had to deal with it.

He pulled himself out of bed to start his very boring routine - the same one he did every single day.

He showered and dressed himself and he was ready to leave his room by ten to six. There was no chance he was going to be late for breakfast today.

He made it down promptly for roll call where they all sat and waited for the hotel owner to bring out the food. How that irritated Adam on a daily basis. Surely if they just turned up at quarter past then the food would all be out?

He tucked into his cereal and then chose a strawberry yoghurt followed by a cup of coffee, and he was all done by twenty past six. But he couldn't go. He then had to sit for forty minutes in virtual silence until the car arrived at seven to pick them up.

They arrived at the office of a supplier at around eight o'clock where they were taken up to a very modern, technologically advanced meeting room and offered very strong coffee, which Adam was incredibly grateful for. He knew it was going to be another long day.

And time most definitely did drag. By ten o'clock they were still in the meeting and Adam's main contribution had been his exceptionally good doodle of Iron Man on his notepad. He'd zoned out the German around him long ago and he was just counting down the minutes until lunch. At least they always had good meals; that was something to look forward to.

But then something different happened. Adam suddenly noticed his phone light up. It was a call from Terence in the UK.

'Excuse me, this is important,' he said, grabbing his phone and stepping out of the room. He couldn't move quickly enough.

'Terence, is everything all right?' he said, enjoying the sound of English.

'No, it's not. Adam, we need you back. I'm sure you're making waves over in Hamburg, but we're going to have to pull you away from the job. We need you back in the UK and we need you on a flight today.'

As Adam resisted punching the air with delight, all he could think to himself was, *Thank you, Emmett.*

ZACK'S ELECTRIC MOMENT

Zack pulled up his car in the office car park, returning from his first lunch break in quite a while. It was Monday and, just as Zack had wished for, all of his colleagues had returned to work. As horrible as it was to see them, at least Zack had been gifted with the pleasure of getting away for his lunch hour.

He dawdled into the building and headed back to his desk where he knew more data inputting awaited him.

Barely anyone had spoken to Zack that day. News had spread that he'd been the only person not inflicted with the awful stomach bug. But rather than anyone question how he'd coped in the office all on his own, there seemed to be this spite towards him that he hadn't been ill when everyone else had.

From his perspective, being off sick had been the better end of the deal. It had been hell on earth manning the office on his own for a couple of weeks, but no one else saw it that way. Not that he ever suspected they would. Any way they could make him uncomfortable always seemed a win for his colleagues.

He really wanted someone to ask him about his weekend. He'd loved every second of his trip to Hamburg.

It had been so much fun. Not only was he very relieved to know that Adam was still his mate, but he was also on the cusp of a wonderful new relationship with Jenny.

She'd spent most of Saturday flirting with him. She'd even wanted them to share a room. It was only because they'd both been so drunk that they'd not ended up in bed together on the Saturday night. Zack was sure of it.

In truth, she hadn't been quite as flirtatious on the Sunday, and she'd looked positively shocked when he'd brought up them joining the mile high club together on the plane journey back. But Zack reasoned with himself that she was a shy girl. Jenny lacked a lot of confidence and Zack decided that it was probably best to take things really slowly.

He'd not seen Jenny as girlfriend material before, but who was he to say no? She was beautiful, fun, ambitious and kind-hearted. He'd be crazy to turn her down.

And if that wasn't exciting enough, even when he'd got home, his smile had got even bigger. He'd stepped into his flat the night before to find Cadence gone. She'd left him a note saying she'd been offered a huge opportunity that she couldn't turn down. She'd told him that she'd managed to get out of the flat on Saturday night and then her agent had called her on Sunday morning with the exciting news.

As a thank you for all he'd done, she'd left him the furniture, but she'd added that she just couldn't resist taking the mirrored coffee table. Apparently it was fast becoming her favourite piece of furniture ever.

Zack smiled just thinking about it. Could it have been any more perfect? Emmett was very good at his work.

'Can you tell me what this is supposed to say?' Arnold said, standing up and moving over to Rachel who sat on the desk next to Zack. He was a well-built member of the sales team who played rugby outside of work and totally scared the crap out of Zack.

'What is it?' Rachel asked in her usual stressed out tone. She had bright red hair and evil eyes.

'It's some message that Zack left for me. If he's going to leave me messages, can you please tell him to write them out properly?'

Rachel glanced quickly at the piece of paper in Arnold's hand and Zack felt his skin prickle. He could feel a moan brewing that was heading right in his direction.

'I don't know. What are you asking me for? How am I meant to read his mind? Who knows what goes on up there? You'll have to ask him yourself. He's sitting right there.'

Arnold sighed and then he moved to stand next to Zack. He whacked the piece of paper down, making Zack jump.

'What does this say?' Arnold demanded to know, pointing to a particular word.

Zack looked at the paper. He'd written incredibly neatly in capital letters. There was no way it was illegible.

'It says electricity,' Zack replied, being careful not to show his irritation. He didn't want to rile the beast further, but not only was the word impeccably clear, it was also the main thing that Energy Biz dealt with. Even if the brickhouse blockhead couldn't read it, no other word would have made any sense in the context.

'Electricity? If you say so,' Arnold scoffed.

He picked up the paper and placed it down on the desk of a fellow sales man. 'Apparently this says electricity.'

Zack focused hard on his monitor, pretending not to be listening. He hated being spoken about like he wasn't in the room, but it was a regular thing he had to deal with in his working day. He'd found ignoring it to be the best way to deal with it.

The colleague shook his head. 'Electricity? Looks more like guiltily to me. Who wrote that?'

'Zack.'

'There you go then. What did you expect?'

'It's a wonder the place didn't burn down last week with him in charge,' Arnold sneered.

'Zack, I need you for a minute,' Rachel announced, standing up. 'Could you join me in the meeting room?'

'Now?' Zack asked, still bitter about the ridiculous comments relating to his tidy handwriting.

'Yes please. You don't need to bring anything.'

Zack followed Rachel to the little meeting room at the back of the office. It was the only meeting room they had and Zack rarely ever had to venture into it.

They both took a seat and Rachel looked at him seriously. She was very pale, but Zack was quite sure it related to her illness. She'd already been sick once that morning. Zack hadn't felt at all guilty for his secret snigger.

'There was a board meeting earlier, as I think you might know,' she started. Zack nodded but he didn't say anything. 'They wanted to discuss the state of things following the dreadful sickness that spread across the company. It was awful, Zack. Really bad.'

'I can imagine.'

'It seems the fact that you managed to look after everything all on your own has been quite an eye-opener to them.'

Zack felt a small buzz. Her words seemed like praise. It was brand new territory for him.

'They've come to the conclusion that they have far too many members of staff,' Rachel continued. 'If you can manage all on your own then why do they need twenty-two of us?'

No, that sounded far more like it. Normality was restored.

'That being the case, they've decided to make you redundant,' Rachel finished.

Zack was stunned to silence. Even though he knew that he'd wished for it, it still came as a huge shock. They were actually making him redundant. The bastards!

'I've been so worried about telling you,' Rachel said. 'It's been making me very sick. I'm still really sick, you know. I'm not better at all. I probably shouldn't even be here. I'm having an awful time of it. You can't possibly imagine.'

'Sorry to hear that,' Zack replied, knowing that he didn't feel even remotely sorry for her.

'What's making it worse is that your situation is really complicated. You don't know what you're doing to me.'

'Complicated?' Zack asked, not liking the sound of it.

'Yes. You're causing us all sorts of issues, Zack.'

'Sorry,' Zack replied, although he hadn't got a clue what he was supposed to have done.

'It's your bloody contract.' Zack could hear his heart pounding in his chest as he waited for Rachel to elaborate. 'It turns out you've been put on four years' notice instead of four weeks by mistake.'

'What?' Zack asked. He was sure he would have remembered that.

'Obviously that's the contract you signed and the board is very worried that you're going to sue them if they don't keep to the terms. Is that something you'd do?'

Zack was lost for words. Four years' notice? That was ridiculous. Surely an error like that would never stand up in court? But then again, they were taking it quite seriously.

'I'd have to consult my lawyer,' was all Zack could think to say. It sounded good, although Zack didn't even know how he'd go about finding a lawyer, let alone consulting one. Or maybe it was a solicitor he needed to ask? Was there a difference? This really was getting complicated.

'I knew it. That's typical of you, being so difficult. We've all been throwing our guts up for weeks and you've totally got away with it, and now you're acting like some sort of victim.'

'Sorry. But you are making me redundant,' Zack reasoned.

'It's better than nearly dying!'

'Did you nearly die?'

'Yes! Yes, I did.'

'But you're all right now?'

'No. All of this stress is making me feel really ill.'

'I'm sorry about that,' Zack said. There was a moment of tense silence before Zack found the confidence to ask his next question. 'Don't I have the right to speak to a legal professional if you're terminating my employment?'

'It's all about you, isn't it. Don't you care about the trouble the company's in? All you can think about is dragging us through the courts to get a few extra quid.' Rachel shook her head and tutted. 'People like you make me so angry.'

'Sorry,' Zack said.

'Because you want to play these games, the board has said they'll honour the four years' notice. Does that make you happy? But you'll need to leave now and then that will be it. There'll be no formal redundancy procedure. You'll just get one lump sum. I have a contract here for you to sign if you agree.'

Zack couldn't believe what he was hearing. A lump sum? Surely he was misunderstanding. 'Sorry, can I just clarify that? In order to get me to walk away without any fuss, are you saying the company is offering me four years' worth of salary? In one go?'

'I knew you'd be like this!' Rachel said with anger. 'I told them you'd play hard ball. You always have to fight for a little bit more, don't you? I think that's a pretty impressive offer, but clearly not for you.'

'I do think that's a good offer,' Zack replied, not sure where this attitude was coming from.

'Knowing you'd be like this, I put together a back-up contract, just in case. Lucky for you, I'm good at my job.'

'A back-up contract?'

'Yes, all right, you can have the lot.'

'The lot?'

'Four years' salary including the two percent annual pay increase year on year.'

'What?' Zack asked. He wanted to jump out of his

chair and do a cartwheel. This was getting better by the second! Instead, though, he forced a very straight face. 'That sounds fair. I can live with that.'

'Money grabbing sod,' Rachel mumbled. 'Sign here.' She presented a short contract that Zack took from her. It detailed everything that she'd just said. As long as he walked away that afternoon and didn't bother anyone ever again, then he could have the lump sum in his bank account by close of play the following day. That included four times his salary and the incremental increases he would have received if he'd worked his four years' notice.

It took all of Zack's will power not to smile smugly.

He signed the contract carefully and then handed it back to Rachel.

'I hope you're happy now,' she hissed. 'That's it then. If you can just log off then you'll have to leave the premises immediately.'

Zack was gobsmacked. As easy as that. He went to thank her when suddenly she grabbed her mouth and darted out of the meeting room.

Zack sniggered. It was such a nasty bug, wasn't it.

He walked back to his desk, feeling a sense of euphoria at how it was the last time he'd ever have to sit at it again.

He flicked through his emails and deleted any non-work ones before grabbing his few personal items.

He didn't bother saying goodbye to anyone and everyone just ignored him anyway. He just headed to the front door with a beaming smile across his face. He was free. He was completely free and he was a very rich man.

Thank you Emmett!

JENNY'S UNEXPECTED VISITORS

Jenny was lying on her sofa that Monday night. It was just after seven thirty and she was trying to concentrate on her new Batman comic that had been delivered that day, but she couldn't stop staring at her phone.

Ever since she'd written that letter to Emmett, she'd not heard a thing from Nathan. He'd texted her throughout Friday night and four times on Saturday morning (to which she'd not sent one reply), and then nothing. But she wasn't feeling safe just yet. She still felt nervous that he was going to call or just turn up.

Could a fictional character that Zack had drawn really make their wishes come true?

Suddenly her door buzzed. She sat up. She knew it. It must be his break from work and, as she'd failed to make any sort of contact with him since Thursday, he'd come around to check she was okay. Why couldn't he just get the hint and leave her alone?

She decided not to answer it. Instead she rested herself back down and she pretended to be engrossed in her book. But the buzzer made its irritating sound again and she knew she had to respond. It was only right to face him.

She dragged her feet to the hallway where she picked

up the intercom.

'Hello.'

'Hi, it's Adam.'

She nearly dropped the intercom receiver on the floor. Had she misheard? 'Adam?' she checked.

'Surprise! Can I come up?'

'Definitely!'

She buzzed him up and then quickly checked her reflection in the bathroom mirror (she looked okay, it would do) before dashing to the door to let him in.

'What the hell are you doing here?' she asked with a big beaming smile.

He dragged his suitcase into her flat and dumped his laptop bag on the floor before hugging her tightly.

'Am I glad to be back,' he said.

She wrapped her arms around him, still unable to believe that he was really there.

'Have you quit your job? You didn't get the sack for being late for breakfast, did you?'

Adam chuckled. 'No, nothing like that. The MD from the UK called me up this morning to say he needed me back urgently. Apparently one of our biggest clients has hit quite a few problems and they'll only deal with me. They told Terence that if I can't be there then they'll be taking their business elsewhere. All I can say is, thank you Emmett!'

'You wished to come home?'

Adam addressed her with a more serious face. 'That was one of my wishes.'

'You had more than one?'

'I had two wishes. Just like you.'

Jenny was puzzled. 'How do you know how many wishes I made?'

'Shall we go through to the living room?' Adam said. He looked exhausted.

'Of course. Can I get you a drink?'

'No, just come and sit with me.'

Adam led Jenny through to the living room and then he plonked himself down on the sofa looking anxious. He flicked through her Batman comic book that was lying on the cushion next to him.

'You don't normally read Batman,' he said.

'I felt like a change.'

'Any good?'

'I've not really started it yet. I'll let you know.'

This was an unusual awkward moment between the pair and Jenny could tell he had something on his mind. She sat on the arm of the sofa nervously, dreading what he was about to say. She had the feeling it wasn't going to be good. Then she recalled her question from a few moments before.

'How did you know that I'd made two wishes?'

Adam looked up at her for the first time. He carefully placed the comic book down next to him and gave her his full attention. 'In the same way that I know we also wished for the same thing.'

Jenny stood up. Why would Adam want Nathan to dump her? That was a bit mean.

'You dropped this on your way out of my room on Saturday,' he said, reaching into his suit jacket pocket and pulling out a folded up piece of paper.

'What's that?' she said, her heart pounding.

'It's your wishes to Emmett. I'm sorry, I didn't mean to read it. I didn't know what it was.'

'No!' Jenny exclaimed. Panic rattled her. He couldn't have read her letter. It was supposed to be a secret. She ran over to her bag that she'd dumped by the telly. She knew the letter was still in the side pocket; it had to be. Or this was some very cruel joke.

'It's fine, Jen,' Adam said, standing up himself.

She checked every inch of her bag, but the letter wasn't anywhere to be found. It really was in his fingers.

The truth was out.

She knew then and there that their friendship was

never going to be the same again. Was she going to lose him? She couldn't speak. She stood up to face him, every inch of her throbbing with the fear of what he was going to say next.

He placed the letter down on the chair next to him and he addressed her quite directly.

'You love me?' he asked.

Even basic tasks like breathing suddenly became impossible for Jenny. The world around her started to become hazy. He knew. That was it, he knew. She stood very still, trying to remain calm. All she could focus on was not falling over. Being able to speak was far too big an ask at that moment.

'Is what you wrote in the letter true?' he asked. His voice was gentle. Maybe he pitied her. It probably made him laugh that a girl like her could ever see herself with a man like him. He was so far out of her league, even Jenny didn't know what she'd been thinking. He was going to end up with a girl like Cadence and all Jenny was good for was a man like Nathan. Sweet and kind and hugely irritating.

She still couldn't speak. But even if she could find her voice, what would she say? If she didn't admit to it then he couldn't laugh at her, or sit her down and give her the 'I like you, but...' speech, followed by 'we'll always be friends,' and topped with 'you're going to find the right man one day, Jen, but that man's just not me.'

'Jen, you need to tell me if this is true,' he tried again. No matter how many times he was going to ask though, she knew he'd never thaw her frozen state. This was too massive for her to talk about.

For the first time since she'd known him, Jenny wanted Adam to leave. The embarrassment was overwhelming and she wanted him to go and for this whole episode to be erased from existence.

He took a step closer and he was now just inches away from her face. Her breathing was jagged, and her heart was thumping so hard it was making her body shake.

'I need to know, Jen. I need to know for a reason,' he said. His words were so soft they were like silk caressing her skin. But still she couldn't speak. What reason could he possibly have? Because he hoped it wouldn't be true? Because he didn't want to ruin their friendship? Because he was getting back with Cadence?

'The reason is...' he started and Jenny could feel the sting of tears about to fall. 'I love you, too.'

For a moment Jenny wasn't sure if she'd died. Her heart had completely stopped beating, her breathing had totally extinguished, and all that was left were her non-blinking eyes glaring at the man of her dreams.

Had he really just said what she thought he had?

She took a breath. It was a joke. He was making fun of her. It must be terribly amusing for him that she'd been in love with him since the first time they'd had their debate about who would win in a fight: Superman or Spider-Man. How she loved their battles. Maybe they'd never have them again.

A few seconds went by where nothing happened. Jenny still couldn't move for the fear that what seemed to be going on was all in fact a ruse.

Then he leaned in. With no warning at all, his lips brushed against hers and then he stood back to see her reaction.

He'd kissed her. He'd just kissed her!

A small smile crept up on her mouth. That had felt good. Had he meant to do that?

He smiled in return before leaning in and kissing her again more deeply.

Jenny took a moment to enjoy it. She wasn't quite sure if she was dreaming or not. It seemed far too good to be true.

Then she realised that it didn't really matter either way, and suddenly she held nothing back. She kissed him in return with all the passion that she'd been saving up over the years. If this was all a joke then she was certainly going to be making the most of it.

After a few moments, Adam wrapped his arms around her, and Jenny lost all her senses. All she could think about was how amazing the kiss was. It was better than she'd ever imagined it would be. She knew he'd be a good kisser, but the feel of his lips - and then his tongue - tickled through every inch of her.

Jenny had no clue how long they'd been standing there for, passionately embraced. It could have been days for all she cared. Finally Adam slowly left her lips, but he didn't step away.

'I love you, Jen,' he said. 'Do you really love me too? Was it true what you wrote?'

She knew the power of words had finally returned. 'Yes. Yes, it's all true. You don't mind?'

'Are you kidding? You've literally made me the happiest man alive! Seeing you with that Nathan killed me.'

'You don't need to worry about him. He's out of the picture now.'

Adam kissed her again and she found herself hoping that it would never end. If a meteor was to hit her flat and they were both on the verge of taking their last breaths, she knew she wouldn't mind. She'd die perfectly happy. How could anything else in her life top this?

'Do you really want to be with me?' she asked, suddenly fearing again that maybe it was all too good to be true.

'Yes. Yes, I really do. I can't believe it's taken us this long to realise it.'

She slid her arms under his suit jacket to get closer to him. She could feel the warmth of his body through his shirt and for the first time the sexual energy between them charged.

That was new. That was incredible.

'You know, I wanted to kiss you so much when we were in bed together a couple of weeks ago,' he said.

'You should have. I really wanted that too.'

'You had a boyfriend! Besides, I was nervous that you'd push me away. I didn't want to lose you as a friend. If only I'd known.'

Jenny snuggled in against him tighter and he rested his head on hers. He was a few inches taller than Jenny and she felt so safe and cosy wrapped up in his arms.

'Do you mind if I have a drink?' Adam finally said, breaking the perfection. 'It's been a long day.'

'Of course not. I'll get you whatever you want.'

Adam looked at her but he didn't let go. Then he moved his hands up to her cheeks and he kissed her again. But this time it wasn't the same. This time it was far more lustful and urgent.

He moved his lips to her cheek and then her neck. She felt her breathing quicken and her toes curl. It was getting exciting.

'There was something else I wanted to do last week as well,' he whispered in her ear and it sent pulses of passion racing through her.

'Oh yeah? What was that?'

Adam scooped her hair in his hands and he kissed her with more fervour than anyone had ever done before. Jenny hadn't even known it was possible to feel so desired. She was worried she might just have an orgasm right then and there.

'I want to make love to you,' he said breathlessly.

Yes, yes, yes! she screamed in her head. How many times had she thought about this moment? But it had never been as good as the reality she was now facing. Adam really knew how to knock her socks off. Suddenly it was seeming well worth the wait.

'I'm not going to stop you,' she muttered, trying not to sound as eager as she knew she was.

'Good,' he grinned, and then he took her by the hand.

He led her into the bedroom but he stopped near the door. He looked at her bed with the duvet half hanging on the floor from where she'd left it that morning and he chuckled.

'You are a messy one, aren't you?' he said.

'Would you have me any other way?' she shrugged.

'Not in a million years.' Then he cupped her face in his hands and he kissed her again. And this time they really didn't stop.

It was another sleepless night for Jenny and Adam, but this one was full of smiles. They made love, chatted, got up to make hot chocolate in the middle of the night, and then they were all over each other again. Despite the fact that they'd known each other for years, they were starting to see each other in a whole different light, and both of them were ecstatic.

Adam's phone alarm went off at seven o'clock where it actually woke them after they'd finally dozed off.

'Morning,' he said, kissing Jenny. She couldn't believe she was waking up next to him again, but this time she knew it wasn't going to be the last time. This was the start of something special.

'Morning,' she grinned.

'I'd better jump in the shower,' Adam said. 'I can't be late today. I'm seeing that client bang on nine o'clock.'

'You can't be late for them!' Jenny ordered. 'They're the people that brought you home to me.'

'They certainly are.'

All the time while showering, dressing and eating breakfast, the couple were still barely able to resist one another, and Jenny still wasn't quite sure whether it was all really true.

She took the breakfast bowls into the kitchen and loaded the dishwasher up, and then she headed into the bedroom to find Adam making her bed.

'You don't have to do that,' she said.

'How does it not irritate you?' he asked with a smile.

'It would irritate me having to make it every day. You

only get back into it a few hours later and mess it up again.'

'How would you feel if we both got back into it again later?' Adam asked.

'You want to stay over again?'

'I have a suitcase full of stuff. What about if I stayed for a few days? I was thinking it might be good for us to have some real quality time together.'

Jenny wanted to jump with excitement, but she kept her cool. 'I'd love that. That would be great.'

He moved around the bed to hug her. Then he whispered, totally seriously, 'Am I your Superman?'

Jenny suddenly felt sick. She'd been going off Superman. But then she remembered how much Adam had always been jealous of her affection for the Man of Steel and she couldn't resist a smile. It suddenly all made so much sense. He really had been jealous.

'I think you're actually more of a Clark Kent,' she said, trying to keep a straight face.

'What?!'

Adam started to tickle her and Jenny shrieked. She hated being tickled. She ran off into the hallway but he ran after her. She couldn't breathe she was laughing so hard.

The fun was instantly cut short when there was a knock at her front door. The pair looked at one another, puzzled.

Jenny gasped. What if it was Nathan? What if he'd been camped out at the door downstairs for hours, waiting for someone to let him in so he could trap her on her own threshold?

The knock repeated. 'I'll get it,' Adam said, reading her fretful expression.

Jenny stood back as Adam opened the door. She poised herself ready to see Nathan's face. Would he be shocked, angry, upset, happy? She could barely look.

But as the door opened, she saw two policemen standing there.

'Hello,' Adam said.

'We'd like to speak to Jennifer Orwell, please,' one of them said.

'Is there a problem?' Adam enquired.

Jenny's heart was pounding. What was going on? She approached the door, grasping Adam's hand as soon as she stood next to him.

'I'm Jennifer,' she said.

She saw the policemen glance down at her grip of Adam before addressing her very seriously.

'We need you to accompany us down to the station to help with some enquiries,' one of them said.

'What sort of enquiries?' Adam asked.

'We're currently investigating the sudden disappearance of Nathan Langley and we believe that you, Miss Orwell, are his girlfriend.'

Jenny instinctively dropped Adam's hand.

'I...' What could she say? She supposed she was still *technically* his girlfriend. They hadn't actually broken up. As much as she wanted to believe that blanking him out of her life counted, she had to concede that maybe her approach did leave a few grey areas.

'We'd like to take you down to the station for questioning.'

'Is she under arrest?' Adam asked.

'Not at this moment. But we do need you to cooperate, Miss Orwell.'

Jenny turned to Adam. What was she going to do? Yes, she'd wished for Nathan to leave her alone, but not for him to vanish off the face of the planet. Or was that what she'd wished for? Suddenly it got very confusing.

'You'd better go with them,' Adam said.

'Will you come with me?' Jenny pleaded.

'You won't be able to join us,' one of the policemen said. 'But you can meet us down there.'

'Can I just grab my bag?' Jenny asked. The policemen nodded and Jenny raced to the living room. With shaking hands, she threw her phone in and checked she had her keys and purse, and then she paced back to the door.

Was she going to go to prison? Flashes of orange overalls blasted through her head. Was this the last time she'd ever step foot in her flat? What were her parents going to say?

'Will you call my work?' she said to Adam.

He nodded and then kissed her quickly before she was guided out by the policemen.

'Don't worry, Jen,' Adam called. 'I'll sort everything. I'll be there to collect you. Just don't worry.'

ADAM'S STICKY SITUATION

Adam couldn't believe what he was seeing. Jenny, being taken away by the police? He had to remember that she wasn't being arrested, but it was clear she was still a person of interest to them.

He rubbed his hand through his hair. This was bad. He knew that Nathan's disappearance was no different to Cadence's and he'd probably show up somewhere at some point soon, but that didn't help Jenny.

What was she going to say? She could hardly tell the truth. She'd definitely be locked up if she said, 'It's all right officer, I wished that he'd go away, and my wishes are currently being granted by a fictional comic book hero who has magically and inexplicably come to life. But don't worry, he'll pop up again. Cadence did.'

Adam took a deep breath. It was going to be fine. All she had to do was answer their questions. They were going to ask her things like where she saw him last and what she'd done over the weekend. She wasn't even in the country so surely she'd be off the hook.

He looked at his watch. It was just after eight o'clock. He really needed to get going. He had to make that meeting with the clients that had brought him home. If he didn't then it might end up with him back in Hamburg and he couldn't risk that. He also knew that would be the last thing Jenny would want as well.

He made a quick mental plan that he'd attend the meeting and then he'd get out of the office as soon as he could afterwards. He'd say he had an errand to run and he'd go straight to the police station to find out what the hell was going on.

He grabbed his suit jacket and his laptop bag and he left her flat, heading straight to his car that was parked on the road right outside.

As soon as he sat in the driver's seat, he grabbed his phone from his pocket. He Googled the number of Jenny's work and he added it to his contacts. It was a bit too early to call them, but he had to try and get hold of them before nine. He'd told Jenny he would sort it, but he also couldn't be late for that meeting.

He began the journey to his office, but his mind was all over the place. He was so worried about Jenny. He felt riddled with guilt that he wasn't there with her, but he knew he'd get there as soon as he could. She just needed to hold on for a couple more hours.

At just after half eight, he was very close to his office so he tried to give Jenny's work a call. He was keeping his fingers crossed that someone would answer.

He pressed the telephone button on his steering wheel and then instructed the car to 'call Heart Attack Marketing'.

Within seconds he was connected and he was grateful to hear it ringing. Then he was even more grateful to hear a human voice.

'Good morning, Heart Attack Marketing, how can we help?'

'Hi, I'm calling on behalf of Jenny Orwell. I'm very sorry to say that she won't be in this morning. Or possibly not for the rest of the day.'

'Oh dear, is she okay?' the female voice asked.

'I hope so. It seems her... boyfriend has gone missing and she's currently at the police station trying to help them... figure out what's happened.'

'Oh no, that's awful! How's she coping?'

'As you can imagine, she's quite shook up.'

'She's only just started seeing him. What a shame. Are you with the police?'

'No, I'm a friend of hers. I'm Adam.'

'Oh hello! She talks about you all the time. It's nice to put a... voice to the name.'

Adam felt a gush of pride. She talks about him all the time. How nice is that! It helped to soften the bitterness he was feeling at having to tell this girl that Nathan was still Jenny's boyfriend.

'One of us will keep you posted,' Adam said. 'Sorry to start your day off with such bad news.'

'Do send Jenny our love, won't you. Tell her we'll be thinking of her. Nathan seemed so nice. I hope he turns up soon.'

Adam gritted his teeth. Nathan was not nice. This whole problem had started because Jenny wanted to get rid of Nathan, therefore he could not be nice.

'Will do. Bye then,' Adam said, hanging up.

He felt agitated, but it wasn't just because he'd had to mention that man's name. It was because he suddenly realised that he didn't actually know what the facts were. It was worrying him that everyone still considered Jenny to be Nathan's girlfriend. Was that still actually the case?

After he'd seen her letter and then Jenny had told him it was all over between her and Nathan, he'd been so happy. Adam had thought no more about it. But now Adam was starting to question exactly what had happened.

Had Jenny actually told Nathan it was over or had she just wished for his disappearance? As Adam thought about it, all he could remember Jenny saying was that Nathan was out of the picture. She hadn't actually confirmed that they'd broken up. It seemed more likely that she'd just wished him away and she was keeping her fingers crossed that it would work. How could she be so silly? How could she be so thoughtless?

Adam sighed. How could he blame her? He was no different. That was exactly how he'd behaved with Cadence. He'd had years to break up with her but he'd never had the guts. When it came down to it, he'd just wished her in the arms of another man and then he'd blamed her for being a cheat. Adam had never once been honest with Cadence.

Maybe he and Jenny really were meant to be together. It seemed they were equally rubbish at breaking up with people.

Adam parked his car in his dedicated parking space right near the reception of his work, and he headed straight in.

He was happy to see his office in exactly the same neat and tidy state that he'd left it in. Although he wasn't quite sure what could possibly have happened in the week or so since he'd been gone.

He set up his laptop, replied to a couple of emails, and then he got the call from reception to say the clients had arrived.

He met them in the meeting room on the first floor and he was instantly relieved to hear everyone speak in English. It made things far easier.

He let the clients lead the meeting, and they started their moaning and whining about prices and customer service and how the product standards seemed to have slipped. It was the same old rubbish, just a different day.

Adam knew these clients and he knew how much they liked to have a good groan about stuff. It rarely ever had any solid grounding, but that made sorting it out so much easier. He just had to butter them up a bit and give them a few freebies, and they normally ended up putty in his hands.

He tried very hard to concentrate, but his concerns for

Jenny did make it difficult. At least he knew his job well, and he was able to calm down his clients' concerns and even get them smiling all within a couple of hours.

He let the junior sales person see the clients out, and then he headed straight back to his desk to grab his things.

As he passed the sales staff on his return he mentioned briefly that he was popping out and he'd be on his phone if they needed him. Then he headed right to the stairs to get out of there and to Jenny as quickly as he could.

He walked through the reception and swung back the glass door of the main entrance, but suddenly he couldn't move. He tried to step forward, but he couldn't get out. It was the weirdest thing.

He stepped back and tried again, but it was like an invisible force field was keeping him locked in.

Oh no! What had he done? What had Emmett done?

'Is everything all right?' the receptionist asked, looking at Adam strangely as he attempted to leave the building.

'Yes,' he replied, trying not to look flustered. 'I think I might have forgotten something. Back in a sec.'

He raced back up the stairs and back to his desk, and he nudged his laptop awake.

He opened his personal folder and looked for the Word document that he'd saved on Saturday. As he waited for it to open, his heart was pounding. What had he actually wished for? How had it all gone so wrong?

The document finally opened and there, before him, he could see his error.

I wish for something urgent to come up in the UK office that means I have to return there ASAP. I then do not want to leave again.

He doesn't want to leave again? What had he been thinking! Was he now trapped?

Could it be that Emmett had taken him quite literally and he'd granted Adam a wish to never leave his work again? What sort of crap was that? He was supposed to be empathising with Adam, not making his life a misery.

Somewhere along the line, their depiction of this superhero had gone massively awry.

This was more like "Emmett the literal wish granting man who is more likely to cock things up for you than anything else", not the caring, empathetic man they'd imagined over drinks that Sunday afternoon.

Although, when Adam thought about it, they had been on their fourth pint when they'd written the character profile. He suddenly started to worry about what Jenny had actually committed to paper. It could have been any old rubbish, they were having such a laugh with it. Little did they know he would come alive to make them suffer.

Then again, Emmett wasn't getting everything wrong. Adam had just spent one of the best nights of his life with the only girl that had ever really mattered to him. He had to concede that without Emmett he and Jenny might have never got together.

Adam breathed slowly. Whether Emmett had good intentions or not, it still didn't help his current situation. He had to get out and he had to get to Jenny.

The only logical thing he could think to do was to wish his way out. Surely that was the only answer.

I wish I could get out of this building and I wish I could get to Jenny. He said it over and over again in his head, hoping that Emmett would be listening somewhere.

After a few minutes of silent chanting, he made the trip back to reception to see if it had worked.

He opened the door again, this time more slowly, and he tried to take a step outside. But once again, to his great frustration, the outside world was blocked by an invisible barrier.

'Forgotten something else?' the receptionist asked, watching him struggle at the door again.

Adam forced a smile. 'You know, it's really not my day today.'

As he walked back to his desk, his head was spinning. He had to think of a way out of this.

Then it occurred to him that maybe their wishes didn't get granted straight away. Maybe he needed to wait an hour or so.

He sat back down at his desk feeling awful. He'd promised Jenny he would be there.

Well, if he couldn't be there for her himself, at least he could make sure she was still taken care of.

He picked up his phone and dialled the only person he knew that would understand.

ZACK TO THE RESCUE

The Star Wars theme tune was loud. Zack opened his eyes slowly and he reached out for his phone to make the noise stop.

He suddenly saw it was Adam calling him and he knew he should take it. There might be problems in Hamburg.

'Hello,' Zack said with a croaky voice.

'Hi, it's Adam. I need your help.'

'Is everything okay?'

'Jenny's been arrested.'

'What?' Zack sat up in bed, suddenly feeling far more awake.

'Well no, not exactly arrested, but she has been taken in for questioning by the police.'

'Why? What's she done?'

'One of her wishes was that Nathan leaves her and it seems Emmett has made him disappear. Just like he did with Cadence. Only this time it's become a missing person's case and Jenny is on their list of suspects.'

Zack took a moment. He was feeling quite hungover so he had to give himself a minute to ponder whether he was just being slow or whether it was right that he didn't have one clue what Adam was talking about.

It was definitely the latter.

'Who's Nathan?' he asked.

'Jenny's boyfriend. Well ex-boyfriend. You know, the bloke I told you about.'

'Her boyfriend?' Zack asked. 'She's got a boyfriend?'

'No! Absolutely not. He is no longer her boyfriend.'

'No longer? I didn't know she'd had a boyfriend at all.'

'It's a long story, Zack.' Zack propped the pillow up behind him so he could get comfortable. Why did he not know about this?

Then he saw sense. He reasoned with himself that if Jenny was looking to start a relationship with him, then the last thing she'd want to do was reveal a boyfriend. Maybe she'd broken up with this Nathan to be with Zack?

Zack felt quite pleased with that idea as he tuned back in to hear the end of Adam's story.

'...currently at the police station and one of us needs to be there to help her.'

'Of course. I'll be there for her,' Zack replied. 'It's not like you can just fly back from Hamburg, is it.'

'Erm, actually... I am back in the UK. I'm in my office at the minute.'

'What? When did that happen?'

'It was one of my wishes. Emmett works fast. So can you get out of work to help her?'

'Hang on, how do you know that Jenny's been arrested? Did she call you?' Zack suddenly felt disheartened that she hadn't called him.

'No, I was at her flat.' There was a momentary pause before Adam added, 'I popped round to see her this morning just to say I was back and then suddenly the police turned up.'

'Oh!' Zack replied, feeling relieved. Jenny probably would have called him. Maybe she'd asked Adam to tell Zack to go and rescue her.

'She was terrified, mate. She really needs you right now.'

'Of course she does.'

'We both need you. You'd know I'd go if there was any way I could.'

Zack paused for a moment. His comment sounded more like Adam was asking Zack to rescue her rather than Jenny had asked Adam to ask Zack to rescue her. 'Why can't you go?' Zack asked with caution.

'That's the other thing. It seems there might have been a small caveat to my wish.'

'What do you mean, caveat?'

'Well, upon wishing to not leave the UK office again, Emmett has apparently taken me quite literally and I'm currently trapped at work. I can't leave the building. It's like that invisible force field, the same that blocked Cadence in your flat. Is she still there, by the way?'

'No,' Zack said, feeling happy at just saying it. 'Good old Emmett. She was gone before I got back on Sunday. She just left a note to say London was calling and she'd see me around sometime.'

'Another wish come true, then.'

'Looks aren't everything, are they?'

Adam chuckled. 'We both learnt that lesson. So please tell me you can get out of work.'

Zack smiled. 'That's not going to be a problem. I made two wishes to Emmett and he granted them both. I got made redundant yesterday!'

'Oh no. Or... congratulations?'

'I got a huge pay off. I certainly celebrated last night, you wouldn't believe it.'

'Good for you, mate. That explains why you sound so rough.'

'Truth be told, you woke me up. It was a late one.'

'Who were you out with?'

'Anyone that was willing to party! You know Miloworth is a sociable place when you're buying the rounds.'

'I bet it is. So you can get down to the police station?'

'Yeah, no problem. Leave it to me.'

'Cheers, mate. I'm really grateful.'

'What are you going to do about getting out of the office?'

'I'm working on something, don't worry. Just look after Jenny. That's all that matters.'

'Of course. She's in safe hands with me.'

As Zack hung up, his head was spinning, and not just from the hangover. It seemed a lot had happened since they'd made their wishes on Saturday. Emmett was proving to be quite a powerful man.

After munching on three slices of toast and marmite, and refreshing himself in the shower, Zack made his way to his car to pick up Jenny.

He waited in the police station for what felt like an age. It was late afternoon before she finally appeared, and she looked most distraught.

'Zack! Thanks for coming to collect me. What a nightmare!' She hugged him tightly.

'Are you okay?' he asked, hugging her back.

'I just want to get out of here.'

'Of course you do.'

Zack led her to his car. He could see her shaking. It was such a shame. They got in the car and he could tell she was fighting back tears.

'What happened?' he asked as he reached out to hold her hand.

'Did Adam ask you to come?' she said.

'Yes.'

'Was he too busy?'

Zack felt immediately irked by this. Why was Adam suddenly so important? 'Let's just say, he's got stuck at work.'

'Oh,' she replied, hanging her head in what could only be interpreted a sheer disappointment.

'Did you not want me to come?' Zack asked, a little defensively.

'No, it's not that. It's...' Zack could see her struggling to find the words.

'What?'

'I guess I just didn't want everyone in the world to know that I'd been arrested.'

'Oh,' Zack said, nodding. He understood. She now had to deal with the fact that Zack knew she'd had a boyfriend. That was clearly something she'd wanted to keep from him. Understandably.

Should he bring the subject up? Yes. It's best to get it out in the open.

'He's your boyfriend?' Zack asked, gently.

'Who?' Jenny replied with a look of horror.

'Nathan.'

'Oh. No!' she insisted, before screwing up her face. 'Well, maybe. Sort of.'

'What does that mean?'

'It's got a bit complicated.'

'Right,' Zack said, squeezing her hand to indicate that he understood.

'What did Adam tell you?' Jenny asked.

'He told me about your wish. Although I bet you wish you'd never met that Nathan now.'

'You can say that again. We started to date a couple of weeks ago, but it quickly became really suffocating. He'd turn up at my work, turn up at my flat unannounced, text me about a hundred times a day. I couldn't handle it anymore, so I wished that he'd leave me alone.'

'My God, he sounds like a right stalker.'

Jenny gazed out of the window, turning her head away from Zack. 'I don't know.'

'What don't you know?'

'His heart was in the right place. He thought I was happy. I never actually told him to back away so I suppose he thought I liked all that stuff.'

'You didn't tell him?'

'You know I'm not good with stuff like that! He was

generally really nice. What was I supposed to say?'

'You're suffocating me. Please leave me alone.'

'I couldn't say that! He bought me flowers and chocolates; it was really sweet of him. Then he sent me these balloons. And I got a kite from him, for some reason. Then there was this blow up Superman thing. Then a Superman toy. And also a really freaky Superman gnome, which I thought was perhaps a little bit weird because I don't have a garden.'

Zack was gobsmacked. 'Do you really like Superman that much? I thought it was more about winding up Adam.'

'No, I do love Superman. I always have. It's just an added bonus that it winds up Adam. The weird thing is, though, that I don't ever recall telling Nathan that I like him. I don't know where he got it from.'

Jenny looked down, unable to face Zack. 'The final straw came just before we went to Hamburg,' she uttered. 'On Thursday night Nathan turned up at my door, but this time he was dressed as Superman. It wasn't even a good suit. It had these ridiculous fake muscles. He looked a right prat. I could have died of embarrassment. I was terrified of what was coming next.'

'Why didn't you tell me?'

'I was humiliated!'

'I could have helped you.'

'I didn't want to talk about it.'

'Is that why your phone kept going off?'

Jenny nodded. 'It was too much. But I knew he meant well.'

'His heart may have been in the right place, but I think we both know he was never going to be the right man for you.'

'No, I'm starting to see that now.'

'Really?'

'I think Hamburg changed a few things for all of us.'

Zack squeezed Jenny's hand tightly again. 'For the

better, I hope?'

She smiled. 'For the best.'

Zack couldn't wipe the smile from his face. 'So Superman outfits are definitely a big no when it comes to dating Jenny Orwell, then?'

'I think they're a big no in any relationship,' Jenny sniggered.

'I have to know. What did you say to him when he turned up at your door dressed up?'

Jenny looked out of the window again. 'I don't want to talk about it.'

Zack tried not to smirk. 'You didn't pretend to like it, did you?'

'I don't want to talk about!'

Zack stifled his laugh as best he could. The images in his head were hilarious. No, it wasn't funny. Jenny had never been good at confrontation. He could see how awkward a situation like that would be for her.

How he wished he'd been a fly on the wall that night!

'Okay, everything else aside,' Zack said, 'we need to sort out your predicament. So you wished that this Nathan would leave you, and now he's completely disappeared?'

'Yes.'

'What did the police say?'

'They asked me loads of things about the time I'd spent with him, where we met, when I'd last seen him. They made me feel really guilty. But, I guess I am. It really is all my fault that he's gone.'

'We need to take a look at what you wrote to Emmett. We need to find out exactly what was said so we can figure out a way around it. Do you know where your wish is?'

Jenny nodded and then Zack could have sworn he saw a little smile dash across her lips. 'It's at my flat.'

'Right, that's our next stop then.'

Jenny opened the front door to her flat and she led Zack straight to the folded piece of paper that was lying on her chair in the living room.

She opened it up and sat down.

'Right,' she started, making very sure that Zack couldn't see what she'd written. Not that he had a problem with that. They had all agreed it would be secret. 'Basically, I said that I'd like Nathan to disappear from my life,' she said before looking up at him. 'See, not disappear completely, just disappear from my life.'

'Is that it?' he asked.

'Well, mostly. I suppose there's a bit more.'

'Tell me everything, Jenny.'

'Okay. So I said that I'd like Nathan to disappear from my life. He's nice but he's not the one for me. Something about me feeling bad breaking up with him. Blah blah blah.'

'What's blah blah blah?' Zack asked.

'It's really not important. Trust me, Zack, don't make me say it.'

'It could be important. I'm not going to judge.'

'Let me just get to what I think is important, then we'll see.'

'Fair enough.'

'Erm... he's far too needy. I just don't want him. Then I ask Emmett to make sure that Nathan doesn't break up with me. That would be far too embarrassing. You know I don't like conflict.'

Zack nodded along but he was in shock. Jenny had gone into so much detail. This was like an extract from her diary.

'Then I said that I'd much prefer it if I didn't hear from him again and could he just vanish from my world.' Jenny looked up at Zack. 'Not everyone's world, just my world.'

'Is that it?'

'No, there's a bit more. I finally finish by adding that maybe I could just say hello to him when I see him in the pub.'

'What pub?'

'That's where I met him: The World's End in town. He's the manager there.'

Zack had flashbacks from the night before. That's where he'd ended up, with all those Sambuca shots. They were a great bunch of students. He'd only meant to pop in for a couple of quiet pints to celebrate, but he'd got chatting and it had all gone downhill. Or uphill, he supposed. It certainly had been a night to remember.

He didn't even know where that karaoke machine had come from.

'I was in there last night,' Zack said. 'There was only female staff.'

'Of course he wasn't there. He's been missing since Saturday afternoon. Apparently he popped downstairs to change a beer barrel and never returned. He just vanished.'

'That's just how it happened with Cadence. Only she was moisturising in the bathroom.'

'What a bitch,' Jenny muttered.

'What?' Zack asked, not sure if he'd heard correctly.

'I don't see anything in what I've written that could explain where Nathan has gone,' she responded.

Zack sat down on the sofa so he could concentrate better. 'Read that last bit again, about saying hello down the pub.'

Jenny scanned her eyes down the paper. 'Maybe I could just say hello to him when I see him in the pub and that would be it.'

'Well, there you go,' Zack said, suddenly seeing it all so clearly.

'What?' Jenny asked, obviously confused.

'You've stated that you only want to see him when you go to the pub. So that's where we need to go.'

'Why?'

'Because it's only when you get to the pub that he'll show up again. It's the only thing that makes sense.'

Jenny shook her head. 'Couldn't I just wish him back?'

'No, it definitely doesn't work like that. Remember, we

can't unwish our wishes. I think Emmett expects us to see things through. It's no good us just changing our minds all the time, willy nilly. He takes us seriously.'

'So from now on Nathan is only going to exist when I go to The World's End pub?'

'No, that's how it sits at the moment. But you have the power to change it.'

'How? If I can't unwish my wish, what am I supposed to do?'

'Well, in your case I'd simply make the wish null and void.'

'What does that mean?'

'You said you didn't want to break up with him. Emmett must have taken that into consideration when he made your wish come true. I bet if you actually do break up with him then everything will sort itself out.'

'I can't do that!' Jenny gasped.

'Why not?'

'What if he hates me? What if he shouts at me?'

'What if you go to prison for his disappearance?'

Jenny sat quietly for a moment. 'Okay, fair point. I guess I've got no choice.' Jenny exhaled sharply. 'I guess I've got to break up with him. Oh bloody hell.'

JENNY GETS SOME GUTS

Jenny was shaking as she walked with Zack to The World's End pub. She really had no clue what to expect. Would Nathan even be there? Even if he was, what would she say to him? Would he blame her for the fact that he'd vanished for three days?

She started to slow down as they approached the door, but Zack pushed her along, refusing to allow her to back out.

She stepped in to find the place fairly quiet. There were just a few customers. It was only early evening on a Tuesday though, it was unlikely to be busy.

'I don't see him,' she said to Zack.

'We're only standing in the doorway,' he replied. 'Go to the bar. Go on.'

Jenny hesitated. There was no way he was going to be there. But if that was the case then what did she have to worry about?

She stepped over to the bar, her heart still thumping hard, and she waited for service.

Suddenly Nathan appeared from a door at the side of the bar. She nearly fell over she was so shocked.

'Darling!' he said with a big smile.

'I take it that's Nathan?' Zack whispered in her ear, to which Jenny just nodded.

'Where have you been?' Nathan asked. 'I haven't heard from you since Thursday. Have you had problems with your phone? I was going to pop by after work tonight to check you were okay.'

'Long story,' Jenny replied. She didn't really know what else to say.

'Nathan!' a girl suddenly shouted. She was in the green staff T-Shirt and she ran up to him with a gasp. 'Where have you been?'

'Changing the barrel. It took me a while, you know how fiddly it is.'

'You've been changing the barrel this whole time?'

'We need to get it looked at. It really should be easier.'

'Since Saturday?'

'What are you talking about? It is Saturday.'

'Can we have a word?' Jenny said to him. She suddenly feared that Nathan hadn't just disappeared for a few days but he'd actually been blanked from existence. Why would Emmett do that?

'No it's not,' the girl replied. 'You've been gone for three days.'

'Please, Nathan, it's important,' Jenny said.

'Of course, darling,' he replied, flashing a peculiar look in the girl's direction.

Jenny gestured for Nathan to follow her and she led him to the back of the pub where they could get some peace and quiet.

'Did you want a drink, darling?' he asked.

'No, I'm fine,' Jenny said.

She felt like throwing up. Zack was right. She needed to break up with him, but she didn't even know where to start. All in all, he was a nice man. Not like her last cheating ex. But maybe if he was horrible then all of this would be a lot easier.

'It's no problem. You look thirsty. You look tired. Are

you okay?'

'I'm fine, Nathan,' she said. All his fussing was making it hard for her to concentrate. She needed to think where to start. What on earth could she say?

'You must be worried that your phone has broken,' he continued. 'I can get you a new one. I have a spare one up in my flat for now and then how about we go shopping tomorrow? We can get you a new fancy one. I'll help you pick it out.'

'That's very kind of you, but it's really not necessary.'

'It's no problem. That's what I'm here for. I tell you what, I'll drop the spare one over tonight after work and then we can make plans for where you want to go shopping. I could tuck you in too. That would be nice, wouldn't it? Your Superman could give you a kiss goodnight.'

'I've met someone else!' she blurted out, desperate to shut him up.

He didn't say a word. He was clearly shocked.

'I'm sorry. I'm really sorry,' Jenny said. 'You're lovely and I really do like you, but I'm in love with someone else.'

'Oh.' He looked very upset all of a sudden and Jenny was worried that he might cry. 'So where does that leave us?'

Jenny couldn't believe it. Was she really going to have to spell it out? This was so hard. 'I want to be with this other man. Not you.'

'What? No! Darling, we're so good together. You must know that. There must be something I can do to change your mind. What we've got is really special.'

'I know. That's why I hope we can still be friends. We do get on very well. But I have to be honest with you.'

'It's Mr Wet, isn't it. I knew it. I saw the look on your face when he left. I shouldn't have interfered.'

'Of course not. I've not spoken to him since he left here all soaked that night.'

'Another man online, then? Have you been dating

online while we've been together?'

'No! Absolutely not. I was totally true to you.' She tried not to fidget. Although, actually, she had been true to him, really. She'd hadn't slept with Adam until she'd blanked Nathan for four days and she'd wished for his disappearance. She couldn't have been much fairer than that.

'Then who is it?' he asked.

She owed him the truth. At least it might give him some closure. 'You know my friend Adam?'

'Yes.'

Jenny waited for it to click, but it clearly wasn't going to. 'Adam,' she said, emphasising her point.

'Yes, I know who he is. What, are you in love with one of his friends?'

'No.'

'Then who?'

'Adam.'

'What about him?'

'I'm in love with Adam.'

'What? No, you can't be. Are you sure?'

'Yes!'

'Really?'

'Why is that so hard to believe?'

Nathan just shrugged. This was getting more difficult by the second.

'When he broke up with his girlfriend,' Jenny explained, trying to get him to see, 'we got talking. We realised... feelings.' That was the best she could do without lying.

'Oh!' Nathan said, nodding and smiling. Jenny hadn't got a clue what that was supposed to mean.

'We both love each other,' she said. 'It's just taken us a while to figure it out.'

Nathan grabbed her hands. 'I see. It's fine.'

'What do you see?'

'I'll be here waiting for you, Jenny.'

'What?'

'Don't worry.'

'I'm not.'

'I think we both know what's going on. I get it. You go. Go and have your fun, and I'll be here for you when you're done.'

Jenny sighed. What was he wittering on about?

She knew she could just leave it there. She'd broken up with him - it was all finished - but suddenly he was annoying her. He just wasn't listening.

'Nathan, it's over between us.'

'For now.'

'Forever!'

'I don't think you really mean that. You've been friends with Adam for a long time and nothing's happened before. I think this is just something you've got to get out of your system.'

'No. No, it's not.'

'Can't you see you're the rebound girl?'

Jenny suddenly felt spikes of rage stab at her. He'd just touched on her biggest fear and now she was ready to explode.

'Even if I am, I still wouldn't want to be with you,' she shouted. 'You're a bloody nightmare!'

'What?' Nathan asked in utter shock.

'You've been suffocating me! I've been desperate to get away from you since the first time you turned up at my office, unannounced. That's why I stopped replying to your messages. There's nothing wrong with my phone, I was just hoping you'd get the hint. Why can't you get the bloody hint like any other man?'

'I...' Nathan seemed lost for words.

'So because you're such a emoron, my friend over there convinced me to be honest with you. Now do you see? Even if Adam wasn't in my life, there would still be no us. No you and me. No darling and Superman. It's over. Permanently. Go and find someone who wants to be showered with attention every fucking moment of the day, because I'm not that girl. We are not meant to be together. Do you finally understand?'

Nathan leaned back, his face pale. 'Bloody hell, Jenny, that was a bit mean.'

'It needed to be said.'

Nathan took a deep breath and he tried to compose himself. 'I have to say, I don't think Adam is good for you. He's making you really angry.'

Jenny stood up, fighting the urge to scream. 'Goodbye Nathan,' she said. 'And also, can you phone your mother, she's worried about you. It *is* actually Tuesday. You somehow got trapped in the cellar, or wherever it is that you change the barrel, and you've bizarrely lost three days of your life. Oh well, shit happens. Just be sure to tell all your friends and family that you're back so I can finally move on.'

Jenny stepped away from the table, not glancing back once. 'Zack!' she called. He was propped up against the bar sipping at a coke. 'We're leaving. Now!'

'Coming.'

Jenny wasn't in the mood for waiting. She marched on, right to the exit. The minute she hit fresh air, she stood back against the brick wall of the building and gasped for breath.

She was still shaking, but she knew it was now the adrenaline racing through her body at how good that had felt. She'd certainly told him! Why had she never realised that conflict could be so releasing? She felt fantastic. She suddenly felt ready for anything.

She had to see Adam. She wanted to tell him the good news. And she also wanted to know what had been so important that he couldn't make it out to see her. Maybe she'd give him a piece of her mind as well!

Zack finally appeared through the doors. 'Did it go all right?' he asked.

'Yes! I did it. I broke up with him. It was difficult at first, but then I found my flow. I'm so glad he's out of my life. Thank you, Zack!'

Jenny threw her arms around him. He really had come to her rescue and she knew she'd be eternally grateful.

She hugged him tightly and then tried to pull away, but he didn't let go. Instead he held her closely to him. Then, without any warning at all, he kissed her right on the lips.

Jenny instantly backed away with shock. That was the last thing she'd expected him to do.

'Sorry, too soon?' he said.

'What?' Jenny was utterly baffled.

'I suppose you have just officially broken up with Nathan. We can take it slow. It's fine.'

'Take it slow?'

'I know we haven't talked about it yet. I have to admit, you caught me by surprise in Hamburg. I didn't know you had feelings for me. But the more I think about, the more we make sense. You're right, we'd be great together.'

'Hamburg?' In the very same second that reality came hurtling towards Jenny, all of her new-found empowerment flushed out of her like water escaping from a smashed aquarium.

'The flirting?' she asked as a small part of her clung on to the hope that he'd deny all knowledge of it. Maybe she'd completely misunderstood the kiss, and actually it was nothing more than some new German friendship thing he'd picked up.

'I was looking forward to us joining the mile high club,' he grinned, shattering that remaining hope. 'Maybe next time,' he winked.

Jenny froze. What was she going to do? It was one thing being honest with a silly man who dressed up as Superman without any prior warning, but telling one of your closest friends that you don't actually like them in "that way" after you've been blatantly flirting with them is a whole different kettle of fish.

Even if she could find the confidence to tell Zack that he'd got it all wrong, how could she explain the truth? She couldn't very well say that she'd been using him to make Adam jealous. That was awful.

It was awful. What had Jenny been thinking? How could she have been so stupid; so cruel? She was certainly paying the price for her insensitivity, that was for sure.

Minutes had gone by and Jenny had said nothing. She was just standing agape, unable to conjure up any words at all that might get her out of the sticky mess that she'd well and truly got herself into.

'It's okay. I understand,' Zack said, breaking the silence. 'You want to be fair. Just minutes after you break up with Nathan, you can't be seen flaunting your new boyfriend in his face. That's not right. I get it.'

'Boyfriend?' It was the only word that Jenny could manage. It was mind-boggling. Putting aside the fact that she in no way viewed Zack as boyfriend material, she'd somehow managed to go from years of singledom to having three men calling her their boyfriend in the space of a week. This was all terribly overwhelming and an absolute nightmare for someone like Jenny. Her immediate urge was always to please people, but pleasing Zack in this instance was going to be very difficult.

'Besides, we haven't even told Adam yet,' Zack added. 'I think he should be the first to know, don't you?'

'Adam?' This was getting worse by the minute. If Zack was to tell Adam that he's dating Jenny then that would surely mess up the only relationship that she actually did want.

Adam! Jenny knew that Adam was the one person that she now needed to speak to. Not only did she need to be honest with him – and she really hoped that he would understand – but she needed some good advice, and fast.

Adam always knew what to do. He was great with people. In fact, he'd probably volunteer to set Zack straight. Have a man to man talk and all that. Yes, Adam would definitely make this horrid nightmare all go away.

'You know, it's been a long day, Zack,' Jenny said,

pulling her best weary face. 'I think I'd better go home. Go and have a lie down.'

'You know, I totally forgot,' Zack said, appearing not to have heard Jenny's declaration of tiredness. 'I bet Adam's still stuck at work.'

'He's still working?' Jenny didn't know whether to feel relieved or angry. She had no idea that Adam was such a workaholic. Was he really going to always put his work before her?

'Yes, he's...' Zack quickly cut himself off.

'What is it?' Jenny nudged.

'You know what, don't worry about it. You've had a massive day and you look like you haven't slept in a week. Adam can wait.'

'Why is he still at work, Zack?'

'As I said, he's just stuck at work. Some big contract has got in the way. It's definitely nothing for you to worry about. Let's get you home.'

Zack grabbed Jenny's hand and they started to walk back in the direction of her flat, but she wasn't concentrating. Suddenly all sorts of worst case scenarios were flicking through her mind.

What if Adam was having to talk himself out of going back to Hamburg? Or worse, talk himself into it after realising what a mistake he'd made with Jenny?

Then the worst thought of all cemented itself in her head. What if Cadence was with him? She could have shown up at his work to talk him into rekindling their relationship. He could be there with her now, having hot, steamy sex on his desk. Repeating their mile high club antics.

'Have you got your key?' Zack asked. Jenny couldn't believe it, they were back at her flat. She couldn't even remember the journey, she'd been so consumed with worry.

'Yeah, I'll let myself in. Don't worry about me, Zack.'

'Nonsense. Come on.'

Zack insisted on not only making sure that she got into her flat okay, but also into her pyjamas and finally under her duvet, where he tucked her in ready for a good night's sleep. She was twitchy with agitation by the time he kissed her on the lips and said goodbye. She had to pretend to be overwhelmed with tiredness just to get rid of him.

The second she heard her front door shut, she leapt out of bed. She knew she had to give it a few minutes to make sure that Zack had properly driven away, and then she was heading straight over to Adam's office.

Wherever that was.

Right, she needed Google first.

ALL BY ADAM'S SELF

Adam didn't even know that he was drumming his fingers on his desk. It had been hours since Zack had last texted him to say that he was still waiting at the police station for Jenny. What could be taking so long? Surely Adam should have heard something by now?

Being trapped in this prison of his own was deeply tormenting. It was bad enough being stuck, but the fact that he'd made a promise to Jenny that he'd be there for her just made the whole situation ten times more horrible. Would she ever be able to forgive him?

He'd wished to be freed so many times that day, but nothing had worked. He'd remembered what Zack had said about not being able to unwish your wishes, and so he'd tried to think differently too.

He'd wished for freedom to get some lunch, he'd wished for freedom to see Jenny, he'd wished that he could go and see his clients, he'd even wished that he could go and see his mother. He'd exhausted every tactic he could think of, but still that invisible force field prevented him from leaving the building. Irrelevant of which exit he tried, he was completely trapped.

In the end, he'd had to get one of his team to get him

some lunch. They were going out anyway, so it wasn't that big a deal, but he hated being reliant on other people.

Overall, his whole day had been quite unproductive. Since his meeting that morning, all he'd done was worry about what he was going to do, wish for freedom, and then faff about at the door looking like a prat. In between all that he'd managed to fit in about half an hour's work, and that was it.

Even though it was now six thirty, he was the only person left in the building, and he had absolutely nothing else to do, he still couldn't find the will power to do any work. All he could think about was Jenny, getting away from this building and how he was going to avoid wishing for anything at all again in the future.

It wasn't unusual for him to be the last one in the office, but he'd never been left there before when it wasn't his own choice. It was wildly frustrating.

He leaned back and sighed. Where was Jenny? He couldn't wait to see her.

His phone rang and he picked it up instantly.

'What's the news?' he asked, seeing that it was Zack calling him.

'She's out. I've got her sorted, don't worry. And we've well and truly taken care of the situation with Nathan, so that should be the end of it.'

'What do you mean you've taken care of it?'

'It's a long story. Don't worry about that for now. What we need to do now is focus on getting you free. I'm on my way over. I'll be with you in a few minutes and I think I might have a way of resolving your problem.'

'Seriously? I hope so, mate. This is torture.'

'Just hang on in there.'

'I'll head down to reception. I'll see you there in a few.'

'Okay.'

Adam stood up and made a beeline for the stairs. He was almost jogging knowing that the chance of freedom could potentially be imminent.

He reached the main entrance and tried to look out. Although the doors were all glass, Adam didn't have a full view of the car park. Outside the immediate entrance there was a small lobby area with plants and benches that had been designed to bring a harmonious feel to the place – apparently. The car park was across to the left.

He stood, willing the agonising wait to end. It felt like forever had passed when he finally saw Zack walking down towards the entrance.

Adam waved his pass at the reader next to the door and it unlocked. He swung it open just as Zack was approaching.

'How are you, mate?' Zack asked as he hopped into the reception. He seemed full of life, bouncing around.

'I've been better. What's the matter with you?'

'I couldn't pop to the loo, could I?'

'Yeah, there are some at the back of reception.' Adam pointed to a door towards the end of the large open space that had "Toilets" emblazoned in gold letters on it.

'Cheers, mate. Look, I know I'm here to help you, but I've got to tell you my good news. I know Jenny would probably want to tell you herself, but I never get to tell you news before she does.'

'What is it?'

'Jenny and I are dating. We've just had our first kiss!'

Adam froze on the spot. Did he just hear that right?

'Back in a sec.'

Adam still couldn't move as he watched Zack virtually skip along to the toilets. Were Jenny and Zack really dating?

Did Emmett have something to do with it? Or was Zack determined to sleep with all of Adam's girlfriends?

Adam was already suffering from tiredness and irritation, and now anger and jealousy had been thrown into the mix. He found himself breathing sharply as he ran his hands through his hair with frustration.

Suddenly he heard a tap behind him. He turned around

to find Jenny standing at the door, knocking on the glass for his attention.

He didn't know whether to invite her in or tell her to sod off.

He decided on the former. He was very curious to hear what she had to say.

He waved his pass at the reader and the door unlocked. Jenny grabbed the handle and pushed it wide open until it held itself in place.

'What are you doing here?' she demanded to know, standing on the threshold with anger in her eyes.

Before he even had a chance to reply though, she followed with, 'Is Cadence here?'

'Cadence?' Adam asked, shaking his head. Was he dreaming? He'd expected her to be annoyed that he hadn't been there to collect her. What did Cadence have to do with it? This was getting more bizarre by the second. 'Why would Cadence be here? I'm completely alone. Well, except...'

But Adam didn't get a chance to finish his sentence, because Jenny strode right up to him and threw her arms around him. She kissed him square on the lips.

'I'm sorry,' she said, still with her arms wrapped around his body. 'It's been a very long day. I'm just being ridiculous. I couldn't work out why you hadn't come to rescue me and I guess my mind started going crazy.'

'Believe me, I'm regretting not being there more by the second.'

'Oh, Adam,' she kissed him again.

'What are you doing?' Zack suddenly yelled from behind Adam. 'You're kissing my girlfriend?'

Adam took a step back. He didn't know what to say.

'I only told you about it two minutes ago,' Zack continued, looking quite upset. 'Is this meant to be some sort of sick revenge for Cadence or something?'

'No Zack, it's not what it seems,' Jenny pleaded.

'You're his girlfriend?' Adam asked Jenny, desperate for

clarification. Surely there had to be a logical explanation. He'd never viewed Jenny as a player.

'I'm not his girlfriend,' Jenny replied to Adam.

'Are you denying what's been going on between us?' Zack asked Jenny.

Jenny just looked to the floor. There was a moment of excruciating tension before Zack pushed past them and stormed off into the car park. Adam was totally lost for words.

'I can explain,' Jenny said, finally looking up at Adam. 'I'm not his girlfriend. I've just cocked up really badly. We need to talk to him.'

Jenny raced out of the building, following Zack, but Adam was still stuck. He exhaled sharply. This was unbearable.

Within a few seconds, Jenny raced back. 'What are you doing? Come on. Please don't be mad with me.'

She darted off again.

Adam placed his cheek on the glass to give himself the best view of the car park. He could just about see Jenny talking to Zack who was sitting in his car, but he had no hope of hearing them.

Then he saw Jenny jogging back towards him. She now had tears in her eyes.

'Please understand,' she said, standing just outside the doorway. 'You're the one I love. Please don't hate me.'

'I don't hate you,' he said, getting as close to the outside world as he was allowed.

'I didn't think Zack would notice,' she pleaded. 'It never occurred to me.'

'Notice what?' Adam asked, still trying to make sense of everything.

'Me flirting with him.'

'You were flirting with him?' Adam felt the rage of jealousy burn in him again. 'Why were you flirting with him? Did you tell him that you'd go out with him?'

'No, of course not. I was trying to make you jealous. It

was some misguided, ridiculous plan. I mean why did you think I was talking about the mile high club?'

'When were you talking about the mile high club?'

Jenny threw her hands in the air. She looked all over the place. 'Oh, you're so frustrating! Look, Zack's going to drive off. Please help me talk to him. Please.'

'I can't...' But Adam's words were lost as Jenny was already racing back over to Zack.

Adam needed her to know what was going on and it was clear that Zack was in no mood for explanations. Maybe he could phone her.

He grabbed his phone from his pocket, but the very second he pressed to call, his phone cut out. His battery had died. This was all becoming some cruel joke.

He pushed his face to the window again to see Zack driving off. Where was he going? Adam needed his freedom. It was getting urgent.

Jenny came jogging back towards to the door.

'I know you're mad with me, but you could have at least talked to Zack,' Jenny said. 'He's really upset.'

'Look Jen, I have no clue what's going on but you need to understand my situation.'

'He told me to tell you to bugger off and sort your own problems out. I tried to tell him it was all a mix up. If you could have just come out and talked to him.'

'I'm trapped!'

'I'm not trying to start some sick love triangle or something. Please believe me, Adam. This is nothing but a mix up. I love you.'

'Right, I get it. I'm just literally trapped.'

'Don't say that. I don't want to lose you. We'll find a way out of this mess.'

Adam could feel his patience wearing so thin now, it was almost non-existent. 'You're not listening, Jen!' he shouted. All that did though was bring on even more tears. 'Please come in and we can talk about it,' he said as gently as he could.

'I don't want to talk in your office,' she snivelled. 'Please, let's go home.'

'It's Emmett! My wish.' Adam was struggling for words, he was getting so irate with the situation.

'You regret wishing that we'd got together?'

'No! I said about leaving the office. I can't leave the office. You've got to understand.'

'You won't even put work aside at a time like this? Oh my God, are you breaking up with me?'

'Of course not.'

'Oh my God!'

Jenny raced off, sobbing. Adam once again forced his face against the window to get a good view and he could just about see her getting into her car. She didn't pull off, though. She just sat there.

She was clearly waiting for him to follow her. He needed to follow her.

Right, it was time for action. This was getting out of control.

He turned on his heels and raced back to his desk. If he could just get his battery charging then he could call her and explain the whole thing.

He darted up the staircase, taking two steps at a time, and then he ran across the floor to his office.

He grabbed his charger from his drawer and plugged it straight in.

He waited patiently for it to spring into life. It seemed to be taking forever.

He looked out the window. He could only see the main car park entrance from his office. Either Jenny was still downstairs or she'd left pretty quickly. How he hoped it would be the former.

His phone finally chimed its hello and he clenched his fist as he waited for it to have a long think.

At last, he was all up and running. He dialled Jenny's number and held his breath.

'Hi, this is Jenny. Please-' He cut it off. It was her

voicemail. He tried again, but he quickly ended the call when he saw her little red Aygo driving away.

He'd missed out. She must have turned her phone off. It was rare that Jenny got upset. This was clearly an overwhelming situation. Whatever was going on.

Adam slumped down in his chair. All he could do was leave her a message and hope she'd pick it up soon.

He dialled again and waited for the beep.

'Hi Jen, it's Adam. You've got it all totally wrong. When I said I was trapped I meant literally. I made a wish not to leave the UK again and it somehow got interpreted that I couldn't leave the office. Emmett's left me stuck in this building. I've been trapped all day. I don't know what's going on with you and Zack, but I believe you when you say it's all a mix up. Please give me a call when you get this so we can sort it all out. It's been an awful day. I need you right now. I love you.'

Adam hung up. He sat for a moment in silence and contemplated his next move.

Should he call Zack?

Maybe he should leave it for a bit. Maybe he should just see if Jenny calls back first. She might call back soon.

This might all be over with really soon.

ZACK'S NEW FRIENDS

Zack was seething. All the way back to Miloworth he hadn't known what to do with himself. He felt utterly humiliated.

Jenny had tried to explain that she'd just mis-aimed her flirting. Apparently she'd actually been trying to flirt with Adam, as implausible as that sounded. Zack had been so sure that he and Jenny were on the verge of a wonderful new relationship. It was mortifying to find out that not only was that not true, but she was actually dating his best mate instead.

In fact both of his best mates were dating.

After driving around aimlessly for about an hour, he eventually pulled into the car park of The World's End pub. He couldn't face going home. He knew he'd just wallow in his own self-pity. Instead he decided that drowning the embarrassment was the best idea. He was determined to make the night before seem like a taster session.

He stepped out of his car, where he'd decided he was leaving it for the night, and he made a beeline straight to the bar to get started.

'You're Jenny's friend, aren't you?' Nathan asked as

Zack waited to be served.

Zack enjoyed a fleeting moment of satisfaction as he saw that his idea had worked. Nathan was still very much present. Emmett must have allowed for the wish to be voided based on Jenny's actions, just like Zack had predicted. At least Zack knew he was good for something.

'Yeah. I'm Zack,' he replied.

'Do you know Adam too?'

Zack felt a small burst of irritation. 'Yes,' he said quite to the point. His plan had been to forget about his so-called mates, but suddenly he could see that Nathan's presence wasn't going to make that easy.

'What can I get for you, mate? Anything you want. On the house,' Nathan said.

'That's very good of you.'

'Well, we're Jenny's friends. We need to stick together. I'm worried about her with Adam. She's been acting very strangely ever since she started seeing him.'

'Tell me about it,' Zack scoffed.

'I don't think he's good for her,' Nathan stated.

Zack took a deep breath. He really wanted to agree with Nathan. It was there on the tip of his tongue to agree with him. But he couldn't. He couldn't deny the truth.

If Zack put his pride aside then he had to admit that he'd never actually viewed Jenny as girlfriend material. They weren't a good match. But she and Adam together made perfect sense. They were made for one another.

In fact, if he was totally honest with himself, Zack had always wondered, deep down inside, if Jenny and Adam would ever get together. They'd always seemed like more than friends. The thought had never bothered him before.

It was only when she'd shown him a speck of interest that his head had turned. He'd needed that interest. It had been a long time since any girl had shown him that sort of interest. Well, except for Cadence, but she didn't really count.

Did he ever really see himself with Jenny? No. That

was Zack's honest answer. Did he have feelings for her? Well yeah, he cared. But, if Zack really thought about it, he'd always seen her more like a sister.

It still didn't make seeing her and Adam together any easier, though. And it still didn't quash his deep embarrassment.

'I'll have a pint of Peroni, if one's going,' Zack said. He might not agree with Nathan, but he'd never turn down a free pint.

'No problem.'

He watched Nathan carefully pour the pint. 'How long have you known Jenny for?' Nathan asked him.

'Years,' Zack replied. He didn't really want to discuss Jenny but now he felt beholden to Nathan.

'You'll look out for her won't you, when I'm not around?'

Zack sighed. 'I always have.'

'I don't know if we can trust this Adam. I'd hate to see Jenny get hurt.'

'Yep,' Zack replied, willing the pint to pour quicker.

The liquid finally filled up the glass and Zack eagerly held out his hand for it.

'There you go, mate,' Nathan said. 'Enjoy.'

'Cheers,' Zack said, grabbing the pint and then moving away from the bar as fast as humanly possible.

To his relief, Zack spotted the group of students that he'd been chatting to the night before.

'Zack!' a few of the group said, inviting him to sit down. 'You're back!'

'Hi everyone.'

Zack took a seat at the end of the table. He'd learnt the previous night that many of the students were studying far away and were only back for the summer. They were mostly school friends, some who were just lazing around and others who had got summer jobs in the local area. They met up in the evening to avoid spending too much time with their parents.

The fun of the previous night seemed long gone, though. They appeared to be having a deep and meaningful conversation about the threat of nuclear technology and Zack's heart sank. He wanted mindless entertainment, not putting the world to rights.

'I've got a question,' Zack announced, determined to bring the heavy debate to a close. He stared at the six faces around him. 'If you could have any super power, what would it be?'

'Why would we have a super power?' one of the lads asked.

'Why not?' Zack asked. 'Let's say we all get one wish but we have to ask for a super power.'

'Who's giving us these wishes?' the same lad asked.

'I don't know. Me. I can grant you any super power. You just need to let me know what it's going to be.'

'You're like some sort of genie now?'

'I get it,' one of the girls said, coming to Zack's rescue. 'It's just for fun. Like, I think it would be great to fly.'

'That's right!' Zack nodded.

'Yeah, flying would be cool,' another lad said, casually shrugging.

'I'd like to fly,' a girl said.

'Yeah, it would be a laugh to fly. I'd say flying too.'

'So we're all going to fly,' the difficult lad said. 'You're right, that was a fun conversation.'

'Would you want to fly too?' one of the girls asked Zack.

'No, I've actually got a really good idea,' Zack smiled. 'You know Doctor Who's sonic screwdriver?'

One lad said, 'Yeah.'

'I was thinking it would be great to have that power, but in my fingers.'

'You want to use your fingers as a screwdriver?' the highly critical lad snorted.

'No, a sonic screwdriver.'

'I don't watch Doctor Who,' a girl said. 'What's sonic

about it? Isn't sonic like sound?'

'Yeah, like when planes break the sound barrier, don't they make a sonic boom?' her friend added.

'So you want a screwdriver that makes a noise?' the awkward lad asked. 'But in your fingers?'

'No,' Zack said. Why didn't they get it?

'Oh my God, talking about fingers, did you hear what happened to Mrs Chuckleberry?' one of the girls asked, and Zack knew that was that.

He sat back in his seat, ready to ignore what was no doubt another conversation about their school. They'd had a few of them the night before. In fact, thinking about it, Zack was starting to remember the antics of his big celebratory night far less fondly.

Why had the super power conversation not excited them? When Adam had brought it up in Hamburg, they'd all had such a laugh. This crowd had no imagination. They were really boring.

Zack gazed across the pub. It wasn't very busy. There were just a few people scattered about and then the group that Zack was with.

Suddenly the television in the corner caught his attention. He could see Cadence on it. She was talking directly to the camera but it was on mute so he couldn't hear what she was saying. It looked like she was presenting something.

'She lives around here, you know,' the lad next to him said. 'If I ever see her... let's just say, I could show her a good time.'

For a moment Zack considered telling all. That would certainly stop the school talk. But he quickly decided against it. Even if they believed him, it was too complicated a story.

'Is she presenting something?' Zack asked.

'Yes, she's doing Snap and Bite,' one of the girls said.

'What's Snap and Bite?' Zack asked.

'That new quiz show,' the lad answered, clearly

bewildered that Zack hadn't heard of it. 'Where people have to put their heads in crocodiles and stuff to win loads of money. Where have you been? Everyone's talking about it.'

'Right,' Zack said, not really feeling overly bothered that he'd missed out.

'Cadence stepped in at the last minute after the original presenter got bitten by that snake. You must have heard about it.'

Zack shook his head. There had been a lot going on for him recently, he'd not had a chance to catch up on the news.

'Have you heard she's a lesbian now?' one of the girls said.

'Cadence?' Zack asked in disbelief.

'Yeah. I saw an interview with her last night.'

'Wasn't she dating some bloke from around here?' the difficult lad queried.

'No, she dumped him.'

'Actually,' Zack started, but he quickly thought the better of it. As much as he wanted to put the group right, it would open a can of worms that he really didn't want to set free. He paused for a second, thinking of what he could say. 'I've not heard about this. Do go on.'

The girl looked at him weirdly before continuing. 'Apparently she's never been happier. She said she just woke up on Sunday morning and decided that it might be best to take a break from men for a while and it's really paying off. You can't blame her. Women are so much easier.'

'I don't think so!' the lad argued, but Zack wasn't listening anymore. He suddenly had a creepy sense of déjà vu. He knew that sentence. He knew it very well. That was what he'd written in his wish. He'd wished for Cadence to take a break from men. But he hadn't meant for her to start dating women!

'Do you really think she's happy?' Zack asked the girl.

'Who?' she replied.

'Cadence. Do you think she's happy as a lesbian?'

The girl shrugged. 'I don't know. But if you see those photos of her kissing her new girlfriend, she looks happy.'

Zack couldn't believe it. A little smirk popped up on his lips. What was going on? What was Emmett doing to them?

He'd definitely need to get his hands on those pictures.

Oh well, at least Emmett was making someone happy. Actually, Emmett seemed to be making everyone happy but Zack. What had Zack done wrong?

'You know who else has come out, don't you?' one of the girls said and Zack knew it was time to tune out again.

He sat back in his seat. He'd not even touched his pint. So much for his crazy night out. All he could think about was his bed.

His phone beeped and he saw he had a text from Jenny.

I'm so sorry, Zack. We never meant to hurt you. I've been a horrible friend. Please can you ever forgive me? It was never my intention to mislead you. I'm in love with Adam, but I love you dearly as a friend and I can't stand the thought of you not being in my life. Please let us know you're OK.

Zack sighed. He knew he couldn't really hate Jenny. She might have made a mistake but she was still one of the best friends he'd ever had. As was Adam. And sitting with those students was making him see what good mates they really were.

I'm OK. I get that it was just a mix up. Shall we just forget about it?

He pressed send and then took a sip of his pint, but it didn't go down very well. Even with free lager, he realised that he wasn't in the mood for socialising after all.

Thank you Zack. I know we have loads to talk about, and we don't want to force you, but if you can find it in yourself to visit us, we need your help. Adam is completely stuck and you're our magician. I hate to ask after we've treated you so badly.

Zack shook his head. He'd totally forgotten about Adam. He really should go and help. As much as he didn't relish the idea of seeing Jenny and Adam, he couldn't leave a mate trapped in a building indefinitely. He had an idea that might help and he knew he had to give it a go.

Of course I'll help. I'm on my way over.

He looked at his pint. It was a waste but at least he hadn't paid for it.

'I'm off now,' he said to the group around him.

'Right, see you.'

'Bye.'

They didn't even seem bothered. They weren't his friends. He'd had one night of enjoyment with them when he'd bought a few rounds in. Now he was just the boring older man.

He knew full well who his real friends were and despite the slight humiliation he felt at having kissed one of them, he could think of nowhere else he'd rather be than in their company.

ADAM'S OFFICE

About half an hour after Adam had left Jenny that voicemail, she finally returned his call. He couldn't have answered his phone quicker if he'd tried.

'Jenny! I'm so sorry.'

'I'm the one that should be apologising. I just got your message. I didn't know you meant literally trapped. I was just so shook up about Zack. What a mess I've made.'

'I didn't think you were going to speak to me again.'

'I wasn't ignoring you. My phone was still switched off from the police station.'

'Oh God, of course. I never even got to ask. Are you okay?'

'It's been a really shitty day, that's for sure. Can I come back and see you?'

'I'd love nothing more.'

That was now half an hour ago and Adam was eagerly waiting in reception for Jenny to arrive. He was flipping between pacing the floor and pressing his cheek up to the window to get a better view, whilst all the time running his hands through his hair with anxiety.

Finally he saw her walking down towards the entrance. He quickly waved his pass against the reader and then swung the door open.

'Hi!' Jenny said, running in and hugging Adam immediately. He wrapped his arms around her. He needed that hug.

After a few moments, Jenny looked up at him. 'Are you okay? You must be going out of your mind.'

'You could say that. What's been going on? Why did Zack think you were dating? He said you'd kissed him. Did you kiss him?'

Jenny sighed. 'It's a long story.'

'I'm not going anywhere. Literally.'

Jenny sighed again and then she looked to the floor. 'I got some advice. I see now that it was really bad advice. I've liked you for a long time, but I never thought you saw me as anything more than a friend, so someone suggested that I flirt with someone else to try and make you jealous.'

'Who gave you that crap advice?' Adam asked, shaking his head.

Jenny hesitated. 'No one you know. Someone at work. Anyway, I just thought the obvious person to flirt with was Zack, so when we went to Hamburg I played up to it a bit. It never occurred to me at all that Zack might think I fancy him. Which I see is ridiculous now, as that was obviously the point.'

'You kissed in Hamburg? Was I supposed to see?'

'No! He kissed me tonight. After he helped me break up with Nathan, he kissed me totally out of the blue and then starting talking about us being in a relationship. I didn't know what to do. I mean, it was awful. So I didn't really say anything and then I came over here to get your advice. I thought we could let him down gently, together.'

'You mean you wanted me to tell him the truth.'

'Yeah,' Jenny nodded, as if it was a good idea. 'I tell you in my awkward "I want the world to swallow me up" kind of way, and then you tell Zack in your cool "I deal with people really well" kind of way. See, we make an excellent team.'

Adam couldn't help but smirk, before he suddenly recalled something that Jenny had just said. 'You've broken up with Nathan? Officially? What happened? Where did he turn up? And what happened with the police? I can't believe I still don't know. I'm really sorry. Your day's been far worse than mine.'

'You can say that again. You might be trapped here, but I've been arrested, I've had to face terrifying conflict, and then I had to tell one of my closest friends that I don't fancy him even though I totally led him on. You realise he'll probably never speak to us again.'

'What terrifying conflict?' Adam asked with concern. 'What did the police do to you?'

'It was horrible at the station. They kept me there for hours and made me feel really guilty. I hadn't done anything. Well, except for wishing that Nathan would disappear. But is that really a crime?'

Adam wasn't sure if he was supposed to answer that or not. Instead he just waited for her to continue.

'But the terrifying conflict came when I had to break up with Nathan.'

'What happened with him? Did he kick off? What did he say?'

'No, it's just not pleasant having to break up with someone. But I had no choice.'

'It was the right thing to do. He needed to know that you'd moved on.'

'No he didn't! I had to tell him because of my wish. I totally screwed things up for myself. Zack said we had to analyse my wish and find a way to break it. You know, to get the police to back off and clear my name.'

'Break it?' Adam asked.

'Yes. We went back to my flat and reviewed the wish step by step. Zack said if I actually broke up with Nathan rather than just blanking him until he got the hint, then it would null and void it all and make everything go back to normal. So we went to The World's End and then, just like that, Nathan reappeared. He didn't even know he'd been gone. And then I broke up with him. Like, properly. It was horrible. Then and there I had to tell him the truth. I mean who has to do that?'

'A lot of people, Jen,' Adam said. 'That's normally how relationships end. Would you seriously have just not told him?'

'It's the twenty-first century. It's widely known that if someone you're dating doesn't speak to you for a week, then it's over. Anyone else would understand that.'

Adam shook his head. 'I'll remember that.'

'Well, it would be different with us.'

'I'd need to give it two weeks of blanking?'

Jenny just looked at him coyly.

'Anyway, how did Nathan take it?' Adam asked. As much as he wanted to be annoyed with her, he actually found it all very amusing. She really was irresistible.

Jenny sighed and shrugged. 'We had a good chat. It took a while for him to absorb the news, but in the end it was... amicable.'

'Good,' Adam said, although he suspected that she wasn't being totally truthful. 'I suppose he couldn't have been surprised. We do spend a lot of time together.'

Jenny didn't say anything for a few moments. Then all she said, straight to the point, was, 'Yes.'

'And that was all it took to break the wish?' Adam asked.

'I hope so. Zack reasoned that because I'd said I didn't want to break up with him-'

'You said what?' Adam asked her.

'I just wanted him to disappear!' Jenny groaned. 'Why has it got to be so difficult?' She folded her arms in a huff. 'I hate all this honesty crap.'

Adam could barely stifle his laugh.

'You're no better!' Jenny snapped, pointing at him for added emphasis.

'How do you figure that?'

'How long did you want to break up with Cadence for?'

Adam went to reply, but he knew Jenny was right. They really were more alike than he cared to say.

Then Adam recalled something else that Jenny had said. 'That reminds me. Why did you think I was here with Cadence earlier?'

Jenny opened her mouth but nothing came out. She stared thoughtfully at him for a few moments. Then she said, 'I think getting you out of here is our first priority. We can talk more about that later.'

Adam nodded. She was right. 'I've tried everything,' he said. 'This is a persistent wish.'

'I think we're going to need Zack's help.'

'He told me to bugger off.'

'But it's not your fault. Let me text him. See if I can get him to come around.'

Adam waited patiently as Jenny exchanged a few messages with Zack, before she eventually turned to him with a smile. He couldn't have been more relieved that Zack was on his way.

Adam made them a cup of coffee to pass the time until about another half an hour later when Zack finally tapped on the window of the reception.

Adam swiftly opened the door and Zack stepped in.

It was immediately tense. No one knew what to say. All three of them just glanced at each other awkwardly.

'Shall we go to my office?' Adam finally said. 'It's more comfortable up there.'

'I get that it was just a mix up,' Zack said.

'I think we owe you an explanation,' Jenny replied.

'You gave me one earlier. I just mis-read the situation. You were actually trying to flirt with Adam. I get it.'

Adam looked over at Jenny. She clearly hadn't told Zack the truth. But did he really blame her? Zack misunderstanding things was probably much easier for him to swallow than being used as a tool in Jenny's game to get noticed.

Adam actually felt quite flattered that she'd gone to so much effort. It was just a shame that it would never have worked. Adam had never seen himself as a man who gets easily jealous.

'Come on, follow me,' he said.

Adam checked that the front door was properly shut and then he led them to the lift. They headed up to the fourth floor to where the sales team sat. He led them past dozens of empty desks, the business of the day still apparent on some of them, and he invited them into his office.

'This is your office?' Jenny exclaimed with wide eyes.

'Yes.'

'I take it you used to sit out there?' Zack said, pointing to the array of desks on the other side of the glass.

'Yeah, I've sat on a few different desks in my time. But I moved in here when they made me Head of Sales a couple of years ago.'

'It's enormous!' Jenny said.

Adam looked around. He'd not seen it as anything other than his office in quite a while, but it was big.

'And incredibly neat and tidy,' Zack added.

Adam shrugged. He'd never understood how anyone could work in a mess. 'Take a seat,' he offered.

There was a table with four chairs around it in the centre of the room and then two further chairs on the other side of his desk towards the back. However, Jenny ignored all other options and raced straight for his massive leather chair.

'This is so comfortable,' she said, rocking back and forth it in, trying it out.

'Don't mess with the settings,' Adam warned. 'It took me ages to get it right.'

'It has settings?' Zack asked.

'It's ergonomic. Top of the range.'

Zack took one of the smaller seats near Adam's desk. 'Of course. Only the best for the Head of Sales.'

'I have back troubles,' Adam justified.

'You do not!' Jenny argued. 'And I don't think you ever will. This is the best chair I've ever sat in. I'm going to get one for home.'

'I bet they're not cheap,' Zack said.

'What would you do with it?' Adam asked Jenny. 'It's not exactly a kick-back-with-a-comic sort of chair.'

'I beg to differ,' Jenny said, looking utterly relaxed. Then she pointed to the chair opposite, next to Zack. 'You can sit there. You're not having this back now.'

Adam smiled. He knew there would be no arguing with her. She'd clearly made herself at home. Besides, her playfulness was softening the tension and so it was very welcome. He took the seat next to Zack, not willing to admit that it was nowhere near as comfortable as the one Jenny had hijacked.

Jenny rolled the chair forward so that she was properly sitting at the desk. Then she addressed Zack very directly.

'I'm sorry if we hurt you, Zack.'

Adam bit his lip. He'd noticed earlier that she was using the word "we" to describe what she had done. Adam could tell that he was going to get pulled into a lot of awkward situations that Jenny was too nervous to get herself out of. Not that he minded really. He wouldn't have her any other way.

'It's fine,' Zack said, putting his hands up. 'I guess I was just flattered when I thought you were flirting with me. You're more like a sister though, if I'm honest. You two are far better matched. I suppose you getting together was only a matter of time.'

'How do you mean?' Adam asked.

'You two have always had a special bond. I've never been as close.'

'What does that mean?' Adam asked. He didn't like the implication that they'd somehow cast Zack aside.

'Well, we say goodbye on a Sunday, and pretty much except for the odd text to talk about a new movie coming out or plans for Comic-Con, I don't hear from either of you until the following Sunday. But when we meet again, you two are completely up to speed with one another. It's obvious that you've been texting all week, or you've spoken on the phone. You've always been really close.'

Adam and Jenny remained silent. He looked over at her, but she was staring at her fingers. What could either of them say?

Adam definitely classed Zack as one of his best friends, but he was starting to realise that Jenny had always been far more. She really was the love of his life. Why had it taken him so long to see it?

'We didn't mean to exclude you in any way,' Jenny said, softly.

'I know,' Zack said. 'Of course I know that. You two have known each other a lot longer and it's never been any different. You're the best friends I've ever had. I'm really happy for you. I mean it. I'm a little embarrassed about what happened, but all in all I'm really pleased. You make a great couple.'

'Thanks, Zack,' Jenny smiled. She reached out to grab his hand and she squeezed it. 'And I should be the one who's embarrassed. It's all my fault.'

'Let's just forget about it,' Zack said before a smile softened his face. 'And just so there's no confusion, I want to make something very clear: I'm going to be best man at your wedding and not some lame male bridesmaid.'

Jenny giggled and Adam expected to feel a sense of horror. Whenever anyone had mentioned marriage before, in any context, he'd always tensed up. But suddenly he felt quite different. He actually felt quite relaxed about it all.

Then that tensed him up. What was that about?

'We can still meet up on Sundays though, can't we?' Zack asked.

'Nothing is going to change,' Jenny said. 'It's the best part of the week. I love our Sundays.'

'But only if we can find a way to get me out of here,'

Adam said. 'As it stands at the minute, we're going to have to meet in my office, not the pub.'

'Right, yes,' Jenny said, sitting up in her new favourite chair. 'Zack, do you have a plan?'

'Jenny told me that you'd broken her wish about Nathan,' Adam said.

Zack nodded. 'We went over her wish – all seven thousand words of it-'

'Tell me about it,' Adam agreed.

'Basically, I figured that if she physically said the words to break up with Nathan, then she'd change the detail and it would make it all null and void. At the end of the day, it's just about looking at the facts.'

Adam felt deflated. That was easy with Jenny's wish; there was plenty to work with. Adam's wish was a little more direct.

'Do you still have what you wrote?' Zack asked.

'Yes, it's on my computer. But I can't see what use it's going to be.'

'Let's take a look first, then we'll see.'

'All right.'

Adam walked around to his laptop. He stared at Jenny so he could take his seat at his desk but she clearly wasn't going to budge.

'It's going to be easier if I sit down,' he said.

'But I'm so comfortable!' she whined.

Adam smirked. Then he tickled her. She shrieked with laughter and jumped out of the seat, at which point he sat down as quickly as he could.

'That's not fair!' she moaned, but with a cheeky glint in her eye.

'Come on, you can sit on my lap,' he said, and without hesitation she did just that.

He wrapped one arm around her and then with the other he nudged his laptop awake. He logged back in and then searched for his letter to Emmett.

'Here you go,' he said, spinning his laptop around to

show Zack the Word document.

Zack took a second to read it. His face looked serious for a moment before he said, 'No problem.'

'Is everything all right?' Adam asked.

'Yeah,' Zack said, but Adam could tell something had bothered him.

'Is there something we can do?' Jenny asked, seeming just as concerned as Adam.

'Yes, it's easy. We just need to honour the terms of the wish.'

'What terms?' Adam asked.

'You said you don't want to leave your job again except for international conferences.'

'So? There isn't another conference until November. I can't stay here until then. That's ridiculous.'

'And what is the definition of an international conference?' Zack asked.

'What?' Adam replied. It seemed pretty obvious.

'There's no detail in the wish. You just say you want to leave for international conferences.'

'So?'

'So, Jenny, invite him to an international conference.'

'What? How?'

Zack reached over and grabbed a pad from Adam's desk. He flicked through to a fresh sheet of paper and then took a pen from the pot. He then handed them both to Jenny.

'Write down that you invite Adam to your international conference which begins now and ends in... two hundred years. That should do it.'

'It can't possibly be that easy,' Adam said incredulously.

'Why not?'

'Because... it's too easy.'

'It's your wish. It's what you wrote.'

'It's worth a try,' Jenny said.

She placed the paper down before her and then wrote, in her spectacularly neat handwriting, exactly what Zack had said. Then she added at the end *I wish to attend* with a line next to it.

'Sign it,' she said, handing the pen and paper over.

Adam hesitated. Was it really going to be that easy?

'All right,' he said. What did he have to lose?

He signed his name before pushing the paper over to the middle of the desk. 'What now?'

'Now we get out of here,' Zack said.

'We can try,' Adam stated.

Jenny stood up releasing him, and then Adam turned off his laptop, tidied up his things and grabbed his suit jacket. As they all left his office, he took one last look around before locking the door.

'Do you always lock your office?' Jenny asked as they made their way back to the lift.

'I have to,' Adam replied. 'I've got all the sales team's personal files in there. The commission rate isn't equal and all hell would break loose if some of them found out.'

'Is that fair?' Zack asked, pressing the button to call the lift.

'Yes, it's totally fair. They don't have equal salaries, nor equal responsibilities, so why should they have equal commission? I've set it all as fairly as I can, but I know the younger ones wouldn't see it that way. They're hungry for it. I want to keep them that way.'

'Like someone else I know,' Jenny smiled. Adam nodded. He'd always been eager to succeed, but he knew something in him was starting to change. Suddenly he wanted far more than money and job satisfaction. Suddenly it seemed like there was far more on offer.

He kissed Jenny's head as they entered the lift.

They stood in silence as they made their way to the ground floor. When the doors opened, Adam stepped out first and he led the way back to reception.

He took a deep breath as he flashed his pass, releasing the door. He pulled it open, keeping everything crossed. He moved his foot forward, expecting it to hit the imaginary wall, but it didn't. It kept going. He was able to step out into the evening.

He punched the air. 'Thank you, Zack. Thank you so much.'

He hugged his mate and then punched the air again with delight.

'You're welcome,' Zack said.

'How did you work it out?' Adam asked.

'I guess I've spent more time with Emmett than you two have.'

Adam and Jenny turned to one another. They were both clearly thinking the same thing. 'Has he been coming round to your flat?' Jenny asked Zack.

'Don't be daft!' Zack laughed. 'I meant because I drew him.'

'Oh!' Jenny giggled.

'But seriously, when you want to get rid of Cadence, you get your mind working,' Zack added.

'Now I can relate to that,' Adam nodded.

Adam shut the door securely behind him and they all walked up to the car park.

'You want to follow me back?' Zack asked Jenny. 'I know you hate using your sat nav.'

'No, I'll just follow Adam. But thank you,' Jenny replied.

'But I only live down the road from you. It'll be easier to follow me.'

Adam felt suddenly awkward. 'It's all right, mate,' he said. 'I'm staying at Jen's tonight.'

'Oh,' Zack said. No one talked for a few seconds. 'Right then. I'll just see you on Sunday.'

'You definitely will!' Jenny grinned. 'Can't wait.'

'Yeah,' Zack nodded.

As Adam unlocked his car he felt very uneasy. He watched Zack pull away with no hesitation and all he could do was hope that everything would sort itself out.

Zack will just need time, he told himself. *Just give him time.*

HAS EMMETT GOT IT RIGHT?

The following Sunday, Zack sat in The Red Lion, waiting for Adam and Jenny. It wasn't unusual for him to be the first to get there and he was sipping at his pint, studying the menu, when they arrived. Their giggling could be heard well before they appeared together, hand in hand.

'Hi Zack!' Jenny said, giving him a quick hug and kiss on the cheek.

'All right, mate,' Adam said, patting Zack on the back. 'Usual, Jen?' Adam asked.

'Yeah, thanks.'

Jenny took a seat opposite Zack as Adam headed to the bar.

'How's the life of leisure going?' Jenny asked.

Zack shrugged. 'I was a bit bored yesterday if I'm honest.'

'Sorry about that. Couldn't you go away or something? How big was the pay out?'

'Very big. Just like I wished for. I've got enough to put a deposit on a house.'

'Wow! Good job Emmett!'

Adam joined then, placing down pints in front of him and Jenny.

'What's Emmett done now?' he asked.

'He's been very good to Zack. It seems being made redundant has really paid off.'

'I'm really pleased for you, mate. About time you had some luck.'

'It's all Emmett, not luck,' Zack replied.

'Or you could say it was lucky that we came up with him,' Adam reasoned.

'What are we doing about that, by the way?' Zack asked.

'What do you mean?' Jenny enquired.

'Well, I've been having a think about it. I have had a lot of time on my hands. Do you still want to pursue it as an idea? Like, still make him into a comic?'

'Definitely!' Jenny said. 'And we now have some real life stories too. It's going to be great!'

'Did you ever send anything off to those publishers?' Adam asked.

'Yes, although I've heard nothing back. But I don't think that should stop us. I've been doing some research. Did you know that we could totally self-publish? We can do it all ourselves, and I reckon between us we've got the perfect combination.'

'How do you mean?' Adam asked.

'Think about it. What else do we need? I can illustrate it, Jenny can bring it to life with her graphic skills, and then you, Adam, can sell it for us. It's like a dream team.'

'I love it!' Jenny said, clapping her hands.

'Where would we sell it? Wouldn't we need to print it?' Adam asked.

'You can do it completely online yourself nowadays. Or there are these companies that do it for you. It's so easy. I've got all the details at home. I'll bring everything with me next week.'

'This would be your dream come true, Zack,' Jenny said. 'You'd finally get your illustrations out there.'

'But it would be all our work,' Zack said. 'I want it to

be the three of us putting it together. I'd just be turning our thoughts into pictures.'

'I'm up for giving it a go,' Adam said. 'But can I just ask that we all agree we're happy with it before we publish anything? I really don't want to be a laughing stock with some lame story about a troubled teenager. We can't have Empathy Man jogging about twenty miles across town only to find out when he gets there that the kid's already been beaten up three times and the bullies have long since buggered off.'

Jenny shook her head. 'Ignore him, he's in a bad mood.'

'I'm not,' Adam argued.

'I wouldn't go to the gym with him this morning. But it's Sunday. I don't know why he can't understand it: Sundays are made for lie-ins. I think it might even be the law.'

'It was nine o'clock,' Adam said, rolling his eyes. 'All I suggested was that we go to the gym before we grab some breakfast.'

'He went on his own,' Jenny informed Zack.

'And she was still in bed when I got back,' Adam added.

'I was watching telly!' Jenny said.

'In bed. Still in your pyjamas.'

'I had to. I'm conserving my energy.'

'Oh yeah, for what?' Adam smirked.

Jenny was giggling as she whispered something into Adam's ear. As he listened, a huge grin spread across his face. 'Oh right!' he said, laughing. 'Well, if that's the case, I think you'd better lie in every Sunday from now on.'

'I'll go order for us, shall I?' Zack said, standing up with urgency.

'I'll come with you,' Adam said.

'No! Please. I mean, I want to buy. I haven't treated my mates yet after my big pay out. Let me get this.'

'Are you sure?' Jenny checked.

'Just tell me what you want. This one's on me.' He seemed quite tense suddenly.

'That's very good of you, mate. I'll have my usual pork then, if that's all right,' Adam said.

'I'm going to have the beef today,' Jenny said. 'Thanks Zack.'

'Back in a sec.'

The second his back was turned, Adam kissed Jenny.

'Love you,' he said.

'I love you, too,' Jenny replied. 'It's so nice being here, having our Sundays, but also knowing I'm going home with you as well. I hated thinking about you going home to Cadence.'

Adam sat back. 'Cadence. I'd actually forgotten about her. Is that bad?'

'At least there's no chance of her turning up today.'

'Yeah, that was really annoying, wasn't it? I hated the way she always had to sit on my lap. She had such a bony arse.'

Jenny burst out laughing. 'See, there's no such thing as the perfect woman.'

'Oh, I don't know,' Adam said, stroking the new blue streak in Jenny's hair.

'It's all working out for us, isn't it?' Jenny said.

'It really is.'

'I can't believe how well Zack's doing too. He said he's going to be able to put a deposit on a house.'

'That's fantastic.'

'All ordered,' Zack said, returning with three pints.

'You didn't have to get a round in as well,' Adam said.

'Yes I did. I want to be able to treat my friends. How often do I come into money?'

'Well, thank you,' Adam said, lifting up his pint. He clinked glasses with Zack and then with Jenny. 'Now we're all together, I want to run an idea past you. You can say no, Zack, but if you've got any extra cash, I was thinking how about we all try and get tickets for San Diego next year?'

'Comic-Con?' Zack asked, his eyes aglow. 'That's the best idea I've heard all year!'

'Hang on,' Jenny said. 'Zack might have money now, but I still can't afford to go. I wasn't serious about being your slave.'

'Don't be stupid,' Adam said, grabbing her hand underneath the table. 'I'm paying for you.'

'You can't do that.'

'Of course I can.'

'Adam, we've looked into it,' Jenny said with a stern face. 'Flights aren't cheap. Then we'd need a hotel.'

'Jen, you're my girlfriend now. We're moving in together. You're going to have to let me pay for some stuff. We'll be sharing everything anyway.'

'You're moving in together?' Zack asked with surprise.

'Not just yet,' Jenny replied. 'Adam's only just given notice to his tenants.'

'They've got to be out in two months,' he said.

'I've got to give a month's notice on my flat, which I'll do in a few weeks, and then we're going to be living in Adam's old house.'

'You mean where you lived before you moved in with Cadence?' Zack asked.

'Yeah. Just for now. Then we'll see how it goes. Maybe it will be better for us to buy a place together further down the line.'

'That seems really fast,' Zack said.

Adam shrugged. 'Not really. We've known each other for such a long time, it seemed the obvious next step.'

'It's really exciting,' Jenny said, the smile getting larger on her face by the second.

'Well, congratulations,' Zack said, but it wasn't full of enthusiasm.

'You're number one on the house-warming party guest list,' Jenny said. 'And we'd want you to stay over.'

All Zack did was nod.

'So are we doing Comic-Con or not?' Adam asked.

'What's the chance of us even getting tickets?' Zack shrugged, his eagerness all gone.

'Well, I've been thinking about that too,' Adam replied. 'Why don't we wish for tickets?'

'What?' Jenny said with excitement.

'If we all wish for the same thing, it's got to come true. We might as well use the power we've got.'

'Let's write it down!' Jenny said. She let go of Adam's hand and then rummaged around in her bag, bringing out a pen and a receipt. She turned the receipt over and poised herself ready to write. 'What shall I put?'

'Do you think this is a good idea?' Zack asked, leaning forward. He suddenly seemed far more engaged.

'It's our dream, mate,' Adam said. 'What more could we possibly wish for? It's not like we've been taking advantage of Emmett. We've been very selective with our wishes so far.'

'And I think it needs to stay that way,' Zack said. 'He's been very good to us. I don't want to take him for granted.'

'I totally agree,' Jenny nodded.

'That's why this wish is perfect,' Adam said. 'It's something we've all wanted for as long as we've known each other. I think Emmett would want to do this for us.'

Zack thought for a second. Then he said, 'All right. Let's do it.'

'Yay!' Jenny said. 'So, what shall I put? We wish to go to the next San Diego Comic-Con?'

'Be specific,' Zack replied. 'Make sure you put our names. Make it really clear.'

Jenny nodded and then she wrote very carefully on the paper.

Dear Emmett

Jenny, Adam and Zack all wish to go to the next San Diego Comic-Con. Could you please help us get tickets so we don't miss out? We can take care of flights and hotels, we just need help with the tickets. As you probably know, it's a very popular event, so we're counting on you.

Thank you so much. You're the best.

Love Jenny, Adam and Zack. xx

Adam shook his head. 'What are you like?'

'What?'

'Why all the flowery stuff? Why not just state the wish?'

'That seems a bit cold,' Jenny replied. 'Emmett's the Empathy Man. He needs to feel how much we want things. He needs to know.'

'I've been thinking about that-' Adam said.

'I'd better go to the loo,' Jenny said, hopping to her feet. 'The food will be here in a sec.'

Adam sat back, taking a gulp of his pint.

'What's happening with your current house, then?' Zack asked. 'Are you and Cadence going to sell it?'

'Yes. We've already started the process.'

'Have you spoken to her?'

'A few days ago.'

'How is she?'

'She seemed really good, actually. She agreed that it was for the best, our break-up. We'd not been happy for... We weren't happy.'

'Did you tell her about Jenny?'

'God no. Far too soon. She doesn't need to know about that.'

'Did she ask about me?'

Adam shook his head. 'There wasn't really time. It was only a quick call.'

'Right.'

'Sorry about that,' Jenny said, returning to her seat. 'But it looks like I had impeccable timing!'

'Who's having the beef?' the waitress asked. Jenny waved her hand and the plate was placed down before her. Zack and Adam's pork dishes were then brought over and they all picked up their cutlery.

Only Adam and Jenny didn't start straight away. They studied each other's plates.

Zack watched with horror as Jenny took one of Adam's Yorkshire puddings and then she replaced it with all of her carrots and two of her potatoes. Then they shared a quick kiss before tucking in.

'Everything all right, mate?' Adam asked, catching Zack's glare.

'Yeah, fine. Miles away,' he said. 'Just thinking how good San Diego's going to be. All three of us together. Can't wait.'

SAD ZACK

Zack had never enjoyed a Sunday afternoon less. Even discussing their Empathy Man comic book had been ruined with soppy talk and a lot of touching. Zack had actually felt relieved when Jenny had said it was time for them to go.

After saying some quick goodbyes, Zack decided to make the short walk into Miloworth town centre. The day certainly wasn't over for him. He needed more to drink. He'd never felt like such a gooseberry in all his life, and he was left with a horrible feeling that things were never going to be the same again.

He headed into The World's End pub only to instantly regret it. It was heaving. As he pushed his way to the bar he noticed a band setting up in the corner. He sighed. That was just what he needed.

'Hi, Zack. What can I get for you?' Nathan asked, just as Zack was contemplating moving on.

He decided he was there now so he might as well have a drink. 'Pint of Peroni, please.'

'Coming up.'

Drink poured and paid for, Zack headed over to the corner of the room, as far away from the band as he could.

He leant against the wall just as music started to blast out from the speakers at the front. It was a deafening mix of guitars and drums attempting to play some sort of rock tune. Zack really wasn't in the mood for it.

Then it got even worse, as some very inebriated lads around him starting jumping up and down. Zack guessed it was meant to be some form of dancing, but it was all he could do just to hold on to his pint.

Just as Zack was starting to think things had got as bad as they possibly could, Nathan suddenly appeared next to him. 'How's Jenny?' Nathan virtually had to shout to be heard above the music.

'She's good, I think,' Zack shouted back, before looking around for some sort of escape.

'Is Adam treating her well?'

'I believe so.'

'You don't need to worry. I told her I'd wait for her.'

'What? Why?'

'It'll never last,' Nathan said.

'Okay.'

'She's known him for years, but it's only suddenly when he breaks up with his girlfriend that they get together. It's a rebound thing. It has to be.'

Zack screwed up his face. Nathan was a sad, desperate man, and all Zack could think about was him appearing at Jenny's door in a Superman costume. What did she ever see in him?

'You should bring her down here with you,' Nathan said. 'Just the two of you.'

'Like a date?' Zack asked with horror. The humiliation of how he'd mis-read Jenny's actions in Hamburg was still quite raw.

'No. I thought you were just friends. She's not seeing you as well, is she?'

Zack sighed. 'No. Trust me, we're definitely just friends.'

'Right. Good!'

'I'm going to go now,' Zack said. He gulped down as much of his pint as he could before handing the glass to Nathan.

'No problem, mate. You'll tell Jenny that I asked about her, won't you?'

'Of course. I bet she's dying to know. She loves all these super men in her life.'

'Great,' Nathan said, patting Zack on the back. 'It means a lot to me. Us blokes need to stick together.'

Zack looked at Nathan. 'You do know that Adam is my best mate, don't you?'

Nathan didn't move for a second. Then he laughed. 'Good one.'

As Nathan walked off back behind the bar, Zack shook his head. No matter how bad things had got for Zack, at least he wasn't Nathan. At least he wasn't an idiot.

Zack gladly pushed his way through the crowd and headed back outside. Although he quite liked the idea of drinking himself into a stupor, he also couldn't face going anywhere else.

How he needed his mates right now. In all his life he'd never had any friends as good as Jenny and Adam. He had so much in common with them and he loved their company very much. They gave him a reason to get through every week and they never judged him, no matter what he did. They were the best friends that he was ever going to have and he knew it. But everything had changed. They were now all loved up and he was like the third wheel, getting in the way, getting all embarrassed.

He knew he'd never lose them as friends, but he also knew the times when they could go out together as a threesome were coming to an end.

How he wished they'd never fallen in love. Why couldn't it be like before, when they were just friends and not all soppy with each other?

Zack decided to grab some beers from the off-licence and then he headed straight home. At least he could relax at home.

The second he got in, he threw his jogging suit bottoms on to get comfortable and then he took a seat on his leather sofa. He stared at his state-of-the-art bookshelf, deciding that maybe he should watch a Blu-ray to take his mind off things.

He stood up and grabbed a Doctor Who box set. If he had time on his hands then he may as well use it wisely. He was going to go back to the Christopher Eccleston days and watch every episode through to the most recent.

Matt Smith was by far his favourite Doctor and Zack was interested in finding out how he actually compared, watching everything in order.

He slipped the Blu-ray into his player before lying down on his sofa.

But within minutes his mind was wandering. What a couple of weeks he'd had. He'd slept with a model who'd turned out to be a controlling nightmare in a beautiful body, and then he'd been led to believe that his best mate fancied him only to be brought smack down to earth again when he'd found out that she actually fancied his other mate. Talk about ups and downs.

Why did Adam and Jenny have to fall in love? As he pressed to play all episodes, he started to wish that everything would go back to the way it was before. He didn't want his friends to be in a relationship. He wanted the Sundays he used to love and treasure. But he knew deep in his heart those times were now all gone and nothing would ever be the same again.

☐

JENNY AND HER SUPERMAN

Jenny watched the clock on the wall. It was Tuesday and she was counting down the minutes to five pm. There were eleven more to go.

She'd found it hard to concentrate that day. Adam had said something the night before which she'd not picked up on at the time, but now she was starting to feel quite upset about it.

She'd cooked a homemade curry especially for him and he'd commented that it was a bit too spicy for his taste. She'd laughed at the time, but now she was wondering what he'd actually meant.

At first she'd considered whether he was subtly trying to tell her that he didn't like her food. They both knew she wasn't great in the kitchen. But she'd made a huge effort, following the recipe exactly, and Jenny thought it had been delicious.

The more she pondered on it though, the more negative her ideas became. He'd said it was 'too spicy for his taste'. What could that really mean? It went round and round her head, and in the end there was only one conclusion that Jenny could come to.

It was obvious that his comment had actually been

more about Jenny in general. He must have been telling her that she was too spicy for him. In short, the colourful streaks in her hair and her brightly coloured T-shirts were great when they were friends, but they weren't right for his girlfriend.

Well, she wasn't going back to her mousy brown hair, that was for sure. He could take his desire for a blander girl and stick it up his nose.

Or maybe it was both? Maybe it was a dig at her cooking whilst also trying to tell her that she needed to be more normal if they were going to start a life together.

He could go to hell!

Five o'clock eventually arrived and she turned off her computer with a rage bubbling up inside. She stood up, said goodbye to her colleagues and then began her short march home.

She arrived back at the front door of her flat, still reeling, when she stopped. She could hear music coming from within.

She knew it had to be Adam. She'd had a key cut for him earlier in the week. But what was he doing there? He didn't finish work until five thirty and it was only ten past.

She unlocked her door and swung it open. He was listening to rock music. Why was that not too spicy for him?

'Adam?' she called, tracking him down in the bedroom. He was making her bed and this instantly sent Jenny's rage off the scale. 'What the hell do you think you're doing?'

'Oh hi!' he said, stepping to the bedside table to switch his Bluetooth speaker off.

'Why are you making my bed?'

'One of us has to.'

'No they don't. There's no law that says you have to make your bed. I'm all ears if you can enlighten me as to how the world is going to be a better place if my bed is made on a daily basis, but until then I think it's just one big, fat waste of time.'

'Don't you think it will just look neater if it's made?' Adam replied assertively.

'That I agree with. But who is it looking neater for? Is the Queen popping around for tea?'

'For me. I want it to look neater for me.'

'Why do you care?'

'I can't stand mess.'

'And that's what I am, is it? Messy?'

'You said it.'

'So I'm a big, fat spicy mess now, am I?'

'What?' Adam pressed the corner of the duvet down and then he moved over to her. 'Why do you keep saying fat? And what the hell is spicy supposed to mean?'

'You called my cooking last night too spicy.'

'Well it was. My mouth was on fire.'

'I know what you really meant.'

'Do you?' he asked with surprise. 'Well, please do tell. What did I really mean?'

'You don't like my hair.'

'What?! How did you get that from spicy food?'

'Isn't it obvious?'

'No. Not at all. That's utterly crazy. Have you been smoking something?'

Jenny was gobsmacked. 'No I haven't! How could you say that? I suppose that's what you think us spicy people do. You prejudiced sod.'

Adam went to argue but he quickly stopped himself. Instead he just shook his head and returned to his bed-making. Jenny watched him as he carefully and precisely tweaked the edges of the duvet. It made her blood boil.

'Why are you home so early?' she demanded to know.

'I took the afternoon off.'

'Why?'

'I couldn't concentrate thinking about the mess of this place. I picked up some boxes. I thought we could have a clear out.'

'Are you joking?'

'No. The boxes are in the living room.'

Jenny stomped to the living room where she saw eight boxes of different sizes stacked up neatly in the corner.

'I don't want to have a clear out,' she said, coming back to the bedroom.

'If we're going to be living together then you need to be neater. I won't tolerate mess.'

'You won't tolerate it?'

Adam opened up her wardrobe and a few items fell out.

'See what I mean?' he said. 'It's an utter disgrace. You live in a pig-sty.'

'How dare you! It may be a little bit scruffy around the edges, but I keep it clean. I just don't believe in hiding everything out of view so it looks like I live in some sort of show home. And I don't see the point of making the bed, only to get back into it again a few hours later. Nobody knows, and quite frankly I think you're the only person in the world who cares.'

'If I'm going to be sharing a house with you then I think my opinion matters, don't you?'

Jenny wanted to scream. What had happened to the nice, caring man she once knew?

'What's this?' he suddenly said, picking up the Superman toy from the floor that Nathan had given to her.

She'd shoved it in her wardrobe as she hadn't known what else to do with it. It seemed mean throwing it out as the gesture had been kind, but she didn't really want the thing. Although she liked reading comics about Superman and watching films, she didn't want a twelve inch action figure of the man sitting in her living room. Nor did she want a blow up version of him either. Thank God she'd deflated that. She'd put it right at the back, behind her shoes. From where Adam was standing she knew he wouldn't be able to see it.

'It's a gift that Nathan gave to me.'

'Nathan gave you a Superman action figure?' Adam

asked with no sense of humour.

'Yes.'

'Why have you kept it?'

'I don't know. I felt bad throwing it out. He meant well.'

'Do you still want to be with him?'

'Of course not!'

'Or is it Superman that you really want?' Adam asked, holding out the figure to emphasise his point.

'How can I want Superman? He's not real. What a stupid thing to say.'

'It's not stupid. How is any other man ever meant to compete?'

'He's not real!'

'You know he's the lamest superhero ever invented, don't you?' Adam said with a venomous tongue.

This sent another bolt of rage through Jenny. 'He's one of the oldest superheroes ever. He's stood the test of time, generation after generation. I don't think that makes him lame.'

'But he has an ultimate weakness.'

'You keep saying that, but it's ludicrous.'

'You've only got to hold a piece of special rock next to him and he's a withering mess.'

'But who has Kryptonite? You say it like it's readily available on the high street. It's not that easy to find.'

'It is easy! You just get a lab to make it up for you or you steal some from Lex Luthor's safe. He never seems short of it.'

'Or I suppose you could shoot some webs at him and he'll give himself up,' Jenny bit back.

'Don't you dare trivialise Spider-Man's powers.'

'How could we forget about the almighty spider sense?'

'It's an amazing ability.'

'Yes, he can sense a man coming up behind him. But what if that man is travelling faster than a speeding bullet? What good is a web then? Superman would have him knocked down before Spider-Man could so much as utter one of his silly quips. He's just a child.'

'Oh, it's Superman's maturity that you like, is it?'

'Well, it would be nice to enjoy the company of a grown-up every now and then.'

'What is that supposed to mean?'

'Superman would like my food. He wouldn't cry about how spicy it is.'

'Then maybe you should be cooking for him instead.'

'Maybe I should!'

'Go on then!' Adam threw the Superman toy at Jenny and he pushed past her. 'But don't you dare come crying to me when someone turns up with a bit of green rock and he's lying on your kitchen floor in a useless heap.'

'I won't!'

Adam stormed to the front door and slammed it shut behind him. Jenny hugged her toy. Superman would never treat her like that. Adam was nasty. How could she have not seen it before?

She placed Superman gently on the carpet and then she grabbed her duvet and scrunched it up as best she could.

That was better! Now it felt like her flat again.

She sat down on the bed and exhaled. She was so angry. Had he left her now? Was that it? She hoped so. She didn't need his overly tidy, jealous of fictional men attitude anymore. She was better off without him.

Then Zack popped into her mind. He was a much better friend. He'd never treat her like that.

She stood up, grabbed her bag and headed out of her flat. It was only about a ten minute walk to Zack's place and she couldn't wait to spend time with her good friend.

She just hoped he was up for a visitor.

ZACK'S JEALOUSY

Zack was just watching David Tennant regenerate as the tenth Doctor, when his buzzer interrupted him. He pressed pause, wondering who it could be at his door.

'Hello,' he said into the intercom receiver.

'Hi, it's Jenny.'

Zack paused. Jenny never turned up out of the blue. He hoped nothing was wrong. 'Hi, come up.'

He buzzed her in and then opened the door. 'Hi Zack,' she said. She looked really miserable.

'Is everything all right?' he asked, gesturing for her to come in.

'Yeah, fine.'

He led her through to the living room.

'Bloody hell, this place has changed,' she said, staring in awe around her.

'Cadence used her time well. I think she fancies herself as an interior designer.' As much as he wanted to be annoyed with Cadence, now that Zack had put his Star Wars posters back, he had to admit that he actually liked the changes. She had a good eye.

'She was only here a week, wasn't she?'

'It felt like years. But I can't deny, I have been feeling

more relaxed sitting in here recently. She had a Feng Shui expert round and I think it might have worked.'

'Or maybe it's just a lot brighter in here now and it's making you more cheery. Those brown curtains weren't great before. It did look dark.'

Zack looked around. Jenny was right. Everything had been a bit brown before. It was definitely lighter now. Maybe it was the brightness that was making him feel better. But he wasn't going to rule out the power of Feng Shui.

'Anyway, what's going on?' he asked, sitting down on one of his armchairs.

'Sorry, am I disturbing you?' Jenny said pointing to the TV screen. 'This is *The Parting of the Ways* isn't it? Are you watching them in order?'

'Yes. I started with *Rose* a couple of days ago.'

'So *The Christmas Invasion* is next? I love that episode!'

'I'm curious to watch the next series as I'm still convinced that Matt Smith is the best Doctor.'

'No! You're so wrong,' Jenny said, smiling. 'Just you wait.'

Suddenly the door buzzed again. Zack was taken aback. He rarely got one visitor, let alone two.

'Hello,' he said, answering the intercom.

'It's Adam, can I come up?'

'Yeah, of course.'

Zack buzzed him in and then he called into the living room. 'It's only Adam.'

'What does he want?' Jenny snapped back, much to Zack's surprise.

Zack met Adam at the door.

'You got a beer, mate?' Adam asked looking like the world was on his shoulders. 'I could do with one.'

'Yeah, come on through.'

Adam walked on to the living room and Zack headed to the kitchen. He opened the fridge to grab three cans of lager when suddenly he heard shouting.

Carrying the beers, Zack followed the noise to find Jenny and Adam glaring at one another fiercely.

'You came over here as well!' Jenny shouted.

'He's my best mate.'

'He's my best mate, too.'

'I thought that was Superman,' Adam snarled. 'You just want to be friends with everyone.'

'Will you stop being so pathetic about Superman. It's getting embarrassing now.'

'You're the one that should be embarrassed. You're in love with a fictional character.'

'What is going on?' Zack yelled in utter disbelief.

'Adam thinks I'm too spicy for him!' Jenny shrieked.

Adam turned to Zack. 'I said her food was too spicy. She put about a thousand chillies in it. A fire-breathing dragon would have found her curry too spicy.'

Zack placed the beers down on the carpet. He couldn't believe it. It didn't even feel like Adam and Jenny, they never argued like this.

'Then he said I was fat and messy,' Jenny added.

'Not fat, just messy. You are very, very messy,' Adam stated.

'It's better than being uptight! "Oh look at me, I've got to polish my shoes every twenty seconds, and there's a very small crease in my shirt." That's you!'

'Will you two stop it!' Zack demanded. 'Where has this come from? Last time I saw you, you were all over each other like lovesick teenagers. What's caused all this tension?'

'She's in love with Superman!' Adam shouted.

'She's always been in love with Superman. What else?' Zack reasoned.

'He doesn't like my hair!'

'I never said anything like that,' Adam insisted.

'I know what you meant,' Jenny hissed.

'Stop it!' Zack said, putting himself between the pair. 'Can one of you please start talking sense?'

'When he said my food was spicy he was actually making a comment about the way I look.'

'He loves the way you look. Don't you, Adam?'

Adam shrugged his shoulders. That was all he did. He'd been stroking her hair last Sunday, whispering sweet nothings in her ear, making her blush. Making everyone blush. But here and now they were like a completely different couple.

'I don't understand why you're so angry with one another,' Zack said.

'He's being really nasty to me,' Jenny said.

'She came home and I was just innocently making the bed when suddenly she started yelling at me.'

'You've got an obsession with making the bed!' Jenny argued. 'It's not healthy.'

'It's not healthy that you can't make the bed,' Adam replied. 'It's like you've got some sort of mental block.'

'This is ridiculous!' Zack shouted.

'It is ridiculous. It's ridiculous that I never knew how unreasonable she was,' Adam said. 'I used to think she was laid back and fun. How wrong can a person be.'

'I'm the most laid back person in the world compared to you!' Jenny retorted.

'Enough!' Zack yelled. 'This fighting has got to stop. All that matters is that you love each other, surely.'

Adam shrugged his shoulders. 'Maybe I don't anymore.'

'What?' Zack asked. Was he joking? He turned to Jenny. 'You love Adam, right?'

'I used to think I did. Now I dread the thought of waking up next to that haughty face. I just want everything to go back to how it was before. I was much happier then.'

'Oh no,' Zack muttered. He suddenly wanted the ground to swallow him up. He was starting to see what had happened. This was all his fault.

'You do love each other,' he said, stepping away. 'I think you need to sit down.'

'I think we should get back to watching Doctor Who,' Jenny said. 'Maybe Adam could learn something about being a decent man.'

'So you've got a thing for Doctor Who now, as well?' Adam asked.

'No, I just know decency when I see it.'

'Mature Superman, decent Doctor Who. You really like exciting men, don't you? No wonder this isn't working. I'm clearly not boring enough for you.'

'Far from it!' Jenny retorted. 'Boring is one word that definitely describes you and your bed-making fantasies.'

'If having standards is too complicated for you, then you're welcome to Doctor Who and Superman. Why don't you invite them round to your flat? And while you're there you could make them your "hotter than the surface of the sun" curry.'

'I might do. I bet they wouldn't whinge about it. I bet they'd be grateful!'

'Sit down!' Zack ordered. He'd never shouted so loudly before, even he was a bit shook up.

He glared sternly at Jenny and Adam until they did as they were told. Then he handed them both a can of lager each, knowing they were going to need it.

'You do love each other. This is a huge mistake. I'm really sorry but I think I might have messed this up for you.'

'You've not done anything,' Jenny said. 'You're the best friend in the world.'

'No I'm not,' Zack said. 'But you have to know, I didn't mean to. It wasn't deliberate. It's not like I wrote it down or consciously said the words. It was just a passing thought. It never occurred to me at the time what I was saying.'

'What are you talking about?' Adam asked.

'The other night, I may have made a wish.'

'What sort of wish?' Adam asked.

'I was feeling sorry for myself. It used to be great just

the three of us, but on Sunday I felt like a complete gooseberry. It made me realise that it's not the three of us anymore. It's more like you two and me.'

'You certainly don't need to worry about anything like that,' Jenny said. 'There's no us two anymore.'

'Don't you see?' Zack said. 'That's exactly what I wished for.'

'What?' Adam looked even more serious, if that was possible.

'I wished - totally forgetting that Emmett might be listening – that everything would go back to how it used to be. I wished that you two weren't in love anymore. Then a couple of days later and you're at each other's throats.'

'That's just a coincidence, Zack,' Jenny said. 'Adam was a prat long before you made the wish. It was only a matter of time before I noticed.'

'You think the world of him, Jenny! You've never said a bad word about each other before. It makes me cringe how much you adore each other.'

'Adored,' Adam stated.

'No! It's my wish. Don't you see?'

'It can't work like that, Zack,' Jenny said. 'It's just taken us a few days to realise it. We never should have got together. We're always going to be better off as friends.'

'I agree,' Adam said. 'Don't feel bad, Zack. Emmett's not that powerful.'

Zack stood up. It was like a horrible nightmare. As much as he wanted life back the way it was before, he couldn't take seeing his best friends break up like that. Their love for one another was far more important than his stupid selfish needs.

'Do you think we can just go back to being friends?' Adam asked Jenny. Zack couldn't bear it. It broke his heart. What had he done?

He darted into his bedroom to think, slamming the door behind him so he didn't have to hear any more of the false words that Adam and Jenny were saying to one another. There had to be a way out of it. His wish could not be final. The big problem, though, was that he couldn't remember what he'd said. He knew that he'd wished it, but it had been a passing thought and not something he'd been concentrating on. He could have actually said anything.

How was he meant to make something right when he didn't even know where it had gone wrong to begin with? He flopped down on the bed under the weight of his guilt.

I wish I knew what to do, he thought to himself. *I wish this wasn't happening.*

Suddenly Emmett appeared before him. His tall, blue clad body stood next to the bed, staring down at Zack. Zack nearly jumped out of his skin. 'What are you doing here?' he asked.

'You wished for help,' Emmett replied in a smooth, caring voice.

Zack suddenly realised what he'd done. He had wished for that very thing. It seemed just saying the word "wish" was becoming highly dangerous.

'How can I stop this happening?' Zack asked.

'You already know the answer to that.'

'No I don't,' Zack replied. He couldn't believe that he was actually talking to Emmett. He looked exactly like his picture; like the man in Zack's head. Was he really there? Could this be a hallucination?

'Yes you do. If you want to end the wish, then you need to end the ability to wish.'

'What does that mean?' Zack said, reaching out his hand to poke Emmett on the leg. He definitely felt real.

'You need to end me,' Emmett replied, seeming not to notice the fact that Zack had just prodded his thigh.

'What?' Zack asked with shock, looking up at Emmett's caring face. 'But won't that end all our wishes?'

'It can't change anything that's already happened. You've already been made redundant and you already have the money in your bank account. Jenny has already broken up with Nathan and Adam has already moved back from

Hamburg. But you know as well as I do that they love each other deeply. This mask that they can't see through has only been put there by your desire for it.'

'You're supposed to be Empathy Man! How can you do this to two people who love each other?'

'No Zack, how can you? I'm empathising with you. They wished to love each other and I brought them together. Then you wished to break them apart and I felt your pain. It was a heavy heart you had, Zack. It was a deep and meaningful wish.'

'I didn't mean to make it, though!'

'I beg to differ.'

'So every time we mutter a wish under our breath, you're going to make it come true?'

'If I believe you mean it.'

'That's ridiculous! I wish all sorts of crap all the time, but most of it is heat of the moment stuff. Who are you to judge what to do with the words in my head?'

'I'm your creation, Zack.'

'No you're not. You were meant to be a fictional character in a comic book. You weren't meant to change our lives like this.'

'Haven't I changed them for the better?'

'No! Okay, maybe. At times. But currently my two best friends are in the next room breaking up, even though I know they love each other. Even I can see they're meant to be together. I hate it, but they're soulmates. I wasn't supposed to interfere.'

'But you did.'

'And now I wish to make it stop.'

'You can't just go back on wishes, you know that.'

'But I want to make it stop!'

'There's only one way now. You wished for everything to go back to the way it was, and I'm making that come true. Any moment now, Cadence will be phoning up Adam, asking for him to take her back. Jenny will encourage him, without meaning to, she just won't be able to resist it, and Adam will listen to his friend because he loves her. But he won't know it anymore, just like he didn't know it before. Then Jenny will go on dozens of disastrous dates again because she won't want to meet anyone else. She'll want to keep herself free for Adam, just in case Cadence dies in a horrific accident or something else just as cheery. So Jenny will be alone and Adam will be trapped in an unhappy relationship, because they'll both be too afraid again to admit their real feelings. And you'll have your friends back just as you like them.'

'I don't want that. That sounds awful. Is that really what happened before?'

'They've loved each other since the first moment they met. They've just both been too insecure to do anything about it, or in Adam's case even realise it.'

Zack buried his head in his hands. He couldn't believe how selfish he'd been. He was ruining their lives. He was supposed to be their mate.

'Okay, Emmett, what do I need to do?'

'End me and end the wish.'

Emmett disappeared and Zack lay back on the bed, breathlessly. Could he really do that?

He jumped up and grabbed his backpack. He took out the drawings of Emmett. There were dozens of them, along with sketches of comic book stories and notes about future ideas.

He felt his heart ache as he stared at the best work he'd ever done. Could he really end it?

ZACK SAYS GOODBYE

Zack sighed. This was incredibly hard, but he knew they couldn't go on like this. This could end in disaster. What if he was having a fight with someone one day and he said, 'I wish you'd just drop dead!' and then they did. He couldn't take the risk. Emmett's power was getting out of hand.

He opened his bedroom door with a small hope that everything had worked itself out and Jenny and Adam had made up again. Maybe Emmett appearing was just a delayed symptom of how much he'd drunk this week and none of it had actually been real.

Adam's mobile phone started to ring and Zack watched through the doorway as Adam pulled it out of his pocket. 'It's Cadence,' Adam told Jenny as he stood up to answer it.

Zack felt a burst of panic. It was all coming true. Cadence was about to ask Adam if they could get back together and Jenny was about to get heartbroken. He couldn't let that happen.

He dashed into the kitchen and opened up the cupboard where everything that he didn't need got dumped. It was the same cupboard that he'd rescued his

Star Wars posters from. He pulled out an old metal mop bucket and he grabbed some matches from a drawer.

He raced to the bathroom as he heard Adam say, 'I suppose in some ways I've missed you too,' down the phone. His heart was pounding.

He placed the bucket in the shower cubicle and squeezed his drawings down to the bottom of it. He took one last look at Emmett's smiling face. He looked so nice and happy. He was meant to help people.

'I don't know Cadence, you need to let me think about it,' Adam said as he paced around the flat on his phone.

Zack knew there was no time now. He lit a match and threw it in the bucket. Within seconds his beautiful artwork was alight. It burned quickly and smoke filled the cubicle. Coughing, Zack quickly turned the shower on to extinguish the blaze, and it soon disappeared, leaving just soggy ash and the odd trace of paper.

Zack turned the extractor fan on and he waved the door to get rid of the smell.

He looked at the mess in the bucket and he felt sad. He stared at it for a few moments with the ache of disappointment.

Then he realised that everything had gone quiet. Jenny and Adam had certainly stopped arguing, and there was nothing but silence now coming from the living room. What if they'd killed each other? What if Cadence was on her way over? He hoped it wasn't all too late.

Zack headed down the hallway, worried what he was going to find. To his great surprise and relief though, he found the pair standing in the middle of the living room, swallowing each other's faces up in a deep, loving kiss.

He felt his whole body relax as he could see he'd been successful. They were clearly back in love again and no major harm had been done.

He left them to it for a moment as he wafted the bathroom door again. The smell of burning paper was slowly going and things were getting back to normal.

He closed the bathroom door, deciding to leave tidying everything up until his friends had gone, and he headed back to the living room. The pair were still locked in a close embrace, but their hands were suddenly getting a bit X-rated.

'I'm glad to see you've made up!' he said very loudly, needing to bring the moment to a close.

They both jumped, as if they'd forgotten where they were. Then they giggled. 'Yes, I guess so,' Adam said.

'I couldn't stay mad at him for long,' Jenny grinned.

'I suppose we have Cadence to thank,' Adam said, turning to Jenny and stroking the blue bit in her hair.

'Cadence?' Zack enquired, as if he had no clue what they were talking about.

'Yes, she just called me,' Adam said. 'You're not going to believe this, but she wanted to get back together.'

'Really?' Zack said, feigning surprise.

'I thought for a moment he was going to say yes,' Jenny explained. 'Then everything sort of clicked.'

'I took one look at Jenny and knew that she was the only one I wanted,' Adam said.

'And I knew I didn't want to lose him,' Jenny added. They kissed each other again and Zack felt the urge to whistle or do something with his hands. This was getting awkward.

Jenny finally stepped back and turned to Zack. 'See, it was nothing to do with Emmett and you thinking you'd wished us apart. We were just having a mad moment. Call it end of the week stress. All couples argue, Zack.'

'I really did enjoy your curry,' Adam said to her. 'If I'm honest, it just made me insecure that I found it hot and you barely seemed to notice. Maybe I need to man up a bit. I'm the one that needs to change, not you.'

'No! You're perfect exactly how you are. I love the fact that you always look so effortlessly smart. You're gorgeous with a wonderfully delicate mouth. There's nothing wrong with that. I was just being over-sensitive. But, to be fair, your last girlfriend was a model.'

Adam smiled. 'She might have been a model, but she was always jealous of you. I don't think you realise just how beautiful you are, Jen. But you're an individual as well. You're like no one else I've ever met and you make every other woman in the world seem poor in comparison.'

Jenny appeared so touched at his words that Zack thought she was going to cry. But before he knew it, they were kissing again.

Zack started to tidy the Blu-rays on his bookshelf. He couldn't bear the embarrassment.

'You know I'd take you over Superman any day of the week, don't you?' Jenny muttered.

'Sorry about that,' Adam replied. 'I guess I was just a bit jealous that you still had a gift from Nathan.'

'I only have it because I felt bad throwing it out. The gesture was kind.'

'It is a really good model. It must have cost him a fortune.'

'I know. But I can't keep it.'

'Well, how about we throw that one out and I get you a new one. One from me. We could get a Spider-Man too.'

'Oh no you don't!' Jenny laughed.

'What?' Adam asked innocently.

'You'll have them fighting. I'll come home from work and Spider-Man will be on top of Superman, punching his face in. Or one morning I'll get up to find Superman on his side with a green pea next to him and you'll be claiming it's Kryptonite.'

'See how much fun we're going to have?'

'Let's go shopping tomorrow!' Jenny said, throwing her arms around Adam and kissing him again.

'Well, I'm glad you've made up,' Zack said, willing the sloppiness to end. Enough was enough.

Jenny stepped over to hug Zack. 'Thanks for being a good friend.'

'I didn't do anything,' Zack said, actually feeling like the worst friend in the world.

'Yes you did. You were right, we really do love each other. And we get why you wished for things to change. We weren't fair to you on Sunday. We both want to be your friend and we both want it to be the three of us, not a couple and a mate.'

'She's right,' Adam said. 'We'll stop being so soppy around you. I promise.'

'You don't need to do that,' Zack said, thinking that it would actually be really great if they did.

'We can't lose you as a friend. We've got San Diego to plan!' Jenny said with a beaming smile.

Zack's heart sank. That wish was now gone too. They were never going to get tickets without Emmett's help. Still, it was a small sacrifice to make to see his friends happy again.

'So, are we watching Doctor Who then?' Adam asked, picking up a can of lager from the floor and sitting on an armchair.

'He's watching them in order. *The Christmas Invasion* is next,' Jenny stated, grabbing her lager too.

'Cracking episode,' Adam said.

'It's a good one, but I still think Matt Smith is a much better Doctor,' Zack said, taking a seat on the sofa next to Jenny.

Adam shook his head. 'For a change, I agree with Jen. It has to be David Tennant.'

Zack took a gulp from his can as he shook his head to argue. 'You can't tell me series six isn't the best one to date.'

Adam turned to Jenny and shrugged. 'He's right, that was clever.'

'But it would have been even better if the tenth Doctor had been in it,' Jenny stated.

'I'll drink to that!' Adam said, raising his can in the air. Zack laughed. It was nice. He had his old friends back. It was exactly what he loved. He just hoped it would last.

EMMETT'S FAREWELL

'What do you mean you've lost them?' Adam asked Zack as their plates were cleared away from their roast dinners the following Sunday in the pub.

'Just that,' Zack replied. 'I don't know what could have happened to them. They were in my backpack, but I've looked everywhere. It's the strangest thing.'

'Could they have been stolen?' Jenny asked.

'Maybe. But who would want to steal drawings of an unknown superhero?'

'Currently unknown,' Adam corrected.

'No, completely unknown. All the work I've done on him has vanished, so that's that.'

'I still have the character profile,' Jenny said. 'We could start again.'

'No,' Zack said, shaking his head. 'I think this is an omen, don't you? We've had a rollercoaster ride with Emmett, but now maybe it's just time to leave it there.'

'How can you say that?' Adam asked with a hint of exasperation. 'This was your dream. This was our dream. Emmett's become part of us. We can't just give in.'

'Hello!' a female voice suddenly sang from across the pub. A petite girl with long dark hair and a pretty face ran towards their table.

Adam stood up, nearly knocking his chair over. 'Lizzy!' He hugged her tightly.

'You decided to come back?' Jenny asked, standing up to join in the hug.

'Surprise!' Lizzy looked absolutely thrilled.

'You can say that again!' Adam said with a smile spread across his face.

'I just got back from Australia this morning. I didn't tell anybody. I just turned up at mum and dad's out of the blue. They were loving it! Then they said you'd probably be down here as it's your normal Sunday afternoon session, and here you are.'

'Sorry mate,' Adam said, seeing Zack looking bewildered on his own. 'This is Lizzy, my sister. She's been in Australia for the past four years.'

Lizzy walked around the table to Zack, as if she'd only just noticed he was there. 'Hi, really nice to meet you.'

Zack stood up with his hand out to shake but Lizzy threw her arms around him and hugged him warmly.

'I'm Zack Harper,' he said. 'I'm friends with Jenny and Adam.'

'Zack! Yes, they've talked about you. So great to finally meet you. This is fabulous, isn't it.' Lizzy looked around at the three faces before her with excitement. 'Jenny, you look fantastic!'

'Thanks,' Jenny said, stroking her now red strands in her hair. 'You too.'

'Are you just home for a visit? How long?' Adam asked.

'No, it's permanent. I'm back for good.' Lizzy sat down on the spare seat next to Zack, and they all settled once again.

'What? That's fantastic news! How come? I thought you were loving it over there.'

'I was. Mostly. But the company I was working for went under and I found myself out of a job. It was like I reached a point in the road where I could easily just pack up and come home or I could try and start a new chapter in my Aussie life. But when I thought about how much I missed you all, there seemed only one option. So I finalised all my bits and got on a plane home.'

Lizzy and Jenny shared a small knowing look, but neither of them said a word.

'I don't mean this to sound bad, but I'm really glad you lost your job. It's great to have you back,' Adam said.

'I want to know what's been going on here,' Lizzy said. 'Mum said you've split up with Cadence. What the hell happened there? Mum's distraught. We were all expecting wedding bells.'

Adam shook his head. 'It's a long story. Let's just say I'm much better off without her.'

'You do look happy. In fact, you look really happy. Maybe some time out for a while is doing you the world of good.'

'Actually,' Adam started. 'I've been seeing someone else.'

'Already?' Lizzy asked, gobsmacked. 'Were you cheating on Cadence?'

'No! Of course not. I'd never do that. But I guess there's always been someone else in my life.'

As Adam placed his arm around Jenny and kissed her on the cheek, Lizzy's mouth dropped open.

'You and Jenny? You two are together?'

Jenny nodded and a huge grin spread across her face. Lizzy screamed and jumped to her feet before skipping around the table and hugging both Adam and Jenny together.

'What happened to Mr Wonderful?' Lizzy asked Jenny.

Jenny just stared at Lizzy but she didn't say anything.

'Not Adam?' Lizzy queried with a look of absolute confusion.

'What?' Adam asked.

'Adam?' Lizzy repeated, this time with her face screwed

up. 'Really?' she sniggered.

'You see why I couldn't tell you?'

'What?' Adam asked.

Then a look of realisation lit up Lizzy's face. 'The bitch was-'

'We'll talk about it later,' Jenny quickly interrupted.

'We definitely will!'

'What's going on?' Adam pushed.

'Nothing. Have you told mum yet?' Lizzy asked.

'No, we've not really told anyone,' Adam replied. 'There's been a lot going on and it's still early days.'

'Can I be there when you tell mum?' Lizzy asked.

'Why?' Jenny asked, a look of concern momentarily haunting her face.

'Because if there's one girl she likes more than Cadence, it's you Jenny. You must know that. You're like the other daughter in her life.'

'Doesn't that make me like Adam's sister?' Jenny asked, screwing up her face.

'No, it makes you like family,' Lizzy corrected. 'She's going to be over the moon that you two have got together. Oh, can I be a bridesmaid!'

'Hang on, Liz, we haven't even moved in together yet,' Adam said.

'Yet?' she asked with excitement.

'We're moving into Adam's old house,' Jenny explained. 'He's already given his tenants notice.'

'This is incredible! Did I come back at the right time or what?'

Adam shook his head and rolled his eyes. 'How about I get you a drink?'

'No, I'll get the next round in,' Jenny said standing up. 'It's my turn. I didn't get chance to buy a single drink last week.'

'Are you sure?' Adam asked.

'I'll come and help,' Zack said.

'What do you want, Lizzy?' Jenny asked.

Lizzy scanned the table. 'You're all on pints?' she checked, to which all of them nodded. 'Same for me then. Whatever you lot have.'

Jenny and Zack walked off and Lizzy propped herself on the edge of Jenny's seat.

'So, tell me about Zack then,' she said.

'What about him? He's a really good mate,' Adam replied.

'No, what's his story? Is he single?'

Adam smirked, clearly not expecting this question. 'Do you like him?'

'Yes! He's gorgeous. He's got that cheeky, sexy face that I always go for.'

Adam chuckled. 'Has he? Well, you're in luck, he's definitely single. In fact, he's not had a girlfriend in all the time I've known him. Well... not really.'

'Are you serious?'

'I think he's quite shy.'

'Aww. Now I like him even more!'

'He's also one of the best. You can't get a nicer bloke than Zack. Plus, you'll be pleased to hear that he loves Star Wars, so you've got loads in common already.'

'No!'

'That's how we met him. Going to Comic Con.'

'Really? He goes to Comic Con?'

'I'm sure I've told you all this.'

'I don't think so. Or I wasn't listening. You never said how cute he was!'

'Sorry, didn't I? And you know I'm always thinking about how attractive my male friends are.'

Lizzy giggled and hit Adam on the arm. 'You certainly don't have any issues finding your female friends attractive.'

Adam couldn't wipe the smile from his face.

'You're going to have to fill me in on how it all happened. Did you dump Cadence for Jenny?'

Adam studied the pint glass before him, awkwardly.

'It's a really long story.'

'It's a good job I'm back then. Now we've got all the time in the world. I want full details!'

'Here you go,' Jenny said, placing down the two pints that she'd carried. Lizzy jumped out of her seat.

'It's fine if you want to sit there,' Jenny said.

'Are you kidding? I want to sit next to Zack.' Lizzy moved around to take her seat as she watched Zack place down the remaining two pints.

'You like Star Wars?' she asked him.

'Yeah,' he answered with trepidation.

'I'm going to ask you the ultimate question now. Please don't say Han Solo, please don't say Han Solo.'

'The best character ever?' Zack checked. Lizzy just nodded. 'For me there's no question, sorry. It's Luke Skywalker.'

'What?' Lizzy hugged him and kissed him on the cheek. 'Yes! No one ever says that. It's all Han Solo, Princess Leia or Chewbacca.'

'No, Luke for me is the heart and soul of the story.'

'He is. That's exactly what I think.'

'There'd be no Star Wars without Luke.'

'Exactly!'

'I can't believe this,' Zack said, turning to Adam with shock.

'It's true, mate. I think she might even be worse than you. We had to watch The Empire Strikes Back over and over growing up. We'd get to the big dramatic ending and then she'd flick it right back to the start and watch it all over again.'

'It's the best movie of all time,' Lizzy stated, as if it was the most obvious thing in the world.

'That's what I think!' Zack agreed with glee.

'You know what, Zack Harper, I think we're going to be new best friends.'

'Excuse me,' a man suddenly said to Zack. He was tall with a beard and a scruffy jumper.

'Yes?' Adam asked.

'You're Zack Harper?'

'Yes,' Zack replied. He looked worried.

'You're not the same Zack Harper who created Empathy Man, are you? I know he lives around here.'

'Yes,' Zack replied slowly.

'Oh my God. Thank you! We've been trying to get in touch with you. I've just been away and I think I must have got your email address wrong. I was going to check it when I got back in the office tomorrow.'

'Sorry, who are you?' Adam asked.

'Sorry, I'm Benjamin. You'll have to forgive me, I'm a little jet lagged. I've just got back from a trip to San Diego.'

'San Diego?' Jenny asked, her eyes widening.

'You weren't at Comic-Con, were you?' Adam followed with.

'Yes, I was actually.'

'You're kidding!' Adam said.

'You must have been really lucky to get tickets,' Jenny noted.

'No, actually, I was there for work,' Benjamin replied.

All three of the friends' pairs of eyes were now glaring at Benjamin with fascination.

'Who do you work for?' Adam asked.

'Bendally Comics,' Benjamin said.

'As in the creators of Jazz Hands?' Adam replied.

'That's us. That was actually my baby.'

'You're kidding!' Adam nearly fell off his chair with excitement, and Jenny and Zack weren't far behind him. 'I love Jazz Hands. He's so different; so fresh.'

'You've read it?'

'Of course I have! I couldn't put it down. Then it got passed between these two like wild fire,' Adam said, pointing to Jenny and Zack.

'It's really clever,' Jenny said, a little in awe.

'I wanted to do something satirical, you know with him dancing through people's problems. I felt it was a strong political statement on how we've become so relaxed about blood and gore on the telly, yet when it happens in real life we're far from ready for it.'

'Exactly!' Adam agreed.

'I liked the story where you mirrored the difficulties of the foxtrot with that earthquake disaster,' Jenny said.

'Yes, that was a favourite of mine too. You know parts of that really happened,' Benjamin said.

'No!' Jenny replied. 'It stayed with me for days.'

'You read Empathy Man?' Zack suddenly asked. 'You actually got what I sent to you?'

'We get loads of material sent to us every day, Zack, but yours was something else,' Benjamin explained. 'It captured me straight away. I love the fact that it's about the little people. The kid getting bullied - it's such everyday sort of stuff we don't touch on enough.'

'That's what I thought,' Jenny said. 'Zack's really talented, isn't he.'

Benjamin looked at Zack. 'I'll say. So are you still interested in speaking to us about it? We'd like to take it further, if you're willing?'

Zack could barely find his voice. 'Yes,' was all he could manage. He was trembling.

'That's great news. Is there any chance you could drop by our office tomorrow? I'd like you to meet my partner. Empathy Man is exactly what we've been looking for.'

'Are you serious?' Zack muttered.

Benjamin reached into his pocket and he handed Zack a business card. 'We're based in Farringdon. Could you get there for about ten tomorrow morning?'

Zack took the card from him with wide eyes. He looked shell-shocked. 'Yes.'

'He's a little shy,' Adam said. 'But his work is phenomenal.'

'I noticed. Well, I look forward to discussing it more with you tomorrow.'

'Thank you very much,' Zack said. 'I'll be there.'

'I'd better get back to my friends,' Benjamin said. 'See you tomorrow, Zack.'

They all said their goodbyes and Benjamin walked off. Then they all let out a tiny squeal of excitement. But not too loud as Benjamin was still in the pub.

'Oh my God, Zack!' Jenny said. 'I'd call that a big break.'

'We'll see.'

'He clearly loved your work on Empathy Man,' Adam said.

'But Empathy Man is not just mine,' Zack said.

'He is now,' Adam said. 'Jenny and I were just playing at it. You've put all the hard work in. Go with it, Zack. Bring him to life for us. Or... just draw him on paper some more.'

Lizzy tried to stifle a yawn unsuccessfully. 'I'm sorry, guys, I'm going to have to go. I don't even know what time of day it is. I'm all over the place. But I want to meet up later in the week. What about we all go out for dinner on Friday?'

'Sounds great,' Adam said.

'You too, Zack,' she said.

'You want me to come too?' he asked.

'I was thinking, maybe we could meet for a drink first. Just the two of us.'

Zack didn't respond. He just looked at her as if she might be joking.

'I want to find out all the news about your upcoming comic book career. And I also think you're pretty hot. I thought maybe we could make it a double date?'

Zack's jaw dropped open. Then he quickly straightened himself up. 'Err... yeah, why not. Sounds good.'

He didn't notice Adam quickly squeeze Jenny's hand before they shared a look of delight.

'Great! I won't have a British phone until tomorrow, so shall I just get your number off Adam and then we can make plans?'

'Definitely. Text me anytime,' Zack replied.

'I might just do that.'

Lizzy kissed Zack on the cheek before standing up. She then hugged Adam and Jenny and said goodbye.

'Bloody hell,' Zack said as soon as she was out of earshot. 'Am I dreaming?'

'It's been one hell of an afternoon for you, hasn't it?' Adam smiled.

'Do you mind me going out with your sister?' Zack checked.

Adam shook his head. 'Are you kidding? I'm thrilled. It's about time she met someone decent.'

'She seems really nice.'

'She is,' Jenny said.

'Do you think they really will take up Empathy Man?' Zack then asked, this time his face full of worry.

'That bloke definitely seemed keen,' Adam said. 'But we need to make sure you're ready. How about I get another round in and then we'll work on your pitch.'

'Pitch? I'll have to do a pitch? I've never done one of them before.'

'Then you're in luck, because I do about fifty a week and I'm about to give you a crash course. All I can say is the world better be ready, as Empathy Man is coming!'

Adam headed off to the bar and Jenny tried to calm Zack down. It really had been the most amazing last hour for him.

Over in the corner, right out of view, stood Emmett the Empathy Man. He was far away from everyone, watching the happy faces of the three friends that he'd helped. It hadn't been the easiest of journeys for them, but the pathway to happiness can't always be straight. Their beaming smiles, though, told Emmett that his hard work had definitely paid off.

As he approached them, just out of sight, he thought to himself how much he really had loved working with them.

But all good things must come to an end and Emmett knew that they needed to navigate through their own lives again now.

'Goodbye my friends,' he said, although they couldn't hear him.

As Zack, Adam and Jenny all laughed over their drinks, they were completely unaware of Emmett disappearing. And they were completely oblivious to the fact that once again their destinies lay back in their own hands.

ABOUT THE AUTHOR

Lindsay is a British author who lives in Warwickshire with her husband and cat. She's had a lifelong passion for writing, starting off as a child when she used to write stories about the Fraggles of Fraggle Rock.

Knowing there was nothing else she'd rather study, she did her degree in writing and has now turned her favourite hobby into a career.

Lindsay has also written the Bird trilogy available from Amazon.